A Will,
a Way,
and a
Wedding

A Will,
a Way,
and a
Wedding

MELODY CARLSON

WhiteFire Publishing

This is a work of fiction. All characters and events portrayed in this novel are either fictitious or used fictitiously.

A WILL, A WAY, AND A WEDDING

WhiteFire Publishing
13607 Bedford Rd NE
Cumberland, MD 21502

ISBN: 978-1-939023-73-5 (print)
          978-1-939023-74-2 (digital)

Chapter 1

On the morning of her thirty-fifth birthday, Daphne Ballinger found herself staring into the bathroom mirror with a mixture of fascination and deep anxiety. Searching her face for any trace of wrinkles, she vaguely wondered if she was about to be attacked by a terrorist. Oh, she knew that she was being melodramatic, not to mention ridiculous, but that silly quote about a single thirty-five-year-old woman's pathetic odds of marriage was unsettling. But, then again, what was the likelihood of a terrorist attack in Appleton?

"Whatcha doing?" Mabel asked from behind her.

Daphne turned to see the eight-year-old, still in her rumpled Hello Kitty pajamas, blinking up with sleepy brown eyes.

"Nothing much." Daphne smiled down at her. "Just trying to see if I look any older today."

Mabel's brow creased as she studied Daphne more closely. "Nope. You still look just the same as yesterday."

Daphne tousled her fingers through Mabel's chestnut hair, making her short pixie haircut resemble a punk-rocker. "Good to know, sweetie."

"Oh, yeah!" Mabel's eyes opened wide. "It's your birthday, Aunt Daphne! I almost forgot. *Happy birthday!*" She threw her arms around Daphne's waist, hugging her tightly as she sang the Happy Birthday song with gusto.

"Thank you, Mabel." Daphne hugged her back. Really, no birthday present could be better than her new role as Mabel's guardian. That was truly the gift that would keep on giving.

"Wait!" Mabel released her. "I got a birthday present for you—I almost forgot." And then she dashed off, her bare feet pattering across the hardwood floor.

Daphne bent down to pet the two cats who were now rubbing against her legs, purring loudly. "Yes, I'm sure you girls are here to tell me happy birthday too," she said wryly. "Unless you're just begging for breakfast." Of course, it was the latter. "Come on, girls."

As Daphne led Ethel and Lucy from the master bedroom, Mabel came bounding down the stairs. "Here it is!" She proudly held out a lumpy looking package wrapped in red and green Christmas paper and with a pale pink satin ribbon wrapped loosely around it. "Open it! Open it now!"

"I can't wait." Daphne took the gift from her. "I wonder what it could be."

"I made it myself," Mabel declared. "With a little bit of help from Aunt Sabrina."

Daphne slowly peeled off the outer layer of paper and more layers of crumpled pink tissue paper until she finally uncovered an oversized mug. Painted and glazed with colorful stripes and hearts and flowers, it declared *Mabel Loves Daphne* in bold rainbow colored letters. "It's beautiful!" Daphne hugged Mabel. "Thank you so much!"

"Sabrina took me to The Potting Shed," Mabel explained. "It's a new store in town where you make all kinds of stuff. At first this mug was all plain and white and boring, but then I got to paint it." Her mouth twisted to one side. "It didn't look real pretty when I got done, but the lady there told me it would look better after it got cooked up. She put it in her big oven after we left and when we went back a few days later it looked like this."

"I *love* it." Daphne held up the bright cup. "I'm going to use it for coffee this morning."

"Yes!"

"I'll go start the coffee and feed the cats." Daphne pointed at Mabel's bare feet. "And you get on your slippers. It's chilly in here."

"Shouldn't I get dressed for school?"

"Today's Saturday."

"Oh, yeah!" Mabel let out a happy whoop as she raced back up the stairs. "Lola and I are going skateboarding this morning."

With Lucy and Ethel fed, Daphne started a pot of coffee. As the aroma of the freshly ground beans drifted through the old fashioned kitchen, she told herself that she had a lot to be thankful for on this milestone birthday. And to obsess over the stupid quote she'd read a few weeks ago was totally ludicrous. Thirty-five was not that old!

"Hello? Y'all here?" A sweet southern voice hailed the house. "Anybody home?"

"Come in," Daphne called out. "I'm in the kitchen."

Sabrina Fontaine, her petite blonde neighbor, entered the kitchen with a large baking pan in her hands. "Happy birthday!" she chirped. "Hot cinnamon rolls to celebrate your big day."

"Yum!" Daphne sniffed the gooey confections. "I just put on the coffee."

Sabrina set the hot pan on top of the stove, pointing to the colorful mug. "Looks like Mabel already gave you her gift."

"Isn't it sweet?"

Sabrina nodded. "You have to wait for my gift." And now she explained how she'd made appointments for both of them. "Two o'clock. For mani-pedis and facials," she said cheerfully. "And then we'll do a little shopping for something special—for your big date with Jake tonight."

"And Jenna's coming to stay with me while you're with Sabrina," Mabel announced as she shuffled into the kitchen with her fluffy pink slippers. "Jenna promised to help me finish up my valentines today."

"That's right." Sabrina cut into the cinnamon rolls, setting them on a platter. "Valentine's Day is Tuesday. That's coming up real quick."

"And Mabel's only half done with her special homemade valentines." Daphne silently blessed Jenna as she poured coffee. Mabel's idea to hand craft all those valentines was very sweet, but each one took so long to make...Daphne had been worried that Mabel might not get them done by Tuesday.

"What time is your date with Jake?" Sabrina asked as she sat the rolls on the little plastic-topped kitchen table straight out of the forties.

"He's picking her up at six-thirty," Mabel said importantly as she flopped into a chrome and vinyl chair. "They're going to The Zeppelin."

"And Jenna's going to baby-sit tonight too?" Sabrina asked Daphne as she sat down. "Because I could always cancel my date with Ricardo if you needed me to—"

"Jake said it was all set with Jenna." Daphne set down Sabrina's coffee and a glass of milk for Mabel.

"Yay!" Mabel made a victorious fist pump. "I get to have Jenna today *and* tonight."

"Thank goodness for Jenna." Daphne set a bowl of last night's fruit salad and some small dishes on the table and smiled. "This looks like the perfect birthday breakfast." Daphne sat down. "Thanks for the cinnamon rolls, Sabrina."

"I'll say the blessing," Mabel offered eagerly.

They bowed their heads, waiting as Mabel said a short grateful prayer and a hearty amen.

"Speaking of Jenna, did you hear the latest news about her step-daddy?" Sabrina's brows arched mysteriously as she looked at Daphne.

"No." Daphne shook her head. She didn't really know that much about Frank Danson. Except that he was quite wealthy and that he'd recently married Jake's ex-wife—and that Jenna seemed to like her new stepfather, which was a relief. "What's up?"

Sabrina glanced at Mabel then shrugged. "Oh, nothing really." It sounded like she was backpedaling. "I, uh, I think he's going to open up a new business or something." As Mabel dished out some fruit salad, Sabrina tossed Daphne a tell-you-later look.

"These rolls are delicious," Daphne told Sabrina, now curious as to what her friend was keeping to herself.

The three of them made cheerful small talk about their favorite birthday memories. Of course, Mabel's favorite birthday was the one she'd had before Christmas. "That was the best birthday party ever!" She beamed up at Daphne. "You wanna have a party like that too?"

"No thanks," Daphne told her. "I like small, quiet celebrations like this better."

Before long Mabel was finished and trotting off to get dressed in the anticipation of skateboarding around the neighborhood with Lola. But as soon as she was out of earshot, Daphne inquired about Frank Danson. "Why are you being so mysterious?"

"Sorry, I didn't think before I spoke. I shouldn't have said a word in front of Mabel."

"Why not?"

"Because I know how she adores Jenna—and it's possible that Jenna will have to move."

"Move?" Daphne felt a wave of concern. "*Why?*"

"It sounds like Frank has acquired a large real estate firm in Miami and plans to relocate there."

"Miami?" Daphne frowned.

"Yeah. That's what Ricardo told me yesterday."

"Do you really think he'll move Jenna and Gwen there? I can't imagine that Jenna would want to leave her school and her friends...not to mention her dad."

"I don't know, but I didn't want to say anything in front of Mabel. She'll be devastated."

"Jake will be devastated too." Daphne solemnly shook her head.

"Maybe it's just a silly rumor," Sabrina suggested. "You know how people love to gossip in this town. And Ricardo catches bits and pieces at the diner. I'll bet it's not even true."

"I sure hope you're right."

"Anyway, I won't mention it to Mabel."

"Thank you." Daphne sipped her coffee. Mabel would certainly be saddened by this news, but what about poor Jake? Miami was a long way from Appleton. He would be lost if his sixteen-year-old daughter moved that far away. And Daphne knew that Jenna was the reason Jake had kept his law practice in this small town for all these years. Especially when he knew he could work in much larger cities.

"I wonder if Jake knows...?" Sabrina said absently.

"If he does know, he hasn't mentioned it to me. But he was away on that business trip last week." Daphne frowned. If the rumor was true and if Jake had heard about it, it would put a definite damper on their evening. And she wouldn't even blame him for feeling blue.

"I'm sorry," Sabrina said suddenly. "I shouldn't have mentioned it to you. I can see it's making you unhappy. Please, don't think about it anymore. It's probably just a small town rumor."

"Yes, I'm sure it is. I don't know Jake's ex that well, but I know Gwen loves Jenna. I can't imagine she'd agree to uproot her from high school and her friends...and her dad."

"You're right." Sabrina got up, carrying her dishes to the

sink. "So...I'll pick you up a little before two, okay?"

Daphne forced a smile. She knew how much Sabrina loved being pampered in a fancy spa, but the truth was Daphne could take it or leave it. Still, she wanted to be a good sport—especially since it was all arranged.

"It'll be fun," Sabrina assured her as if reading Daphne's doubtful thoughts. "And when we're done, you'll feel like a new woman, Daph. *Trust me.*"

Daphne patted her petite friend's shoulder. "You know that I trust you, Sabrina. I'm sure I'll enjoy it. Thank you for setting it up."

Yet as Sabrina left, Daphne wasn't so sure she could trust her good friend. More specifically, she didn't *want* to trust her—at least not in regard to the rumor she'd just shared. Because if Frank and Gwen were truly moving Jenna to Miami, Jake McPheeters would have no reason to remain in Appleton. And Daphne wasn't sure that she was ready to tell him goodbye.

Chapter 2

By the time Jenna was dropped off by her mom, Daphne had pushed her worries about Miami into the back of her mind. And since Jenna looked as happy and chipper as ever, Daphne felt certain it was just a rumor.

"Mabel is so thrilled that you're babysitting her both today and then again tonight—she's nearly beside herself." Daphne led Jenna inside.

"Happy birthday." Jenna handed Daphne a large yellow envelope then peeled off her parka. "Sabrina told me."

"Thank you." As Daphne took her coat, she mentioned Mabel's valentine project.

"Mabel already told me about it. Sounds like fun." Jenna unwound a colorful scarf from around her neck. "I haven't made old fashioned valentines in ages. I might even make some for my friends too."

"*Jenna—Jenna—Jenna!*" Mabel sang out as she raced down the stairs "You're here *at last.*"

"Sabrina said to come at 1:45." Jenna grinned at her. "And I'm five minutes early."

"But I've been waiting for you forever!" Mabel grabbed Jenna by the hand. "Come to the kitchen—my valentine making stuff is all in there and I really *need* your help!"

"How does it feel to be so needed?" Daphne asked as she hung up Jenna's coat.

"Kinda nice." Jenna laughed as Mabel eagerly tugged her along.

Daphne opened the envelope, slipping out a pretty card with a picture of sunflowers on it, and taking her time to read the sweet message. "Thank you for the card, Jenna," she said as she joined them in the kitchen.

"You're welcome."

Daphne spotted Sabrina through the kitchen window. She was putting something in her car. "Looks like Sabrina's almost ready to go." Daphne grabbed her jacket from the hook by the laundry room. "You've got my cell number, Jenna. And the other numbers on the fridge."

"Yeah, we're fine," Jenna said. "Have fun!"

Despite her reservations, Daphne hoped it would be fun—or at least tolerable. As she hurried out to Sabrina's car, she had a flashback to the time she'd had a seaweed facial in New York and ended up looking like something from a horror film. Who knew she had an allergy to algae?

"Y'all ready to get beautified?" Sabrina asked as Daphne got into her car.

"I guess so." Daphne smiled uneasily then pointed at Sabrina's doggy carrier in the backseat. "Tootsie's going to the spa too?"

"I just didn't want to leave him home alone all afternoon. Especially since I'll be gone tonight too." Sabrina backed out into the street. "You don't mind, do you?"

"Not at all." Daphne was used to Tootsie by now. Even his little pink tutu didn't bother her anymore—although he had on a bright red sweater today.

"The spa lady said it was all right—especially since I'm such a regular customer there. And I promised her that Tootsie wouldn't make a ruckus or run hog wild." Sabrina laughed. "As if I'd let him. But you know how spa folks are. They want to keep the place calm and quiet. Can't blame 'em for that."

"I must admit I'm a little wary about the spa." Daphne explained about her seaweed allergy several years ago. "I don't want to look like the creature from the Black Lagoon for my date tonight."

Sabrina laughed. "Don't you worry, I'll tell them you're extra sensitive, and make sure that they use the gentlest of products on you. When we're done, you'll be pretty as a picture or I'll throw a sweet little hissy fit."

"Well, I don't want you to—"

"No fretting, Daphne. This is *your* day." Sabrina glanced at her. "And I'm not surprised you've got sensitive skin, honey. All that naturally red hair and your peaches and cream complexion, it's no wonder. Don't worry, they'll treat you right or we'll know the reason why."

Daphne couldn't help but chuckle at her small southern friend. Sabrina was unlike anyone Daphne had ever known and, in many ways, Daphne's exact opposite. Where Daphne was tall and often felt awkward, Sabrina was short and spirited. And where Daphne was somewhat shy and insecure, as well as fashion-challenged, Sabrina was bold and confident and something of a style diva. Despite their many differences, Daphne felt thankful for the unexpected friendship and she knew that, where it mattered, she and Sabrina were actually a lot alike.

"Did Jenna mention anything about moving to Miami?" Sabrina asked as they were getting out of her car to go into the day spa.

"No. And she seemed like her usual cheerful self." Daphne reached for her purse.

"I'll bet it was just idle gossip," Sabrina said as she got Tootsie's carrier out. "Wish I'd never mentioned it now."

"We'll just forget about it then." Daphne sighed. "And we won't repeat it to anyone."

"You got that right." Sabrina led the way to the front door of the charming old building. "Now—let the fun begin!"

After a couple hours of surprisingly delicate pampering, Daphne really did feel prettier. Not to mention more relaxed. And all without the slightest reaction.

"Thank you so much," she told Sabrina as they waited in the parking lot for Tootsie to do his business along the curbside strip of grass. Daphne examined her nails, which were painted a soft luminescent shell pink. At least she wouldn't ruin them gardening since it was only mid-February.

"I'm so glad you like it, Daph. You look like a million bucks with the cosmetics that gal put on you. I really should take your picture while you're trying on clothes." As Sabrina extracted a hot pink doggie-do baggie from her purse, Daphne tried to think of a gentle way to put the brakes on this intended shopping expedition. She simply did not need any new clothes—she could easily wear one of the dresses she'd worn at Christmastime. But how to tell Sabrina?

"Good boy," Sabrina told Tootsie as she stooped over, deftly picking up after him.

"The time at the spa was so great," Daphne began cautiously, "I just don't want you to feel you still need to take me shopping, because I have plenty of—"

"You are not going to deprive me of the best part of my day, are you?" Sabrina waved her pink parcel in the air before dropping into the nearby trash can. "You know how much I love to shop. And I already found the perfect place to get you something really special. Please, do not tell me you want to quit now." She produced a small bottle of rose-scented hand-sanitizer, giving herself a generous squirt and vigorously rubbing her palms together.

"Okay—okay." Daphne shook her head. "Show me what you found."

"There's this new shop right here in Appleton," Sabrina explained as they got into her car. "I met the lady who owns it. She's from Germany, and I swear she could pass for Heidi Klum's older sister. Her name is Erika Schwartz. And she was so disappointed not to open her business before Christmas, but she just couldn't get everything ready in time. Anyway, it's called The Chic Boutique—isn't that cute? And I feel we should do our part to make her feel welcome—and to support local businesses."

"I've seen that shop. Looks like they fixed it up really nice, but I haven't been in there yet."

"Well, I promised Erika I'd bring you shopping there for your birthday today. She's expecting us."

As soon as they walked in the door of the shop, with Tootsie still wearing his little red sweater and now on a leash, Erika greeted all three of them like dear old friends. "Velcome, velcome," she said with a thick accent. "Thank you so much for coming to Chic Boutique."

And suddenly, like being caught in a whirlwind, Daphne was being shown dresses and skirts and tops and all sorts of things—most of which she wouldn't want to be caught dead in. But with an armload of garments, she was shown to a hanging chamber made of colorful curtains. And then both Erika and Sabrina took turns shoving various items at her. As the swaying dressing room moved from side to side, Daphne could almost feel her head spinning. She honestly did not understand how so many women, particularly Sabrina, found shopping fun. To Daphne, it was just plain old hard work.

"I know you're trying to help," Daphne said as she modeled

a dress with far too many details. "But you need to remember, I like more classic styles."

"She means plain clothes," Sabrina told Erika.

"Classic." Erika nodded at Daphne. "I understand vat you mean."

"But you're so dramatic looking," Sabrina protested. "All that beautiful auburn hair and your height. You could be so flamboyant."

"You are right, Sabrina," Erika said quietly as Daphne returned to the swaying chamber. "Your friend is tall like fashion model. She vill look good in anything."

"That's the *problem*," Sabrina said in a hushed tone. "She will wear almost *any*thing."

"Oh?" Erika sounded confused. "That's not good?"

"Yes, I guess it is. But we want to make her look very *beautiful* for tonight," Sabrina said. "Not only for her birthday, but she has a big date too."

"*Big date?*"

"You know...she's having dinner with a *man.*" Sabrina chuckled. "A very handsome man."

"Oh, dat's goot. Ve vill make her even more beautiful."

It was close to five o'clock when they all agreed that a cream colored cable-knit dress with a wide leather belt meant to be worn low on her hips was perfect. "It looked so boring on the hanger, but it really does look good on you." Sabrina conceded as she snapped some pictures with her phone.

"It shows off her figure," Erika said with a pleased nod. "Good for big date."

Daphne felt her cheeks warming and nearly pulled the plug on the dress but knew that would mean trying on more clothes. Instead she returned to the swaying chamber and, eager to be done with this, handed it over to Sabrina.

"And you want the belt too?" Erika asked hopefully.

"Absolutely. And those suede pumps too," Sabrina declared.

"No," Daphne called out as she pulled on her jeans. "I've got some boots that will look great with that dress. They're the same color as the belt too."

"Oh, yes," Erika agreed. "Boots vould be goot with this dress. Daphne is right."

Relieved that Sabrina was talked out of purchasing the shoes they'd insisted she try on with the dress, Daphne hurried to change into her own clothes then pretended to browse the racks while Sabrina and Erika handled the purchase.

"Happy birthday!" Sabrina declared as she handed Daphne the garment bag.

"You're too generous." Daphne called out goodbye to Erika as she held the shop door open for Sabrina and Tootsie.

"The truth is I have ulterior motives," Sabrina confessed as they went out to the car.

"What do you mean?" Daphne asked.

"I don't want to lose you," Sabrina confessed. "I want you to marry Jake and then you and Mabel will remain across the street from me—and we will all happily grow old together."

Daphne laughed. "Well, at least you're being honest about it. And, for the record, it sounds good to me too."

"You know, I've been giving this whole thing a lot of thought lately, Daphne." Sabrina started her car. "For a while I was really miffed at your grandmother for the way she wrote out her will. I mean, it just seemed wrong and selfish for her to insist you must get married in order to inherit her estate. But the more I thought about it, the more I began to understand. She simply wanted to ensure that you were happy."

"You mean happily married." Daphne frowned. "And yet she never chose to marry herself. Doesn't that seem a bit ironic?"

"Yes. But it just proves that she understood what it felt like to grow old alone. Even with her big house and beautiful car and those two cats, I suspect she was lonely. And I'm sure she didn't want the same for you."

"But what if the stipulations in her will tempted me to marry the wrong man? Out of plain desperation? How could that make me happy?"

"Your grandmother must've known you were far too sensible to do something foolish like that. Not to mention you're too honest. No, Daphne, the old darling trusted you to make the right decision. That's why she wrote it out the way she did. It was for your own good."

Daphne sighed. "Well, I've actually had similar thoughts, Sabrina. Still, it sure hasn't been easy. And seeing the months of the calendar turning over is unsettling. You know I have less than three months now."

"Believe me, I know. But here's what I'm thinking, Daph. It's sort of like I'm an ambassador."

"An ambassador?"

"You know, like a diplomat or delegate. I'm representing your grandmother. I like to think that old Daphne Delacorte or Daphne Ballinger or Penelope Poindexter—whatever handle she went by back then—anyway, I like to imagine that she sort of selected me to help you. Sort of like your fairy godmother." Sabrina laughed. "I know it sounds silly."

"Well, you make a sweet fairy godmother." Daphne chuckled, envisioning Sabrina in a fairy godmother costume, complete with sparkling wand and tiara—oddly enough it wasn't hard to imagine.

"Anyway, I don't mind helping you. Not one bit." Sabrina made a loud sigh. "I just hope we're not wasting our time on Jake." Sabrina parked her car in her own driveway. "I'd hate to be barking up the wrong tree. Especially when time is precious."

"What do you mean?" Daphne turned to peer at her. "I thought you *liked* Jake."

"I do like Jake." Sabrina's forehead creased. "But I'm worried that rumor is true—that Frank really does plan to move Gwen and Jenna to Florida." She bit her lip as if she didn't want to say more.

"But you said earlier that you didn't think—"

"The truth is—I texted Ricardo while you were having your facial, Daphne."

"And...?"

"He confirmed that it's true. Frank told him himself. Straight from the horse's mouth."

"Oh...." Daphne felt her spirits plummeting.

"So—since I'm playing fairy godmother—I want to give you some advice." Sabrina looked at her with sincere blue eyes.

"And that would be?"

"Guard your heart, my friend."

Daphne just nodded.

"We all know how much Jake loves his daughter—and that he could easily relocate his law firm to just about anywhere."

"Including Miami," Daphne said quietly.

"So keep that in mind," Sabrina said soberly. "Don't let yourself fall into something that will ultimately hurt you."

Daphne nodded. "I will keep that in mind, Sabrina."

"Sorry to be such a wet blanket on your birthday." Sabrina's lower lip protruded ever so slightly. "But I just want the best for you." She reached over to squeeze Daphne's hand. "I considered not telling you that it was true. But it didn't seem right to keep it a secret."

"Thanks, I appreciate that." Daphne managed only a stiff smile. "And don't worry about me, it's still been a great day. And I'm sure that dinner with Jake will be pleasant and fun. We've been friends for a while. I'll just enjoy his company. And I'll guard my heart too."

"Good for you."

They both got out of the car then Sabrina rushed over to hug Daphne. "Happy birthday, honey."

Daphne thanked her again and, with her new birthday dress in hand, hurried across the street to her house. But as she went up the walk, where the tulips were just starting to open and bloom, she wondered if this would still be her house by her next birthday. And if it weren't, where would she be—what would she do and how would she take care of Mabel?

Chapter 3

Instead of going home until 6:30, Jenna opted to remain at Daphne's. "I can just read or something," Jenna said after Daphne sent Mabel up to clean her room. "I don't want to be in the way or anything."

Daphne gave her a sideways hug. "You are never in the way, Jenna. You're always welcome here. If Mabel had her way, you'd be her roommate."

"You look really pretty," Jenna told her. "Did you have fun at the spa and shopping?"

Daphne shrugged as she kicked off her shoes and flopped on the sofa. "It was okay. But the truth is I'm not really into the froufrou. It's more of Sabrina's thing."

Jenna laughed. "That's just like me. My mom loves all that stuff, but I could take it or leave it."

Daphne felt certain that Jenna was unaware of Frank's plan to relocate his new family, but the journalist in her couldn't help but sniff around. "So how is it going in your new house, Jenna? Do you feel all settled in?"

"I guess so. I mean, it's a really fabulous house. It has a great pool that'll be cool this summer. And I have the whole top floor completely to myself. Kinda like living in my own apartment. Mattie is totally jealous. Although it does make for good sleepovers. And she's excited about the pool too."

"Sounds nice."

"Yeah. And Frank is okay. I mean, he's not really like a dad. But then I don't need him to be a dad since I already have one." Jenna grinned. "I kinda had to have a talk with him about that."

"How so?"

"Well, he'd gotten the idea that he should act *fatherly* toward me." Jenna wrinkled her nose. "And, hey, it was sweet and everything, but totally unnecessary. And a little weird. Anyway, I set him straight and I think he was actually relieved. I told him I'd rather just have him as a friend and he was good with that."

"So he doesn't have any other children? I know he's a bit older than your mom, but I thought I'd heard he'd been married before."

"Nope. He and his ex-wife never had kids."

"Who never had kids?" Mabel asked as she came hopping into the living room.

"My step-dad—Frank."

"Oh." Mabel sat down next to Daphne. "But you're his kid, aren't you?"

"Yeah, kinda." Jenna smiled.

"Kinda like I'm Daphne's kid now." Mabel snuggled up next to Daphne.

Daphne wrapped an arm around Mabel, squeezing her closer. "So, tell me the truth. Did you really clean your room that fast?"

Mabel nodded with a somber expression. "You can check it if you want—even under my bed, and I laid out my church clothes like I'm s'posed to."

"Good girl." Daphne turned to Jenna. "We call it the Saturday Night Special. Mabel cleans her room up really nicely and then we order pizza."

"Did you order it yet?" Mabel asked eagerly.

Daphne glanced at her watch. "Not yet. But I will. And I better get dressed too. Sabrina will throw a fit if I don't put on the dress she got me for my birthday."

Both girls urged her to go get changed. Daphne wasn't sure if it was because they wanted to see her dressed up or because they wanted their pizza, but since the clock was ticking, she got moving.

By six-thirty, the pizza was on its way, Daphne was dressed in her new outfit, and both girls had given their approval. "The boots look just right," Jenna agreed after Daphne told them about the shoes Sabrina had wanted to get. "And there's Dad now."

"I'll get the door," Mabel yelled as she raced for it.

"Happy birthday!" Jake announced jovially as he came into the foyer with a large bouquet of the most beautiful roses Daphne had ever seen. They were a warm peach color with tinges of red around the edges, and each bloom looked perfect.

"Thank you!" She happily took the vase, pausing to sniff them. "They're beautiful."

"I was glad you weren't working at Bernie's Blooms today," he said as he leaned over to kiss her on the cheek, "otherwise I couldn't have surprised you very well."

"Did your mom get her gift okay?" Daphne savored the thrill from the peck on the cheek as she set the bouquet on the marble topped table in the foyer.

"Oh, I totally forgot," Jenna exclaimed. "Grandma McPheeters's birthday is today too."

Jake gave his daughter a kiss on the cheek as well. "Maybe you could call her. She'd love to hear from you."

"I'll do it right away." She turned to Daphne. "Isn't it cool that you and Grandma have the same birthday? She's my favorite grandma."

"Well, then I'm honored," Daphne told her.

Jake paused to look at Daphne. "Well you look absolutely

gorgeous, birthday girl. You ready to go?"

"I am." Daphne reached for her good coat, allowing Jake to help her into it. "The girls have pizza coming," she told him. "So they're all set."

"And a movie!" Mabel exclaimed as she eagerly herded them to the door. "Jenna brought a movie about penguins for me. You guys have fun!"

Jake laughed. "Looks like we're not needed here."

"Have a happy birthday dinner," Jenna called out with Mabel echoing her.

Daphne thanked them both, and suddenly it was just her and Jake, heading out into the frosty dark night toward his car. And yet she didn't feel the least bit cold.

"Have you had a good birthday so far?" he asked as he opened the passenger door for her.

"It's been delightful," she said as she slid into the seat. "No complaints."

As Jake closed the door and walked around to the driver's side, Daphne tried to make a decision—should she mention what she'd heard about Frank's plans to relocate, or should she just keep quiet? She supposed it was possible that Jake didn't even know yet, although that seemed unlikely in a town this small. Except that Jake had been away on a business trip. Plus there was that tiny possibility that Ricardo was wrong. And Jenna hadn't seemed to know anything about it. Or else she was simply hiding it well. And maybe Daphne was just making a mountain out of a mole hill. That was possible.

"You're being awfully quiet," Jake said as he slowly drove down her street. "Something on your mind?"

"Oh, no, not really. I mean, well, there's always *something* on my mind." She laughed nervously. "Guess it just comes with being a writer."

"Thinking about the advice column?" he asked.

"No, but I probably should be." She considered the *Dear*

Daphne letters she'd selected to use for the column. They would probably have to wait until Monday now, but since they weren't due until Thursday, that shouldn't be a problem.

"How's your novel coming along?"

"Mostly it's just been sitting lately. You know how I've been helping out at Bernie's Blooms. That's taking some time. By the way, was Olivia working today?" Daphne felt a wave of concern for her old best friend. About to have her first baby, Olivia had sounded a bit distraught the last time they'd talked.

"Olivia was there and—these are her words not mine—she is as big as a house. Although I must agree, she's got quite a baby bump going on."

Daphne laughed. "Well, Olivia is short so the baby makes her look pretty round. How did she *seem* though? I know she's getting pretty impatient, and her due date is still a couple weeks away."

"She seemed a little distracted and frazzled to me. I had to tell her several times what I wanted. That reminds me, she told me to tell you she's got something special for your birthday, but that you'll have to wait."

"Oh, she shouldn't have gone to any trouble. I would understand completely."

"Maybe she meant the baby," he joked. "She could be going into labor right now. Imagine having Olivia's baby born on your birthday. Would she name it after you?"

"Goodness, I hope not. At least I hope she's not having it tonight anyway."

"It's very generous that you're helping her with the birth, Daphne. She told me you're her coach and that you've been going to the classes with her. She seemed very appreciative."

"Yeah, Jeff just wasn't much into the whole Lamaze thing. And if her sister Bernie was alive, well, I'm sure she'd be doing it with Olivia. It seemed right that I should help. And it's actually been kind of interesting. Who knows...I might even use it in a book someday."

He chuckled. "But not in real life, eh?"

Daphne felt her cheeks warming. Was he asking her if she wanted to have a baby? And, really, thirty-five wasn't too old. She knew women who had waited to nearly forty to begin their families. "I wouldn't mind using it in real life...I mean if the timing was right and everything seemed to fit."

The car grew silent now, and Daphne suddenly regretted the direction she'd allowed their conversation to take, but she couldn't think of a graceful exit. And so she stuck her foot in her mouth.

"I heard a rumor," she blurted. "About Frank Danson."

"Oh?" Jake blew out what sounded like an exasperated sigh. "So word is already spreading—why am I surprised?"

"Then you know about it already?"

"That Frank plans to relocate to Miami?"

"Yes." She felt a mixture of relief and dread. "So it's really true then?"

"Unfortunately."

"Oh, dear." She pursed her lips, wishing she hadn't mentioned it.

"How did you hear?"

She explained about Sabrina and Ricardo. "I'd hoped it wasn't true."

"You and me both."

"When did you hear about it?" she asked meekly.

"Last night. Gwen sent me a text."

"Oh...."

Now there was another lengthy silence, and it wasn't until he pulled into The Zeppelin that she spoke. "Are you okay with it?" she asked quietly.

"*Okay?*" He let out a long sigh.

"Well, I'm sure you're not okay with it, Jake. I just meant, well, was it hard to hear...?"

"Yep." He parked the car then turned to look at her, and immediately his strained countenance softened. "But let's not allow it to spoil this evening, Daphne. I hadn't planned to even mention it to you. If you don't mind, I'd rather not talk about it at all."

"That's fine." She nodded. "I totally understand."

But as they walked into the restaurant, it felt like the old proverbial elephant in the room. How could they just ignore it? So, as they waited for their table, Daphne went over a number of other possible conversation topics, lining them up in her mind in the hopes she could pull them out as needed. As much for herself as for Jake. Because it really would be nice to enjoy this evening together. Who knew when they'd do it again...if ever.

By the time they were seated at a secluded table near the fireplace, Jake seemed to be in good spirits again. He told her a bit about his recent trip and how he'd been enjoying doing some legal consultation work. "It started up last fall, and I thought maybe it was just a fluke, but it seems to be continuing. This corporation has branches all over the country."

"And you like traveling a lot?"

"Well, I thought I did...at first. But I'm not so sure now. Flights all seem to be overbooked and people are generally rude. Plus, the airlines want to charge you for every little thing. Honestly, I won't be surprised if they start putting a credit card slot on the restrooms before long."

She laughed.

"Then there's all that security nonsense." He told her about witnessing the body-searching of an elderly woman who could barely even walk. "Meanwhile, this guy who seriously looked like a terrorist just sailed right on through. As much as I'm not into profiling, I had to just scratch my head over that one."

They continued to chat congenially throughout the meal. Just like old friends. And, Daphne reminded herself, that was just what they were. Well, not really *old* friends since she'd only met Jake last May when he'd handled her grandmother's will. Of course, at the time, she thought the old woman was actually her great aunt. Anyway, Jake had been a good friend then, and he was still a good friend now. And as much as she wished it could grow into something more, she felt uncertain. Despite his cheerful conversation, she could see that he was troubled. It showed in his serious dark eyes. This news about Jenna moving to Miami was troubling him a lot.

By the time dessert arrived—a complimentary piece of German chocolate cake for her birthday—Daphne knew she had to broach the subject again. And so after blowing out her candle, after making a wish that was more for Jake than it was for her, she spoke up.

"I know you don't want to talk about Jenna moving to Miami," she began carefully, "but I think it's because you don't want to spoil my birthday."

He shrugged. "It's not a happy subject, Daphne. Not for me anyway. Naturally, Gwen is over the moon about it—acting like she just won the lottery. And she's certain that Jenna will be ecstatic too—when she tells her." He sighed. "And who could blame Jenna if she were happy about it? Miami compared to Appleton? What teenage girl wouldn't be thrilled?"

Daphne wasn't so sure, especially after talking to Jenna earlier this evening. "I don't know...leaving her friends and her school, it may not be that easy."

"Like Gwen pointed out last night, Jenna will be doing that before long anyway. For college."

"That's true, but it's still a ways off."

"I remember when I took Jenna to Kauai for spring break a couple years ago. She absolutely loved surfing. She was sad to leave and she told me she wanted to live near a beach someday. Even talked about going to college in a beach town. No beaches around here."

"That's true." She felt surprised that Jake seemed to be adjusting to this idea. As if he really was trying to accept it—although his eyes were sad.

"Moving will be an adjustment for her...but she'll get over it. Not sure that I will though." Suddenly Jake looked so downhearted that Daphne regretted bringing up this depressing subject. What had she been thinking? Now it was time to encourage him.

"I'm curious," she began slowly, "would you ever consider relocating? Would you want to move to Miami? I do remember how you said you'd only remained in Appleton to be here for Jenna, to watch her grow up. I know this little town wasn't your first choice."

He barely nodded as he dipped his fork in the cake. "That's partly true. When Gwen and I split up—all those years ago—I promised Jenna that I would never quit being her dad. That kept me here. But then I got used to it."

"And everyone knows that your law career was always secondary to Jenna." This was one of the things she'd always admired most about Jake—his commitment to being a devoted dad.

"That's true."

"Well, Miami is a big place. I'm sure your law practice would flourish down there. Lots more potential than here in little Appleton. And I hear the weather is lovely." Daphne felt like she was intentionally sabotaging her own future. And yet she couldn't stop herself. How could she possibly be happy with Jake if he was miserably missing his daughter?

He frowned. "Believe me, I've considered that possibility."

"And it's not that long until Jenna starts college." She tried to keep a positive tone in her voice. "These last years with her are precious."

"Just a year and a half," he said glumly.

"Girls need their dads during the turbulent teen years,"

she said with all sincerity. "I don't know what I'd have done without my dad during my last years of high school. He was like my rock."

"Really?"

"Well, I didn't have a mother. And as much as I loved Aunt Dee, she seemed a bit old and stodgy to me by the time I was seventeen." She sighed. "It's kind of a shame that I didn't know as much about her as I do now. I probably would've turned to her more." She looked back into his eyes. "But teenage girls really do need their dads, Jake. I think you know that."

"I guess I do. At least I like to think so." He smiled sheepishly. "Although I sometimes feel like I need Jenna more than she needs me."

"I can understand that. I feel that way about Mabel at times. Oh, I realize she needs me, there's no denying that. But I never would've guessed how much I could need a child in my life. Not until I had her." And maybe she would be needing Mabel even more now—if Jake did decide to move to Miami. Had she really just encouraged him to do that? And yet, how could she have done anything else?

"After all you went through to keep Mabel, I'm sure you can understand how much you'd miss her if she was taken from you."

Daphne felt a small lump in her throat. She wasn't sure if it was for Jake or for herself—or perhaps both of them. "Yes...I would." She forced a smile. "But you really should be thankful, Jake."

"*Thankful?*" He grimaced. "What for?"

"That you have the sort of job you can do *anywhere*. Not everyone has that." She smiled even bigger. "You've been proving you can take your job with you by traveling for consulting. Maybe that's why you've gotten so interested in it recently. Almost like it's preparing you for what's next in your career."

His brow creased as he slowly nodded. "You know, that actually makes some sense."

"And can you imagine what fun it could be to take Jenna surfing in Miami?" She hoped the restaurant's dim light would conceal her misty eyes.

"I'm not sure the surfing is all that good down there, but the truth is I wouldn't mind doing some surfing myself." His eyes lit up ever so slightly. "I enjoyed it in Kauai."

"And I'll bet Gwen won't want to go surfing with Jenna."

He chuckled. "You got that right."

Daphne began talking about all the wonderful opportunities that would probably be awaiting him and his daughter if he relocated his law firm to Miami. She kept her voice cheerful and bubbling—almost as if imitating Sabrina. She rambled on about the adventures that he could share with Jenna in the last of her teen years, keeping her smile luminous and effervescent, talking about chances of a lifetime and how this was a decision he'd never regret—because he was doing it for his daughter. But the whole while she tried to sell him on Miami, it felt as if her heart was breaking, crumbling into a thousand little pieces.

Chapter 4

By Monday morning, Daphne grew weary of keeping on her brave front in regard to Jake. And so as soon as Mabel was at school, she carried her coffee mug over to Sabrina's house and let her hair down, telling Sabrina the details of her birthday date and how she'd managed to convince Jake that he should relocate his law practice to Miami.

"So I got to enjoy the first and last date—all in one night. How's that for efficient? But, really, it's probably for the best. I mean, not to drag it out. Better to just cut my losses and move on, right?" Daphne let out a long, sad sigh. "Jake and I decided that it probably wasn't wise to continue dating...under the current circumstances." Actually, it had been her suggestion, but he'd had no problem agreeing to it.

"This is exactly what I was afraid of." Sabrina refilled Daphne's mug. "That you'd get hurt by *that* man."

"It's not Jake's fault," Daphne said defensively. "It's not as if he *wanted* them to move to Miami."

"I know, I know." Sabrina sat back down. "It's just that I had a bad feeling about the whole thing."

"Yeah, you warned me." Daphne took a sip.

"It's always dicey going out with a man who's been married before—especially with kids involved. I know that from personal experience. I've already told you that Edward had been previously married. And even though his kids were nearly grown, they sometimes played havoc with our marriage." She laughed sarcastically. "Not that our marriage was in great shape to start with, but I've already told you about all that."

"I didn't know that Edward had children from his first marriage."

"Yeah, two girls. And it wasn't really his *first* marriage either. Oh, he told me it was, but I learned later that he'd been married in his twenties—only for a couple years. So I was actually wife number three." She shook her head. "And I found out that he'd cheated on his other wives the same as he did to me. Anyway, as much as I like Jake, I was worried for you. You really don't need a man with baggage. Especially now that you have Mabel to care for. You need a reliable, dependable guy. Someone who's ready to fit into your world, Daphne. Jake is obviously unable to do that."

Daphne almost regretted sharing her heartache with Sabrina now. "But it really isn't Jake's fault," she said for the second time. "It's Gwen and Frank who want to move to Miami."

Sabrina put a hand on Daphne's shoulder. "I'm sorry, Daph. I probably sound like I'm throwing out the baby with the bathwater."

Daphne couldn't help but laugh at that image in regard to Jake.

"But I'm desperate for you to find your Mr. Right."

Daphne just nodded. She wouldn't admit it, but she thought she had already found him. It was hard letting that dream die. And maybe she was wrong to give up on Jake. Maybe there was another way around it. What if they truly were meant for each other?

"But I want you to know that I am not giving up on finding you the right man, Daphne. In fact, I discussed this very thing with Ricardo just yesterday."

"You've really been seeing a lot of him, haven't you?"

Sabrina's whole face lit up. "Every chance I get! And I don't want to count my chickens before they hatch, but I think I'm really falling for that man and, unless I'm mistaken, I think he might be falling for me too. It's been so amazing." She giggled. "Seriously, I know I'm not everyone's cup of tea. Goodness knows I'm a little quirky. But it's not like I can change that. Not any more than a tigress can change her stripes." She chuckled.

"I wouldn't want you to change," Daphne told her. "I love you just the way you are, Sabrina. You're like a happy ray of southern sunshine."

"Thanks. I think Ricardo likes me for who I am too." Sabrina held up a long fingernail polished in sparkling silver. "But back to what I was saying. Yesterday, I told Ricardo that I was concerned about you getting hurt and that it sounded as if Jake planned to follow his daughter to Miami—and I asked Ricardo to help me."

"To help you how?"

"By helping us. To find your Mr. Right."

Daphne rolled her eyes. "I'm not sure I want any more help. It seems the harder I try, the worse it goes. I'd rather just wait...let time take its course...and if I'm meant to get married by May, well, maybe it will just happen. After all, I've given this whole thing to God. It seems like a lack of faith for me to go running ahead trying to find Mr. Right. And, quite frankly, I'm tired of looking. I'd rather just focus on my life as it is. Caring for Mabel, finishing my novel, helping Olivia to have her baby." Daphne patted her sweatshirt pocket to make sure she'd tucked her cell phone in it. "Did I tell you that she texted me last night? She thought she was in labor but it turned out to be Braxton Hicks."

"Braxton Hicks? Who in the world is that and does Jeff know?"

Daphne laughed. "It's a pre-labor thing. Kind of getting the muscles ready to give birth. I learned about it at the Lamaze class."

"So does that mean she'll have her baby soon?"

"Hard to say. I guess it can go on for a couple of weeks. Olivia told me she's determined to work every day this week. She hopes that the physical exercise will push her into labor. She's eager to hold that baby in her arms."

"Well, it is exciting, isn't it? Thinking about Olivia with a baby. And it's so sweet that you're helping her with the birth. You be sure and call me as soon as you know she's in real labor."

"Of course. After all, you're my backup for Mabel." Daphne slowly stood. "Thanks for listening to me whine a little, Sabrina. I actually feel better now."

"Well, like my mama used to always tell me, he's not the only fish in the sea. You be patient, and I'm sure the right fish will swim along." She winked. "And maybe some of your friends will help direct him your way."

Daphne grimaced but said nothing.

"Don't you get all worried. I promise I won't make a big deal about it. You just go on living your life like you said—and we'll just see how it goes, okay?"

Daphne made a stiff smile. She knew it would do no good to protest this. Sabrina would likely do as she pleased anyway.

On Tuesday morning, Mabel had all of her valentines finished and neatly stowed in her backpack. Dressed in her red Christmas dress and brightly striped leggings and boots, she looked very festive as she handed Daphne a homemade valentine. "I made this one for you." She smiled shyly. "I hope you like it."

Daphne looked down at the ornate card. It was trimmed with lace and glitter, but it was the words written in purple felt pen that took her by surprise. She read them aloud. "Happy Valentine's Day, *Mom*. Love Mabel." She turned to Mabel with misty eyes. "This is for me?"

"I know you're not really my mom," Mabel said quietly. "But you feel like a mom to me. I wondered if it was okay to call you Mom instead of Aunt Daphne."

Daphne bent down and, scooping Mabel into her arms, she kissed her cheek. "It's more than okay, Mabel. It's wonderful. I'm honored that you want to call me Mom." After a long hug, Daphne pointed toward the kitchen. "I have a valentine for you too," she said. "In there."

Mabel ran into the kitchen, letting out a happy whoop. "A *real* box of chocolates just for me?" She clutched the heart-shaped box to her chest. "I won't eat them all at once either. I promise."

"I'm sure you won't." Daphne watched as Mabel picked up the card, slowly opening the envelope and reading it.

"This is so beautiful. Thank you, Aunt—I mean, *Mom.*" She grinned.

"And there's something else." Daphne pointed to the small box wrapped in pink paper and tied with a purple ribbon.

"This is the best Valentine's Day ever!" Mabel exclaimed as she reached for the box, carefully removing the paper then opening the small white box. She gasped as she stared at the silver heart-shaped locket. "Does this really open up?" she asked eagerly. "I've always dreamed of having a heart necklace that opens up."

"It does." Daphne helped her to open it, revealing two tiny photos inside. One of Mabel and one of Daphne. "You can put different pictures in it if you—"

"*I love it!*" she declared happily. "Can I wear it to school today?"

"I think it's okay—just for today. Maybe not for everyday though." Daphne slipped the chain around her neck, securing the latch. "You wouldn't want to lose it on the monkey bars."

"Yeah, I'll wear it for special days and for church." She beamed at Daphne. "But today *is* a special day. Thanks, *Mom!*"

Daphne hugged her again. "Happy Valentine's Day, sweetie."

Daphne looked up from her desk to observe a florist truck stopping in front of her house. The van wasn't from Bernie's Blooms, but the large bouquet being carried by the delivery man was pretty spectacular looking. Daphne watched as he carried it up to Sabrina's door and, although she couldn't really hear her, Daphne imagined how Sabrina's happy shriek must've sounded.

As she shut down her computer, Daphne tried not to feel sorry for herself. Of course those flowers wouldn't be for her. Who would send her a valentine today? After all, hadn't she systematically rejected every chance for romance that had come her way this past year? Even to the point of encouraging Jake, the one man she'd had real interest in, to follow his daughter to Florida. Why should she receive flowers?

As she waited for the screen to go dark, she felt certain the bouquet was from Ricardo and, really, Daphne was happy for Sabrina. For both of them. She hoped that Sabrina was right—that they were both falling in love. They did make a sweet couple.

Glad to be finished with this week's advice column, Daphne pushed back her chair and gave her neck a good stretch. Time for a break. Maybe she would give herself the afternoon off from working on her novel. The weather was so nice today, she might even spend some time weeding in the garden. If the predictions for an early spring were correct, she should probably get a head start on it.

Daphne paused to admire her own beautiful bouquet on the marble-topped table in the foyer. The cheerful peachy roses still looked fresh and pretty. She could pretend that they were for Valentine's Day too. No need to go around being a sad sack today. She had much to be thankful for. A warm rush ran through her as she remembered Mabel's valentine—and how she wanted to call Daphne *Mom*. Really, what could be better?

As Daphne turned on the gas to heat the kettle, she felt her phone buzzing in her pocket. Removing it, she saw that the text was from Olivia. Thinking it was probably a Valentine's Day greeting, she scanned down then quickly turned off the stove and texted Olivia back. Hitting speed dial, she called Sabrina. "Olivia's in labor," she said quickly as she ran to her room to slip on a pair of loafers. "Her doctor said it's the real deal. I need to get to the hospital right now."

"That's great. I'll pick Mabel up at school. You let me know when the baby comes and I'll bring Mabel over to the hospital to see her."

Daphne thanked her then hurried out to her car. As she drove to the hospital, she prayed for Olivia and the baby. And she asked God to help her be a good birthing coach too. She had expected to be nervous, but by the time she made her way to the OB/GYN area, she was literally shaking.

"Get a grip," she told herself as she hurried down the hall to the nurses' desk, inquiring about Olivia. Before the nurse could answer, Daphne spotted Jeff frantically waving to her from a nearby room.

"How is she?" Daphne asked after she greeted him.

"She needs you." Jeff jerked his thumb into the room. "I'm useless at this kind of stuff."

"Yeah, I hear you faint at the sight of blood," she teased.

"What can I say?" He shrugged, clearly embarrassed. "Thanks for coming."

"Olivia," Daphne exclaimed as she came into the room.

"You're going to have a Valentine's baby!"

"Yes." Olivia made a huffing sound. "Help me!"

For the next few hours, Daphne remained by Olivia's side, helping her to breathe through the contractions, feeding her ice chips between them, encouraging her that it *wouldn't be long now.* Jeff turned out to be worse than useless with some less than helpful comments. And when Olivia exploded at him for telling her to "buck up," Daphne gently but firmly excused him from the room. He didn't seem the least bit offended by this.

Shortly before six o'clock that evening, a healthy baby girl entered the world. Daphne was surprised by her own tears, but then she'd never seen a miracle like this before. "I can't believe it," she said over and over as the nurse whisked the wailing infant away.

"Is she okay?" Olivia asked in a hoarse voice.

"She's perfectly beautiful," Daphne assured her, using the damp washcloth to swab Olivia's flushed face and offering her a drink of water. "You did great, Livvie. What a trooper."

"I'm so glad it's over with." Olivia closed her eyes. "I've never done anything so difficult. Thanks for helping me."

"Seven pounds, six ounces," the nurse announced.

"Go look at her for me," Olivia urged Daphne. "Make sure she's really okay."

Daphne went over to watch as the baby was bathed and the bottoms of her tiny feet were inked and printed onto a card. Finally, she was diapered and dressed and wrapped snugly in a pink blanket. "Here." The nurse placed her in Daphne's arms. "Take her to Mommy."

As Daphne stared down into the wide dark blue eyes, it felt like she was looking into eternity. "She's beautiful," she whispered as she set her in Olivia's arms. "Happy Valentine's Day," she said quietly. "I'll go get Jeff."

Relieved to hear that he was finally a father, Jeff picked up a bouquet of pale pink roses and hurried to his wife's side,

MELODY CARLSON

apologizing profusely for his earlier ineptness and exclaiming over the baby. Naturally, Olivia completely forgave him, and Daphne snapped a few family photos. But standing back and watching the couple happily reunited with their sweet little newborn, Daphne suddenly felt like a fifth wheel.

"I need to call Sabrina and check on Mabel," she told them as she stepped away.

"Tell them to come see her," Olivia called out. "I want everyone to meet my little Bernadette."

Daphne smiled. Of course, Olivia would name her baby after her sister—a lovely young woman who had died too soon. Perfect.

Before long Sabrina arrived with Mabel. Both were eager to see the newborn and congratulate the parents, but shortly thereafter Sabrina asked to be excused. "I told Ricardo I'd go out with him tonight if Olivia's baby made it on time," she whispered to Daphne. "You don't mind, do you?"

"Of course not." Daphne thanked her for watching Mabel then said her own goodbyes to Olivia and Jeff. "Enjoy your little valentine," she called out as she and Mabel left.

"I wish we could have a baby too," Mabel said longingly as they went past the nursery window.

Daphne tried not to laugh. "Well, you really need both a mommy and a daddy to have a baby, Mabel. Anyway, that's the best way to start a family."

"But you're a mommy and you have me," Mabel said as they walked through the lobby. "And we're a family. Even without a daddy."

Daphne laughed as she grasped Mabel's hand, swinging it as they exited the hospital. "You're exactly right. We are a family. A perfect little family—just the two of us."

Chapter 5

Daphne and Mabel decided to have a quiet dinner at home that night. Together they made Mabel's favorite meal. "Mac 'n' cheese 'n' peas." They had just sat down at the kitchen table when Daphne noticed Ricardo parking his SUV in Sabrina's driveway. As he got out, she could see that he was dressed up. Wearing a dark suit, he looked quite handsome, and the spring in his step suggested he was anticipating a fun evening with Sabrina.

"Look at Sabrina." Mabel pointed out the window. "She's got on her new dress."

Daphne turned to see Sabrina stepping onto her porch. With her blonde hair in an up-do and wearing a happy smile and a pink dress with a flowing skirt, she looked delicate and pretty as she waved to Ricardo.

"She looks like a fairy princess," Mabel said dreamily.

"They make a gorgeous couple, but we probably shouldn't stare." Daphne lowered the shade.

"Yeah, they probably wanna kiss or something." Mabel giggled.

After dinner, Daphne helped Mabel with her homework. When that was done, they watched half of an old Disney video together. "We'll have to finish it tomorrow," Daphne announced, ignoring Mabel's protests as she clicked the TV off. "It's already a little past your bedtime, and tomorrow's a school day." She herded Mabel up the stairs, supervising as she brushed her teeth.

Then as Mabel got ready for bed, Daphne sat down on the chair, taking up the book she'd been reading aloud at bedtime. It was the same book that Aunt Dee used to read to Daphne when she was a girl, spending a night in this exact same bedroom—*Little House on the Prairie*.

"This was a great day," Mabel said as she pulled on her nightgown. "The kids liked my valentines, and Olivia had a baby girl." She came over to Daphne, fingering the silver locket. "But this was the best part. I love my heart necklace."

"Turn around," Daphne said, "and we'll take it off so that it doesn't get broken while you're sleeping. I know how much you toss and turn."

"Yeah. I don't wanna break it ever." Mabel spun around.

Daphne removed the locket and set it on the dresser as Mabel hopped into bed. Then Daphne sat back down and read a chapter, and as tempted as she was to continue, she knew that little girls needed their sleep. And so she listened to Mabel's prayers, kissed her goodnight, and turned off the lamp.

As Daphne went downstairs, she knew she had every reason to be perfectly happy. And in so many, many ways, she truly was...and yet it felt that something was missing. But perhaps it was simply how her life was meant to go.

She sat down to read but found herself too distracted. She wondered how Olivia and Jeff were doing with their new baby. Then she thought about Sabrina and Ricardo out for their Valentine's Day date. And then she thought about how Mick Foster had recently gotten engaged to the beautiful Julianne

Preston—they were probably having a good celebration. Even her dad, who'd gotten married last fall, was probably enjoying a romantic evening.

She picked up the pretty journal and matching pen from the side table. It had been a birthday gift from Olivia, and Daphne was determined to put it to use—although she had never been good at journaling. Instead of writing a journal entry, she found herself writing a Dear Daphne letter.

> *Dear Daphne,*
>
> *I feel like the only person in the world who cannot find romance. It seems that all my friends and relatives are out enjoying Valentine's Day tonight. And I am home alone. Oh, I'm not really alone. I have a precious little girl sleeping in her bed upstairs. But my heart feels lonely. Here is my question: Is it possible that I have some secret desire to live my life as a spinster? The reason I think this is because I have managed to push away every single man that has shown the slightest interest in me. Am I crazy? Or am I simply destined to live my life as a single woman? And if that's so, why am I feeling so sad about it?*
>
> *Anxious in Appleton*

Without giving her words a great deal of thought—the same way she sometimes answered the real *Dear Daphne* letters for the advice column—she started to write.

> *Dear Anxious,*
>
> *First of all, you are not the only person in the world who doesn't have a romantic relationship. Millions live perfectly contented lives as single people. So stop feeling sorry for yourself. Secondly, you need*

to count your blessings—starting with that precious
little girl. But as to your question about spinsterhood
and whether you are secretly sabotaging your life—I
would have to say no. If you had truly loved any of
the men that you claim to have "pushed away," I
suspect you would have welcomed them with open
arms. Perhaps you just need to be more patient until
the right man comes along.
  Daphne

Daphne set down her pen with an exasperated sigh. "Oh, poppycock!" she said as she tore the pages she'd just written, crumpling them up into a tight wad that she chucked into the fireplace. "Daphne doesn't have all the answers."

She stood up and got the fireplace matches and, lighting a long stick, proceeded to burn the silly letter. As she watched it burning, she thought of the men that had walked into and out of her life this past year. Harrison Henshaw, the attractive architect she'd met speed dating, but who had seemed more interested in himself than her. Then there'd been Mick Foster, although she'd never been sure if his flirting was sincere or not, but never mind because he was engaged now. And Mick's friend Collin—well, Daphne couldn't shake that guy off quickly enough. Even Ricardo had seemed interested in Daphne at first—or maybe it was Daphne's dad who had been trying so hard to get them together. But now Ricardo seemed to be smitten by Sabrina. And then there'd been Mabel's uncle—Daniel had actually proposed to her shortly before Christmas... and she had rejected the handsome marine. But at least they were pen-pals now. But Daniel hadn't been her only proposal since moving to Appleton. Her old beau, the man she at one time thought she couldn't live without, had shown up with marriage on his mind. But when Ryan Holloway showed his true colors, she sent him packing.

Then there was Jake. Well, actually he'd been in the running since the first day she'd met him. That day when he'd told her the ridiculous conditions of Aunt Dee's will—and told her the truth about who Aunt Dee had really been. As much as Jake had sometimes aggravated her—probably more due to the crazy will than anything else—her heart had always done a happy little flip whenever she saw him. And now she had driven him away too. She wiped a stray tear from her cheek and chided herself for being so silly and sentimental. Maybe she really needed to take *Dear Daphne*'s advice and simply be more patient. Really, what choice did she have?

The next two weeks passed by in a whirl of busy activities. Between parenting Mabel, filling in at Bernie's Blooms, writing the *Dear Daphne* column, working on her novel, which was nearly done, visiting Olivia and her new baby, getting some gardening in...Daphne's life was full. So full in fact that she had little time to feel sorry for herself in regard to Jake. So when he popped into Bernie's Blooms in early March, inviting her to meet him for coffee, she felt pleasantly surprised. Was it possible that he'd changed his mind about going to Miami?

"Olivia is coming in at two," Delia told him. "Will that work for you?"

He smiled brightly. "Perfect. See you at two."

When Olivia came to the shop, she had Baby Bernadette with her. Of course, Daphne had to spend some time cooing to the tiny cherub, and then she told Olivia about her coffee date. "Well, it's not really a date. Just meeting for coffee." She glanced at the clock. "But I better go."

Daphne attempted to quiet her nerves as she walked down the street toward Red River Coffee Company. She wished that this were a date, that she was meeting Jake to gaze fondly in his dark brown eyes, but she knew that was silly. From what she'd heard around town, he'd already sold his law firm. Although rumors were sometimes wrong...or people could change their minds. Still, as she went into the coffee shop, she was determined not to get her hopes up.

Jake waved from a table in back, pointing to the second coffee already on the table. Of course, he'd ordered a latte for her. She fixed a smile on her face and, acting as if nothing whatsoever was wrong, strolled toward him. They exchanged greetings and sat down and, for a long moment, neither of them spoke.

"You're looking good," he said cheerfully. "But then you always look good."

"Thanks," she said, suddenly feeling self-conscious.

"I'm going to miss you, Daphne."

"So, you really are going then?" She felt her heart sinking.

His brow creased. "You said it was such a great idea—you encouraged me—I thought you—"

"Of course, it's the right thing to do." She forced a bigger smile. "It's just that I'll miss you, Jake."

Jake didn't say anything, just gazed at her with a sad expression.

"I mean, you've been a good friend to me," she said quickly, worried that she'd said too much about missing him. "But I do think you've made the right choice. I haven't seen Jenna lately, but I'm sure she's thrilled that you're going to Miami too."

He nodded grimly. "Jenna was pretty upset when Gwen told her they were moving. But when she heard I was relocating too, well, you were right, Daphne, it made a huge difference. I meant to call you and thank you for our little counseling session, but I've been so busy getting everything in order to leave. My plan is to get out there before spring break—that's when Frank plans to move them out. I want to be settled in my apartment by then. It's just a tiny one bedroom, but Miami real estate is pretty spendy. Not like in good old Appleton.

And although I listed my house here, with your step-mom as a matter of fact, it'll probably take until summer for it to sell."

"It sounds like you really have been busy."

"Trying to get everything worked out, which is one reason I wanted to meet with you today." He pulled a business card out of his pocket and slid it across the table to her. "I've handed your case over to Warren Thornton."

"My case?" She frowned at the card.

"You know, Dee's will and the estate and all that. I totally trust Wally, and I made it clear that this was a very special case. He understands all the details of it."

"Oh..." She picked up the card, studying it as if it were very important. So that was why he wanted to meet with her—to hand her off to another attorney.

"I have to admit that it's kind of a relief to pass this onto someone else, Daphne. It hasn't exactly been easy. I mean, being friends with you—and dealing with Dee's will."

She nodded. "I know. But thank you for all you've done, Jake. I really do appreciate it." She slipped the business card into her purse then took a big gulp of her coffee, scalding her tongue, which caused her eyes to get watery. "Oh, that's hot." She set down the cup and grabbed a napkin, blotting her lips. "I burnt my mouth."

"Can I get you some ice water?"

"No, I really should go. Olivia is at the shop by herself with the baby, and I'm not sure she's really up to that yet." She abruptly stood.

"Okay." He stood too, looking at her with what seemed like sadness in his eyes. "Wally will take good care of you, Daphne. If you need anything or have questions, feel free to call him...or call me."

"Thanks. And I hope your move to Miami goes smoothly. I'm sure you've got a lot to do, Jake. I don't want to keep you from it." And then, knowing she had real tears in her eyes, she hurried out of the coffee shop, practically running down the street.

When she burst into Bernie's Blooms, Olivia was helping a man at the cash register, but Daphne could hear Bernadette crying in back. "I'll go check on the baby," she said as she rushed toward the backroom. And then, rocking the wailing infant in her arms, Daphne allowed her tears to flow too.

Chapter 6

Daphne was surprised to see that it was already the second Tuesday of March, which meant tonight was critique group. And since Sabrina had insisted on hosting tonight, Daphne would need to get a babysitter. Unsure whether Jenna was available, she decided to give her a call before school that morning.

"Yeah, I'd love to come over. I've been missing Mabel a lot."

"I thought you were probably pretty busy...I mean with school and everything." Daphne couldn't bring herself to mention the move.

"You mean with *moving,*" Jenna said with a slightly bitter edge.

"I know it's coming up soon."

"Too soon, if you ask me. Frank's already in Miami, and Mom says we have to join him as soon as spring break starts."

Daphne arranged to pick up Jenna at six-thirty...then realized this meant she needed to break the sad news to Mabel. Best to just get it over with, she thought as she pulled on her coat to walk Mabel to school. Like pulling off a Band-Aid.

"Jenna is going to stay with you tonight," Daphne said as they left the house.

"Yay!" Mabel started doing her happy dance.

"But I need to tell you something that you're not going to

like," Daphne began.

"*What?*" Mabel asked in alarm.

"Jenna is going to be moving far away—in about a week. This might even be your last chance to spend time with her."

"No!" Mabel stopped walking, planting a foot and folding her arms in front of her. "Jenna can't move away."

"I know how you feel, sweetie." Daphne wrapped an arm around her, nudging her to continue walking. "I don't want her to move either."

"Why does she have to move?" Mabel demanded.

Daphne gave a simple explanation and even mentioned that Jake was moving too.

"Jake *and* Jenna?" Mabel's frown grew bigger. "That's not fair."

So Daphne explained how Jenna would need her dad nearby, and how Jake would want to be around for Jenna's last years of high school.

"I want them to stay here in Appleton," Mabel declared. "I want everyone I love to stay here."

"I know." Daphne nodded. "I do too. But unfortunately that's not how life works. Sometimes people have to go away."

Mabel peered at her with troubled eyes. "You won't ever go away, will you, Mom?"

It still tugged at her heartstrings to hear Mabel calling her that. "No, Mabel, I will never go away from you, not if I can help it. Wild horses couldn't drag me away."

Mabel smiled. "Are there any wild horses around here?"

"Not that I know of." She used a finger to wipe a stray bit of oatmeal off Mabel's chin.

Mabel didn't look entirely convinced of this as they continued walking. To be fair, a lot of people had left Mabel already. Her dad abandoned her at birth. Her mom died of an overdose. Her grandmother recently passed away with cancer. Even her uncle had to leave in order to finish his tour of duty in the Marines. And now Jenna and Jake were going too. It was no wonder she was concerned.

When they were in front of the school, Daphne knelt down, wrapping her arms around Mabel. "I love you, Mabel, and I'm your mom now, and I never plan to leave you. Okay?"

Mabel nodded somberly. "Okay."

"I'm sorry Jenna has to go, but at least you've enjoyed getting to know her. And we can keep in touch with email and stuff."

"Can we have pizza tonight?" Mabel asked meekly.

"Of course."

"Can I stay up a little bit past my bedtime?"

"I think that would be okay."

Mabel brightened. "Thanks, Mom."

"Have a good day, sweetie." Daphne kissed her cheek and then watched as Mabel ran up to greet a friend who was going into the building.

Consoling herself that Mabel was probably more resilient than most eight-year-olds, Daphne headed back toward home. She was slightly surprised that Mabel was so concerned over Jake's leaving too, but then she realized that Jake had gone out of his way to befriend Mabel some time ago. Naturally, she looked up to him. And Daphne knew it was important for Mabel to have good father figures in her life. Perhaps it was time to invite her dad and Karen over for a Sunday dinner again—for some grandparent time.

As Daphne went back to work in her office, she felt relieved to know she wasn't hosting the critique group tonight. Mostly because she'd neglected some housekeeping chores lately. Nothing too serious, and only because she'd been busy helping Olivia at the flower shop—but she didn't want to feel pressured to scramble to get everything in apple-pie order in time for the group.

Especially now that she was so close to finishing her novel.

She'd been encouraged to learn that Olivia had hired a part-time girl over the weekend. This gave Daphne more time to devote to writing. Her plan was to finish the novel by the end of the week and start working on edits next week. She'd already started querying agents and had been invited by a couple of New York agencies to send a completed manuscript. She knew that her bio, as well as her sample chapters, was garnering a little bit of attention. Not so much her stint writing for the *New York Times*, but her "anonymous contribution to a national advice column" (that she explained couldn't be disclosed without a contractual agreement—advice from Jake).

Daphne's hope—and maybe it was unrealistic—was to contract her first novel and earn enough money to allow her to remain in Appleton with or without Aunt Dee's sizeable estate. And with May quickly creeping up, she knew she needed to make a plan for her financial future. Jake had made it clear that, even though she'd "inherited" the *Dear Daphne* column, the agreement had only been for a year—and the proceeds from the column were tied into the estate. After the year expired in May, Daphne could lose the syndicated column along with everything else.

Daphne had already started a vitae that she planned to take to the local newspaper as soon as her novel was finished. She hoped to secure a position on the writing staff. And Olivia had offered her a fulltime position at the flower shop, but she could only afford minimum wage. Not enough to live on with a child to support. So Daphne had declined. Still, she was not giving up. There had to be something out there for her. A way to support herself and Mabel. But it was hard not to feel discouraged or anxious.

Daphne usually tried not to dwell on these things—she knew it was better to pray than to worry—but as the days kept marching past, it was hard not to give her future some serious consideration.

And now, instead of working on her novel, like she wanted to, she knew she needed to finish up the last letter for this week's advice column. She'd selected the letter last week, but now that it was time to wrap it up, she wasn't so sure she wanted to answer it. In fact, parts of the letter hit rather close to home. Probably why she'd picked it in the first place. She paused to read it again.

Dear Daphne,

I will turn forty this summer and I have never been married or engaged or even in a romantic relationship that lasted more than a couple of months. And I hate to sound conceited, but I am reasonably attractive and fairly well educated and some people find me rather amusing. I have a fantastic job, a nice apartment, and some great friends. But everyone around me keeps telling me that I should be married by now. And to be honest, I agree with them. I had always planned to be married by the time I turned thirty.

The problem, according to my best friend, is that I am way too picky. She says that I don't give guys a chance. I think it's because I've got this preconceived notion of what my man should be like. I have imagined him and dreamed of him for years. He is my own special prince and naturally, he is perfect and wonderful, handsome and smart, and he is head over heels in love with me.

My friend tells me I'm living in a fairytale fantasy that can never come true. She keeps urging me to date these average, ho-hum, boring guys—men that I feel no attraction to. She tells me that I should just settle with the best guy I can find and work to create a good life out of it. I think that I might rather

remain single than to do that. What do you suggest?
Prince-less Princess in Portland

Dear Prince-less Princess,
I am guessing by your letter that you might be
a Type A personality, that you love perfection and
like keeping your world under control. It sounds as
if you've created yourself a nearly perfect life—and
there is nothing wrong with that. The only problem
is that no one is perfect—not even you. If you are
waiting for your Mr. Right to show up in the perfect
package that you have imagined for all these years,
you will probably have to wait forever. Or if he does
show up, you will probably discover (before long)
that he is not as perfect as you'd expected. Perhaps
that has already happened to you in one of your
short-lived romances.
Should you settle for an average, ho-hum, boring
guy? My answer would be a definite no. You would
probably be miserable, and the guy would be as
well. You need to ask yourself if you could really
be happily married to an imperfect man—because
that is all that is out there. And if you cannot accept
that, than you would be better off to remain single.
And your letter suggests that you are contented
with being single. So unless you can adjust your
expectation for a "dream prince," you might as well
keep sleeping.
Daphne

As Daphne added this letter to the others and sent it on to
the manager who handled the syndication, she told herself
that she was not really like the prince-less princess. Yes, she
had rejected a number of suitors, but it wasn't because they

weren't "perfect." It was because she hadn't fallen in love with any of them. She felt certain that she could fall in love with an "imperfect" man. In fact, she probably already had. The problem was that he hadn't returned her feelings.

Still, as she opened up her novel document, instead of focusing on the last chapter like she wanted to do, she continued to ponder the main question in the letter. About settling. Was Daphne willing to settle if it secured her future? Wouldn't that be the selfless thing to do? In order to provide for Mabel? Shouldn't she at least consider it? What if being idealistic and holding out for "true love with her prince" landed her and Mabel in the poorhouse? Oh, she knew there was no such thing as a poorhouse anymore, but what if Mabel had to go without because Daphne was too stubborn to settle?

These answerless questions were disturbing—and distracting! Daphne knew she needed to just give them to God. Praying for him to direct her path and to provide for her and Mabel, she handed her worries to God then got back to work.

Mabel had mostly recovered from her sadness and shock by the time Jenna hopped into the car with them that evening. And it probably helped that Daphne had given Mabel a little pep talk about not making Jenna feel too bad. "She's not happy about the move either," Daphne had confided to Mabel. "So we should probably try to be encouraging to her."

To Daphne's relief, Mabel was her usual bubbly self, telling Jenna about the plans for the evening. "And Mom said I can stay up past my bedtime too."

"Just half an hour," Daphne reminded her. "And that's only if you're all ready for bed—in your PJs with brushed teeth." She smiled to herself, knowing this actually meant Mabel was only staying up an extra fifteen minutes since it usually took her that long to get ready for bed.

The pizza truck arrived shortly after they got home, and before long Daphne was headed for Sabrina's. She still thought it was amusing that Sabrina wanted to write a romance novel, but she was impressed with Sabrina's discipline to stick with it. Her friend was already starting her third chapter and, really, it wasn't too bad.

Ricardo, who was working on a cookbook for men, was already there, making himself useful in the kitchen. And Spencer arrived shortly after Daphne. As much as she had enjoyed getting acquainted with Spencer, after Jake set her up on that blind date last fall, she hadn't felt any attraction to him. Although as she greeted him, inviting him into Sabrina's living room, she wondered if he was the kind of guy she could "settle" with if it was her only way to preserve her inheritance and care for Mabel.

Spencer was a nice man. Polite, well spoken, congenial, and thoughtful. And he wasn't a bad writer either. She liked the direction his suspense novel was taking. As she handed him a cup of coffee with cream, she vaguely wondered what it would be like for two novelists to be married. And in the next instant she chided herself for thinking such a thing.

Before long, Mick and Wally arrived and the critiquing began. As she listened to the members of the group taking their turns to read, it occurred to her that, since the inception of this group not so long ago, everyone in here had become romantically involved with someone. Everyone except her and Spencer. Mick was engaged. Wally was dating Ricardo's mother. Ricardo and Sabrina were dating each other. Only Spencer and she were still single. Did it mean anything? Certainly not. But it was interesting.

After Spencer read his short chapter, she was the first one to offer critique. Daphne mostly praised his work, only offering a couple of suggestions for improvement. "I'm so impressed," she said finally. "You're writing seems to be getting better and better."

He beamed at her. "Thanks, Daphne. That's encouraging."

When the critique group wound to an end, Daphne helped to clear the coffee mugs and dessert plates, rinsing them in the kitchen sink. She was just finishing up when Spencer joined her. "I really did appreciate your kind words," he said quietly. "It means a lot coming from you since you're the most seasoned writer of the group, and I admire your skills immensely."

"Well, thank you." She smiled at him as she dried her hands.

"And I didn't want to sound overly effusive about what you read tonight," he lowered his voice, "because I don't want to make anyone else feel slighted, but it was really very good. I'm sure that you'll find an agent to represent your work. I'll bet that your novel will be published by next year."

"That would be amazing." She sighed. "And most welcome. Thanks for saying that."

Now the others came into the kitchen, and talk shifted to the news that Mick and Julianne had set a wedding date. "We want to have it before the nursery and landscaping business gets too busy," he explained. "And that means we can't wait very long. Julianne decided on the second Saturday in April. It won't be anything fancy. Just a small ceremony and a reception in the barn, but you're all invited." He laid down a piece of paper. "Julianne is sending save-the-date messages this week, so if you could write down your email addresses or phone numbers, she can get something to you."

"That's so exciting," Sabrina told him. "I'm sure it'll be a gorgeous wedding in that wonderful barn of yours. I can't wait." She glanced at Ricardo, and Daphne could tell Sabrina was hoping that they'd go together. Daphne figured she'd probably need to go on her own, but at least she could take Mabel. And maybe that was how it was going to be from here on out...maybe it was time to just get used to it.

Chapter 7

When Daphne got home from critique group, she realized that she hadn't really made a plan for getting Jenna back to her house. She also knew that Gwen wouldn't appreciate being called to come get her. And so she called Sabrina, hoping she might catch Ricardo before he left since his SUV was still in the driveway. He probably wouldn't mind giving Jenna a lift. But by the time Sabrina answered, the SUV was already heading down the street.

"Sorry to bother you, but would you mind popping over for a few minutes while I run Jenna home? I totally forgot she need—"

"Not at all. I'll be there in a jiffy."

Two minutes later, Sabrina arrived and Daphne and Jenna left. "I couldn't tell you how devastated Mabel was to hear you were moving," Daphne confessed as she backed out of the driveway. "I encouraged her to put on her brave face for you tonight. I hope she did."

"She was fabulous. I should take lessons," Jenna said glumly.

"Are you getting used to the idea yet?"

"I suppose I'm *used* to it, I just don't like it. I hate leaving my friends and my school."

"Your dad said you like to surf. That's lots easier to do in

Miami than Appleton," Daphne offered brightly.

"Yeah, surfing would be fun." Jenna's tone lightened. "I'm so glad Dad's decided to move too. He just left to go down there on Monday, but you probably knew that already."

"I knew he was getting ready to leave." Daphne felt the sting of sadness to think he was gone—gone without even telling her a final goodbye. But then, why should he?

"I don't know what I would've done if Dad wanted to stay here in Appleton. I mean, besides being totally miserable. It'll make it easier having him around. Someone I can crash with and complain about how much I hate living there."

"Maybe you won't want to complain. I mean, lots of people would love to live in Miami. Close to the beach and so warm year round. I'll bet you'll end up liking it."

"That's what Mom keeps saying."

"And maybe you'll invite friends like Mattie to come down and visit you."

"That'd be cool." She nodded. "I hadn't even thought of that."

"At the very least it should be a great adventure. And since you want to be a writer, you really should welcome seeing new places, meeting new people—it makes for good story fodder."

"I guess so."

"And before long you'll be in college anyway. You can live where you like."

"Are you sad that my dad's gone?" Jenna said abruptly.

"Oh, well...yeah, sure. He's been a good friend to me."

"I thought you guys were *more* than just friends."

"Well, I suppose we might've been...but we never really got the chance."

"And now you never will?"

"Never say never." Daphne forced a smile.

"Hey, maybe you and Mabel could move to Miami too."

Daphne chuckled. Somehow she just couldn't imagine that, but she didn't want to discourage Jenna. "Yeah, maybe I'll sell my new novel for a boatload of money and then we could live anywhere we want."

"Would you want to move to Miami then?" Jenna sounded doubtful.

"I'm not sure." She sighed. "To be honest, I got pretty tired of the big city life when I lived in New York. And I'm really fond of Appleton. Plus Mabel has her friends and her school to consider."

"*See*! It's the exact same for me—my friends and my school are here *too*! But my mom won't even acknowledge that. She keeps telling me this is the opportunity of a lifetime. For *her* maybe."

Daphne had never heard Jenna be this vocal or negative, and it was somewhat alarming. It probably really was good that Jake had gone down there.

"It's like since I'm not eighteen, I don't get a vote. Like I don't matter. I have no life, no opinion, no say whatsoever. Seriously, it makes me wanna scream and pull my hair out."

"I'm so sorry, Jenna." Daphne glanced over at her as she stopped for a traffic light.

"Yeah, me too." Jenna sort of collapsed into herself now, folding her arms across her chest with an exasperated sigh.

Daphne wasn't sure what to say. There seemed nothing to say that could change anything. Maybe it was time to change the direction entirely. "I, uh, I told Mabel that maybe we could stay in touch with you, Jenna. I realize you'll be busy with your new school and whatnot, but if you don't mind, we'd like to send you a note now and then—just to connect. Mabel loves you so—"

"That'd be cool. And I'll write back too. I promise."

"Great." Daphne pulled into the drive-around in front of the big house, which now had a FOR SALE sign in front. "I know spring break is next week, Jenna, so if I don't see you before you leave, I hope it all goes well for you. You'll be in my prayers."

"Thanks." Jenna reached for her bag.

"And thanks for being such a good friend and babysitter for Mabel." She grinned. "If you need references, just give them my number."

"I don't actually do much babysitting anymore. Except for Mabel. She's a special case. I doubt I'll do it at all in Miami." Jenna wrinkled her nose. "After all, my step-daddy is rich, I don't need to earn money."

"Oh." Daphne nodded with uncertainty. "Well, I appreciate it even more now."

Jenna blew her a kiss. "Take care, Daphne. And stay in touch."

Daphne blew a kiss back. "You too, sweetie!"

As Jenna jogged up to the house, Daphne felt another wave of sadness rushing over her. Similar to how she'd felt when she parted ways with Jake. Perhaps not as deep, but for some reason it felt even more final. As if this was really it. They were leaving Appleton for good. She remembered how Mabel had protested this news just this morning, how she'd stomped her little foot and rejected the whole thing as unfair. Well, that was exactly how Daphne felt as she drove back home. It was all unfair.

Daphne invited her dad and Karen to come over for Sunday dinner after church. Partly to reassure herself—and Mabel—that they still had loved ones around. And partly because Karen had fixed them a meal the last time they'd gathered.

"Why don't you call Grandma Karen *Mom?*" Mabel asked as they were setting the dining room table together. Mabel had eagerly accepted Daphne's dad's invitation to call them Grandpa and Grandma, although she added the "Karen," probably out of respect for her grandma who had died last fall.

"I don't know." Daphne carefully set a stack of Aunt Dee's

best china plates on the table. "I never really thought about it before. I just call her Karen."

"Is it because she doesn't feel like your real mom?" Mabel looked up with sympathetic eyes.

"I guess that could be it."

"You've never told me anything about your real mom. Except that she died when you were a little kid. Just like me. But do you remember her?"

"I don't have a lot of memories, but yes I remember her." Daphne set the plates in front of the chairs. "She was very kind and gentle, and she had a really sweet voice."

"Kinda like you?"

Daphne smiled at Mabel. "Well, I'd like to think I'm like her. But I really don't look much like her. I take after Aunt Dee."

"And Aunt Dee was really your grandma," Mabel added.

"That's right. But I never knew that until this past year. So I still think of her as my great aunt."

"I can't remember hardly anything about my mom."

"Oh...?"

"Except this one time when I ran out into the street and she grabbed me by the hand and jerked me back to her. It hurt my arm, and I thought she was being mean, but I guess she was keeping me from getting run over by a car."

"So maybe she saved your life."

Mabel's eyes grew larger. "Yeah, I guess so."

"Well, God bless your mommy for that."

Mabel just nodded. "Do you think Mommy is with Grandma in heaven?"

Daphne felt uncertain. "I'm not a real expert on that sort of thing, but I do know this—God loves us more than we can ever understand. And he loves to forgive us and to welcome us into his kingdom, so it seems like he would happily do that for your mom."

"That's kind of like what Pastor Andrew said when he came

to talk to our Sunday school class today."

"He talked to your class?"

"Yeah. Joselyn had a question about heaven last week and Miss Conrad didn't know the answer, so Pastor Andrew came today. And he said something kind of like what you said."

Daphne felt relieved.

"Pastor Andrew said there will be lots of good surprises in heaven. Like people we didn't think would be there. And he said it will be like Disneyland, only way, way, way better." Mabel frowned. "But I don't know what Disneyland is really like 'cause I never went there before."

"It's been a long time since I've been there, but as I recall it was pretty amazing. But I can imagine how heaven would be way, way, way better."

"Do you think my mommy and your mommy are friends up in heaven?" Mabel set the last pieces of silverware down.

"Wouldn't that be fun if they *were* friends?" Daphne smiled to think of it. "That's just how I'm going to imagine them from now on."

"And Grandma Vera too?"

"Yes. And Aunt Dee. They're probably all up there having some fantastic tea party right now."

"Or flying through the air with the angels?"

"That sounds like even more fun." Daphne glanced out the front window to see Karen's yellow Mustang pulling into the driveway. "There's Grandpa and Grandma Karen now. You go greet them at the door, and I'll go check on the oven."

As she hurried to check on the roast, Daphne chuckled to herself to think of those women gathering together in heaven—it was pretty amazing to think about. She stuck in the meat thermometer and, feeling like the roast was done enough, turned off the oven. Pot roast was one of her dad's favorite meals. And it wasn't even that hard to make. Aunt Dee had taught her how to do it when she was just a little older than Mabel.

"Smells good in here," Don Ballinger said as he came into the kitchen.

"Hey, Dad." Daphne gave him a hug then took his coat, hanging it by the door that led to the laundry room.

"Is that what I think it is?" He nodded to the stove.

"Pot roast and potatoes and carrots and onions," she told him.

"And it's not even my birthday." He smacked his lips.

"Speaking of birthdays, thank you for the gift certificate." She kissed him on the cheek. "I plan to use it next week."

"That was Karen's idea. She thought you'd like to try out that new dress shop—what's it called—the Cheap Boutique?"

"*Chic* Boutique." She laughed. "And Sabrina actually took me there already. The clothes are really nice and the woman who owns it is great too."

"Isn't she though?" Karen said as she joined them. "I just love that little Erika. I hope her shop does well enough to stick around awhile. I hate seeing businesses come and go in this town. We need stability."

"But you're a realtor," Daphne reminded her. "When people come and go, doesn't that give you the opportunity to sell property?"

Karen smiled. "Good point, honey. I guess that's like making lemonade from lemons."

"Speaking of lemonade, Mabel made us some Hawaiian punch." Daphne winked at Mabel.

"Yeah, you want some?" Mabel offered eagerly. "I get to serve it if you do."

Daphne offered coffee and tea as well, but everyone agreed that Mabel's Hawaiian punch sounded good, and while she filled the glasses Daphne had set out, Daphne led them into the living room where she'd put out a plate of crackers and cheese. She would've made something fancier, but she knew her dad's taste leaned toward simple and traditional.

"So how's retirement going?" Daphne asked her dad as she sat across from them.

"It'll be going better when it's warm enough to golf a little," he said as he reached for a cracker.

"Poor Don," Karen said. "He can see the golf course from the condo, but it's not open yet. He's like the kid with his nose pressed to the candy store window."

"It's like a big tease." He frowned. "Makes me want to become a snowbird and head down south."

"But spring is right around the corner," Daphne pointed out as Mabel came into the room with two glasses of punch. Fortunately, she'd taken Daphne's advice and not filled them too full.

"This is for you, Grandma Karen," Mabel said politely. "And for you, Grandpa." She handed the second one over.

"You're quite the hostess," Karen told Mabel. "Impressive."

As Mabel returned for the other glasses, Don went on to complain about the golf course's condition. "Canadian geese have been wreaking havoc all winter, and I haven't seen them even touching the putting greens yet."

"Yes, but the course is scheduled to open in a couple weeks, so it'll be ready," Karen assured him. "But speaking of snowbirds," she turned to Daphne, "you probably heard about Frank and Gwen Danson moving to Miami."

"I did," Daphne said. "And I saw you got the listing for their house when I dropped Jenna home from baby-sitting Mabel."

"I also got the listing for Jake McPheeters's house," she said.

Daphne just nodded, not wanting to admit she knew that as well.

"Well, I just showed it yesterday, and I have a very good feeling about the couple. I expect an offer will come in this week."

"How nice." Daphne tried not to grimace at this news.

"But the Danson house will take more time. Goodness, that place is a mansion. Not easy to sell real estate in that price range."

"But worth the effort when you do." Don winked at her as he nudged her with his elbow.

"Here you go, Mom." Mabel handed Daphne a glass of punch.

"Mom?" Don echoed.

"That's right," Daphne said quickly. "It was Mabel's idea and I agreed wholeheartedly." She patted the seat beside her. "Right, Mabel?"

Mabel nodded, and Don broke into a large grin. "Well, that's just wonderful," he said. "Warms my heart to hear that."

They continued making congenial small town small talk, but all Daphne could think about was the fact that Jake's house might be sold by next week. She had secretly hoped that his property would just sit on the market and that, in time, Jake would decide he missed Appleton too much to remain in Miami—and that he would come back. Of course, she knew that was selfish, not to mention unrealistic. Best to just let it go...let him go...move on.

Chapter 8

On the first Monday of spring break, Daphne and Mabel woke up to heavy gray skies and the forecast of rain for the entire week. To make matters worse, Lola would be gone the whole time—visiting her grandmother. Plus, Daphne had been so focused on finishing and editing her novel that she didn't think to book any spring break activities for Mabel, and now they were all full.

"It's just not fair," Mabel complained to Daphne and Sabrina as the three of them hovered together on Daphne's porch after grabbing the mail in the pouring rain. "Spring break is supposed to be fun." Mabel frowned up at the dripping eaves. "What can we do that's fun?"

Sabrina's brow creased as if she was trying to think of a solution and then she raised a finger in the air. "How would you like to do some babysitting?"

"Babysitting?" Mabel looked interested, followed by dismay. "But I'm only eight. How can I baby-sit?"

"Tootsie is bored too," Sabrina explained. "I'll pay you five dollars to go over there and play with him for an hour."

"Five dollars?" Mabel's eyes grew wide. "Really?"

Daphne started to protest, but Sabrina hushed her. "Yes," Sabrina told Mabel, "if it's okay with your mom."

"Please, Mom," Mabel begged.

Daphne shrugged. "Sure, why not."

"You know where his toys are," Sabrina said. "Just make sure he gets a lot of exercise and has fun."

"I will!" Mabel said eagerly. "Can I go right now?"

Daphne gave her permission, and Sabrina told her to lock the door after she went inside. Then they both watched as Mabel carefully crossed the street and ran up to the house. "Got any coffee?" Sabrina asked after Mabel was inside. "We can keep an eye on my house from your kitchen."

Before long they were settled at the kitchen table and Daphne was expressing regrets for not being a better mom. "It just never occurred to me that I should plan for activities during spring break. It wasn't until I called Lola's mom, hoping to set up a sleepover, that I found out how it's done."

Sabrina chuckled. "Hey, I remember being let out on my own during spring break. My friends and I would make our own fun by running wild and terrorizing the neighborhood. But kids aren't allowed to do that these days."

Now Daphne told her about what Mabel had said about Pastor Andrew comparing heaven to Disneyland. "Only heaven is way, way, way better," she quoted Mabel. "I wish I'd planned something like that." She frowned. "But the truth is I can't afford it. I really need to start budgeting and planning for what happens after May."

Sabrina's brow creased. "Oh, Daphne, you can't let May come and go without getting married. You just can't."

"I don't see how I can avoid it, short of marrying someone that I don't love—and I don't want to do that. Besides, it's not like the men are lining up at my door."

"But they could be. You still have options. What about Harrison? He was really into you and you just—"

"Enough." Daphne held up her hand like a stop sign. "I really don't want to go there, Sabrina. I've given the whole business to God, and if I'm meant to find someone before...well, before it's too late, then it will happen."

Sabrina pursed her lips, and Daphne could tell that she was biting her tongue.

"Now if you want to give me any advice, tell me what I can do to make Mabel's week more pleasant." She looked outside at the gloomy rain, which seemed to be coming down even harder now, and just shook her head.

Sabrina pulled out her phone. "I have an idea."

Daphne waited while Sabrina did some searching. What she was searching for was a mystery, but her expression was intense. Daphne got up to get the coffee pot, refilling their cups with what was left. "I suppose I should make a list of all the indoor activities we can do. Arts and crafts, puzzles, cooking, videos...." She sat down. "Except we do those things all the time. I wish I could think of something special."

"I've got it!" Sabrina held up her phone.

"What?"

"We're going to Disney World!"

"Disney World? Are you nuts? I can't afford that."

"You don't need to."

"What are you—"

"I just texted my friend in Orlando, and she's offered us her guest house for the whole week."

"*Really?*" Daphne blinked. "But there's still airfare and—"

"I have a bunch of air miles that I never use. I'm going to see what I can get." Sabrina stood, smiling brightly. "It'll be easier to do that from my computer at home."

"Are you kidding?"

"Not in the least." She finished the last of her coffee. "I'll let you know how it goes, but you might want to start packing your bags."

"*Seriously?*"

"Absolutely." She was heading for the door. "But I won't tell

Mabel. Not until I know it's for sure."

"Sabrina, this is crazy. We can't just—"

"Yes, we can," she insisted. "You're done with your book, right?"

"Yeah...I already sent it to the agent who was most interested."

"So you're free to go?"

"Well, yes, but—"

"And you don't have a problem with going to a warm sunny place for a few days, do you?"

Daphne glanced at the dismal weather. "No, not at all."

"And Mabel wanted to go to Disneyland. This is Disney World. Even better, right?"

"Yes, of course, but—"

"No buts. We're doing this for Mabel." Sabrina winked as she opened the front door. "And if we have fun while we're there, even better, right?"

Daphne just nodded. Sometimes Sabrina was a bit like a southern tornado—she took off and there was no stopping her. But she was a sweet tornado.

"So you're good to go then?"

Daphne felt a smile spreading over her face, and she knew she was pulled in. "Oh, Sabrina, it would be fabulous. Do you really think you can use your mileage to get tickets?"

"I'll give it my best shot."

"And if you succeed, I've got an idea." Daphne giggled. "We won't tell Mabel where we're going until we're at the airport! Can you imagine how excited she'll be?"

"And I'll record it on my phone," Sabrina said with excitement.

"Great. I can share that with her Uncle Daniel. He'll love it."

Sabrina crossed fingers on both hands. "Wish me luck!"

Daphne clasped her hands together. "I'll be praying!"

Daphne could barely contain herself as Sabrina drove them to the airport later—*the same day*. To Daphne's pleased surprise, Sabrina hadn't only secured the plane tickets using her airline miles, she'd also gotten a special deal that included a rental car and Disney World passes. Although Sabrina acted as if the whole trip was "practically free," Daphne knew that probably wasn't the case, and she intended to reimburse her friend as much as possible.

Sabrina had called Daphne with the good news while Mabel was still entertaining Tootsie, explaining that the only seats available to Orlando departed at 3:25 *today*, and like a whirlwind, Daphne had packed their bags. Then, with Mabel still at Sabrina's, Daphne snuck across the street and slipped them into the trunk of Sabrina's car.

Now, after an hour long drive, they were just coming into the airport. Sabrina had led Mabel to believe they were going to an indoor shopping mall, and since Mabel was engrossed in using Sabrina's iPad, she didn't even realize they were at an airport until they were getting their bags out of the trunk.

"We're going to fly in a plane," Daphne explained. The plan was not to tell Mabel about Disney World until they boarded the jet.

"I get to ride in a real plane?" Mabel shrieked. "*For real?*"

"That's right," Sabrina said as she put Tootsie in his doggy carrier. "Won't it be fun?"

"I've never ever been in a plane before," Mabel said with excitement.

Daphne handed Mabel her little wheeled pink bag. "And we have to spend the night away from home, so I packed you a bag."

"I'm going on a plane and spending the night somewhere else!" Mabel was grinning from ear to ear. "This is the best spring break ever!"

Mabel was thrilled about everything in the terminal, so much so that Daphne knew that if all they did was fly around and come back, she would've been happy. But after they were seated, finagling a bit to get seats together, and after Tootsie's doggy carrier was stowed beneath the seat and Sabrina had her phone out and ready, Daphne made the announcement.

"Mabel Myers, Sabrina and I have something to tell you. This is not just a plane ride, this is a plane ride that is taking you to Disney World!"

Mabel's eyes were huge, but she didn't say a word.

"And maybe you don't know this, but Disney World is even bigger than Disneyland."

Mabel just nodded and then exploded with a shrill shriek of joy that made the other passengers jump. "*I'm going to Disney World!*" she cried out. "In a real plane! *This is the best spring break ever!*" The passengers laughed, commenting on Mabel's first plane trip. Meanwhile Sabrina continued to record and finally, still wearing an ear to ear grin, Mabel hugged them both. "I'm so happy I think I'll burst!"

"Oh, I hope not," Daphne told her. "You'd miss out on Disney World."

By the time they landed in Orlando, picked up the rental car, and navigated to Sabrina's friend's house, it was nearly late, but Mabel was still awake and in good spirits. Though as soon as they got settled in the guest house and Daphne tucked Mabel into one of the twin beds in the little bedroom that the two of them would be sharing, she was out like a light.

"I think she'll be sleeping in tomorrow," Daphne said as she closed the door.

"Her and me both," Sabrina said as she poked around in the kitchen. "I'm heading for bed too."

"I want to thank you again," Daphne said as she gathered up

her things to move to the little bedroom. "I still can't believe you pulled this off."

Sabrina waved her hand with a big grin. "I must admit, it felt kind of like being a magician."

"Or a fairy godmother."

Sabrina laughed. "Well, I just hope y'all sleep well, but I wish you'd taken the master suite."

"No, we'll be fine. I wanted you to have that."

"Tomorrow you'll meet Ruthie." Sabrina removed a bottle of water from the fridge. "I've known her most of my life and, let me tell you, she's a hoot and a half."

"I'm looking forward to it." Daphne looked around their lovely quarters. "This guesthouse is much nicer than I expected. Far better than staying in a hotel."

"Wait'll you see the rest of the place. It is really swanky."

As Daphne went into the bathroom to get ready for bed, she felt mixed emotions. On one hand, she was very grateful to Sabrina for this luxurious spring break week. On the other hand, she felt guilty. Was she setting Mabel up to expect a lifestyle that she wouldn't be able to deliver?

For all Daphne knew, she and Mabel could be living in a shabby one-room apartment on the grungy side of town after May passed by with Daphne still unwed. Still, she told herself as she pulled on her pajamas, this was a once in a lifetime opportunity for both of them. Mabel had seen enough of life to understand that. And while they were here, they might as well enjoy it to the fullest. What would come would come... not much she could do about it now anyway.

Chapter 9

"**A**re we in Florida now?" Mabel asked sleepily the next morning.

"Yes." Daphne laid shorts and a t-shirt on the bed for her. "We're in Orlando, and that's in Florida."

"Can we see Jenna while we're here?" she asked hopefully.

"Probably not, sweetheart. Miami is a long way from Orlando."

Mabel frowned. "But Miami is in Florida, isn't it?"

"Yes, but it would be quite a drive."

"But we have that rental car. Can't we please go—"

"Good morning," Sabrina called out cheerfully. "Y'all ready to soak up some of this fabulous Florida sunshine?"

"I am," Daphne called back. "Mabel's still getting dressed."

"Wait till Mabel sees this pool," Sabrina said enticingly.

"A real swimming pool?" Mabel's face lit up.

"Yeah, and it's pretty nice."

Mabel was hurrying to pull off her pajamas now.

"Come out when you're ready," Daphne told her as she went to join Sabrina.

"Isn't it just picture perfect?" Sabrina waved to where she'd pulled open the drapes, revealing a gleaming turquoise pool with a large, beautiful stucco home on the other side.

"It's gorgeous." Daphne went over to peer out. "Look at those palm trees, they're enormous."

Sabrina slid open a door, waiting for Tootsie to burst out in front of her. "I put some coffee and toast and orange juice out there. Ruthie stocked a few things in the kitchen for us, but we'll probably need to do some shopping today."

"Oh my, this is heavenly," Daphne declared as she stepped onto the sunny patio. "I feel like I'm really on vacation now." She sat in one of the wicker chairs and sighed happily.

"*Wow, wow, wow!*" Mabel exclaimed as she rushed out of the guesthouse. "This is so cool! Our very own swimming pool! Can I get in right now?"

"Well, it's not our *very own* pool." Daphne glanced at Sabrina. "We're guests here and we should probably talk to the lady of the house first." She pointed to Mabel. "Plus you don't have on a swimming suit."

"Ruthie said to make ourselves at home. She had some things to do today." Sabrina waved her hand. "But I know she meant with the pool too. I sure plan to use it."

"Did you pack my swimming suit?" Mabel asked hopefully.

"I did."

"*Yippee!*"

Daphne put a hand out to stop her from going back inside. "But you need to have a little breakfast first. Sabrina made some toast, and there's orange juice."

It didn't take long for Mabel to have some toast and juice and then there was no holding her back. Soon she was splashing happily in the shallow end. "I want to get her into swimming lessons this summer," Daphne told Sabrina. "She's never had any instruction."

"At least she's not scared of water." Sabrina sipped her juice. "I had a terrible fear of pools when I was her age. All because I fell into a pond when I was a toddler. After that I kept a safe distance from all forms of water. Didn't get over it until I was in junior high school and a girl teased me and called me a chicken. I begged my daddy to get us one of those above-ground pools and then I forced myself to get in it every single day. By the end of that summer I was swimming like a fish."

"I can just imagine you doing that," Daphne said. "You have such great determination, Sabrina."

Sabrina pointed to where Mabel was trying to hold her breath underwater. "Mabel has great determination too."

Daphne laughed. "Yes, she's been practicing holding her breath in the bathtub. She has me count for her sometimes."

"After all she's been through, she needs some determination."

"Which reminds me." Daphne told her about Mabel's suggestion to see Jenna. "She did not want to give up on it either."

"She sure loves Jenna." Sabrina pulled out her phone. "How far is it to Miami anyway?"

"I'm not sure, but Orlando is in the north part of Florida, and Miami's down south."

"About three and a half hours according to this." She held up her phone. "One way."

"The round trip alone would eat up most of a day." Daphne shook her head. "And what would we even do? Say *hello Jenna* then turn around and drive back."

"Yeah, it seems a little crazy." Sabrina continued messing with her phone, and Daphne watched in amusement as Mabel, with her nose plugged, went down again. "It's so lovely here, I wouldn't mind just staying here all day," she said with contentment.

"I was thinking the same thing," Sabrina agreed.

"So maybe we shouldn't head for Disney World today."

"Our Disney passes are good all week."

"And I don't feel compelled to drag Mabel to all the other amusement parks and tourist traps around here." Daphne gave Mabel two thumbs up as she popped out of the water. "I think one nice long day at Disney World should be plenty."

"If we went tomorrow, we'd still have Thursday to spend relaxing here. Then we fly home on Friday morning."

"Sounds like a plan." Daphne waved at Mabel as she climbed out of the pool them jumped back in. "And I doubt she'll mind."

So for the rest of the morning, they just hung out by the pool. Then they went out for lunch, did a little shopping, then came back to enjoy the pool with the plan to barbecue burgers on the guesthouse grill later.

"Hey, there's Ruthie." Sabrina waved to the brunette approaching them, taking a moment to introduce her to Daphne and Mabel.

"Thank you so much for letting us stay here," Daphne told her. "It's been just wonderful."

"I love your pool!" Mabel exclaimed.

"I'm so glad." Ruthie patted Mabel's still damp head. "Maybe if my kids see you in it, they'll be enticed to come out and use it for a change."

"You have kids?" Mabel's eyes got wide.

Ruthie nodded. "Drew and Mila. Drew's ten and Mila's seven."

"Why don't they like swimming in their very own pool?" Mabel's brow creased.

"That's a good question." Ruthie chuckled. "Maybe because it's always here and they take it for granted. But lately they've complained that the water's too cold."

"It's not too cold," Mabel declared. "Not once you get used to it."

"Well, if they see you in it, I bet they'll want to join you." Ruthie nodded to where Daphne had started setting out their dinner ingredients. "I'll leave you ladies to your dinner. Max and I have a fundraiser to go to tonight." She tipped her head to one side. "In fact, I was going to have a babysitter come, but—"

"Why don't you let me watch them for you," Sabrina offered

eagerly.

"Yes, yes," Mabel agreed. "Maybe they'll want to play with me."

Ruthie grinned. "Perfect." She put an arm around Sabrina. "Come on into the house and I'll fill you in on everything."

"And we can catch up," Sabrina said happily.

After Ruthie and Max left, Sabrina and the kids came over to meet Daphne and Mabel. Before long, all three kids were splashing and playing in the pool.

"Mabel's in hog heaven," Sabrina said as they sat in the lounge chairs watching them.

"So am I." Daphne sighed happily. "Almost makes me wish I lived down here."

Sabrina turned to her in alarm. "You wouldn't consider leaving Appleton for this, would you? I mean what if Jake proposed to you—would you leave Appleton to live in Miami?"

Daphne shrugged. "I don't know, but since that's not likely, you don't really need to worry about it. Besides, you know how much I love Appleton. I can't imagine Miami being the kind of place to bring up a little girl."

"Lots of people do it."

Daphne just shook her head. "I'm a small town girl at heart. Believe me, I found that out in New York City."

Sabrina looked relieved as she leaned back into the lounge. "Me too. Oh, I can enjoy a bit of the big city from time to time, for shopping, theater, and restaurants. But the rest of the time I'd rather live in a town where people know my name."

Daphne agreed with her on that, but what Sabrina said about Jake did set her to thinking. What if he had proposed marriage to her, inviting her and Mabel to live in Miami with him? Would she have considered it? The truth was, she was considering it now. And that was unsettling!

To Sabrina's relief, Ruth and the kids volunteered to watch Tootsie the next day. And so, early in the morning, with Daphne behind the wheel, Sabrina playing navigator, and Mabel singing Disney songs in the backseat, they headed for Disney World, arriving there just as the gates opened.

With a "walking breakfast" they started their journey through the pristinely maintained amusement park. Sabrina proclaimed it picture perfect, and Daphne couldn't disagree. Everything in the park was attractive and clean and clever.

Daphne wasn't sure which was more fun—seeing the wonders of this place with her own eyes or seeing it through Mabel's. The spellbound girl was amazed by absolutely everything—from shaking hands with a smiling Cinderella and Snow White to riding on the Seven Dwarfs' mining train. After spending most of the day in the Magic Kingdom and then the Animal Kingdom, Daphne could tell that Mabel was wearing down a bit.

Since it was nearly five, Daphne thought they could call it a day, but before she could voice this, Sabrina's phone chimed and Sabrina held up her hand. "I have to take this." She stepped away from them with a mysterious expression.

"What's that big thing?" Mabel pointed to the big gleaming globe structure across the way.

Daphne explained how the Epcot featured countries from all over the world. "It's sort of like traveling to foreign lands but staying in one place."

"Can we go?" Mabel asked with renewed energy.

Just then Sabrina came back with an interesting twinkle in her eyes.

"You look like the cat that swallowed the canary," Daphne teased. "What's going on? And who was that?"

"That was Jake."

Daphne blinked. "Jake?"

"Yes. I texted him yesterday, telling him that we were here

in Orlando. And guess what?"

"What?" Daphne felt unexpectedly nervous.

"Jake and Jenna are going to meet us."

"I get to see Jenna!" Mabel exclaimed, hopping from one foot to the other.

Daphne was dumbfounded. "Are they coming all the way up here from—"

"They were already in Cocoa Beach," Sabrina explained. "They'd been doing some surfing. And then they drove up to Cape Canaveral early this morning. Sounds like they arrived here around noon and right now they're in Epcot."

"That's where we're going!" Mabel was jumping up and down. "We decided that, didn't we, Mom?"

Daphne just nodded.

"Then off we go. I'll text Jake back for a place to meet."

Feeling flabbergasted, Daphne was speechless as Mabel grabbed her hand and started tugging her toward the gates. She felt no less confused after the bus ride that delivered them to the gleaming silver globe. What on earth did Sabrina think she was doing setting up a rendezvous like this?

"Jake says they'll meet us in Japan if that's okay."

"*Japan!*" Mabel echoed. "I've always wanted to go to Japan!"

"Lucky you." Daphne told her then lowered her voice as she turned to Sabrina. "But why are you doing this?"

Sabrina grinned as she sent a confirming text. "You know that Mabel wanted to see Jenna. So I texted Jake on the off chance that we could get together. I'd suggested we meet in the middle. But turns out they were already halfway here. And Jenna wanted to visit Epcot." She patted Daphne's back as if to reassure her. "It was perfect. Don't you think?"

Daphne shook her head in wonder. Leave it to Sabrina, the perennial fairy godmother.

After the initial awkwardness of exchanging greetings and hugs with Jake and Jenna, Daphne felt herself relaxing a little.

And together the five of them toured the Japanese section as well as several of the other countries until they all decided that everyone was probably hungry for dinner. And because Jenna and Mabel liked the look of the Mexican restaurant, they decided to eat at La Hacienda de San Angel.

"This is such a great surprise," Jake said after they were seated at a big round table. "It feels like homecoming week."

"Do you like living in Florida?" Mabel asked Jenna with sincere interest.

"It's been pretty fun so far." Jenna told Mabel about the past couple days of surfing with her dad. "But school starts next week." Her mouth twisted to one side. "Not sure how that'll go."

As Daphne sipped her iced tea, she didn't know why she felt so uneasy. Really, what was the big deal? Just friends meeting up. But she suspected her angst was related to Sabrina's question yesterday. Would Daphne give up Appleton to be Jake's wife? Not that he was asking—for Pete's sake! But the question still nagged inside of her, and every time she locked eyes with Jake, she felt herself melting inside and grew worried that the answer was "yes." Although she doubted she'd ever get the chance to say it—and that was probably for the best.

As they ate, everyone chattered away like a big happy family. Daphne tried to feign as much interest and enthusiasm as the others, but the truth was she felt strangely disconnected, and as much as she enjoyed seeing Jake—and as much as she wanted to just stare at him—she would be very relieved when this surprise encounter ended. It was the very definition of *bittersweet*.

"It's almost time for the fireworks," Sabrina announced as they finished up dinner. "We can't miss that."

Before long, they were positioned along a retaining wall overlooking the lagoon, all watching in awed wonder as the huge, colorful fireworks, accompanied by magical music, filled the dark sky. It was gorgeous! By now Mabel was clinging to

Jenna like glue. Meanwhile Sabrina was standing a little off by herself, capturing the sparkling images with her phone. And Jake was standing shoulder to shoulder by Daphne—so near she could feel warmth radiating from him, as well as her own personal fireworks going off inside her. At one point she turned to look at him, curious as to whether he felt what she felt. And to her pleasant surprise, he was gazing directly at her with a happy smile.

"I can't believe I'm here with you right now," he said with a startling, quiet intensity.

"I know," she said in a slightly shaky voice. "I kind of thought I'd never see you again."

"That would be lousy." He reached over to push away a strand of hair that had blown into her eyes, brushing her cheek with his fingers and sending a pleasant tingle down her spine. But in the same moment a loud boom in the sky made her jump, and she let out an embarrassing squeal.

"Easy there." Jake slipped an arm around her shoulders as if to steady her.

She giggled nervously. "Isn't it beautiful?"

"Yeah." He nodded, turning his attention back to the sky, but leaving his arm around her.

Despite the cool night air, warm feelings were rushing through her and bouncing all around inside. But she told herself he might just be acting in a big brotherly way. She shouldn't take this too seriously. And yet she wasn't buying it. Jake seemed just as attracted to her as she was to him.

But too soon the fireworks display was over with and Jake's arm slid away and he shoved his hands in his pockets. They all visited for a bit, remarking on the show. But announcements were being made that the park was closing and now they began to walk. It was time to say goodbye. More hugs were exchanged and Jenna promised to write to Mabel and they parted ways.

"Well, that was sure nice," Sabrina said happily as they

walked along a well-lit walkway. She nudged Daphne with an elbow. "You enjoyed it too, didn't you?"

"Of course." Daphne reached for Mabel's hand, not wanting to lose her amongst the crowd that grew thicker as they neared the park exit.

"And you're glad I contacted Jake, aren't you?" Sabrina's voice had a slight teasing tone to it.

"Sure. It was great seeing both of them." But as they walked, Daphne felt uncertain. Maybe it wasn't that great after all. What sort of price would she pay for allowing herself to experience those delightful feelings tonight? Would she be tortured over a relationship that would never be allowed to bloom like she wished it could? Or if it somehow managed to bloom, would she regret having to choose between Jake in Miami and her peaceful quiet life in Appleton? And what about what was best for Mabel? That weighed heavily into all this. She sighed as they got into the car.

Why did her life never seem to run smoothly?

Chapter 10

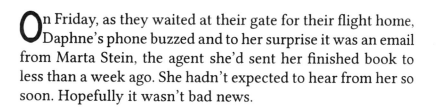

On Friday, as they waited at their gate for their flight home, Daphne's phone buzzed and to her surprise it was an email from Marta Stein, the agent she'd sent her finished book to less than a week ago. She hadn't expected to hear from her so soon. Hopefully it wasn't bad news.

> *Hey Daphne,*
>
> *I received your finished manuscript on Tuesday. I read most and skim-read the rest last night. I absolutely love it. Brilliant! My literary agency would like to represent you. I'm attaching a contract for you to print out and sign—if you are in agreement and wish to become my client. Please, return this to my assistant, Amy Walters, at your earliest convenience. I can't wait to start shopping this delightful book and I know right where I'll start. Great work, Daphne. I could be wrong, but I feel this has 'bestseller' written all over it.*
>
> *Sincerely,*
> *Marta*
> *Marta Stein Literary Agency, New York, NY*

Daphne stood up and started dancing around—similar to Mabel's "happy dance"—as she reread the email. She wanted to be sure she hadn't read it wrong or simply dreamt it up. But sure enough it was true. Marta Stein wanted Daphne's novel! "This is fabulous!" Daphne exclaimed happily.

"What is?" Mabel asked, staring at Daphne with big eyes.

"What's up?" Sabrina came over to stand with them.

Daphne told them both the good news and then they were all hugging and dancing around. "My friend here is about to become a bestselling novelist," Sabrina explained to a curious onlooker. "She's got a big New York agent who loves her book."

"You'll be famous!" Mabel told Daphne.

"Well, I don't know about that." Daphne stared down at her phone again, just to be sure the message was still there.

"We need to celebrate." Sabrina pointed to a coffee kiosk. "I'll buy a round of iced mochas for everyone." She grinned at Mabel. "Yours will be sans caffeine."

While Sabrina, with Mabel to help her, got their mochas, Daphne responded to Marta's post, promising to sign and return the contract as soon as possible. She felt slightly lightheaded as she hit send. It felt like her dreams were about to come true!

Before long, Daphne was flying high as she was flying high. Maybe this was her answer—her book would sell and hit the bestsellers list and she wouldn't even care whether she got Aunt Dee's prickly inheritance after all. In fact, if she made enough money, perhaps she could just buy Aunt Dee's house. Hopefully the attorney that Jake had gotten to handle the will and estate would price it graciously. Maybe Jake could encourage him to do this.

Thinking of Jake made her want to talk to him again. And now she felt she had a good excuse to contact him—to share her good news. She was tempted to call him now but decided an email might be more appropriate. Anyway, she knew he'd be happy for her.

As soon as they got home, even before unpacking, Daphne dropped her bags in the foyer and ran to her office, printed the agency contract, signed it, and slid it into a Fedex envelope. Although it would have to wait until tomorrow, at least it was ready to go. As she set it by the front door, she whispered a quick prayer—asking God to bless this new chapter in her life.

Although it was still rainy and dreary in Appleton, both Daphne and Mabel were happy to be home. And it felt good to make a fire in the fireplace that night. "I know it's not the same as Florida with a swimming pool," Daphne told Mabel as she slid in the DVD the Mabel had picked out, "but it is cozy."

"I love our home," Mabel said contentedly. "Florida was fun to visit, but I wouldn't want to live there."

"And why not?" Daphne sat down next to her on the sectional, reaching for the bowl of popcorn.

"Because Lola is here in Appleton," Mabel proclaimed. "And my school is here, and I love Miss Simmons. And I love my ballet school, and I love Grandpa and Grandma and all our neighbors and—because *this is our home!*"

Daphne smiled. "Yes, it is." And hopefully it would remain their home too. If Daphne could just get a book contract, maybe it would be possible.

On Saturday, Mabel was thrilled to get a phone call from Lola and an invitation to spend the afternoon at her house. "Can I go?" Mabel begged eagerly.

Daphne was happy to agree. Not simply because Mabel had been dearly missing her BFF, but also because Daphne thought an afternoon on her own sounded blissful. After she dropped Mabel at Lola's, Daphne suddenly missed her childhood best friend too. Oh, she knew Olivia's life had taken a different route than Daphne's—married with a baby. And that Daphne sometimes felt more comfortable with Sabrina these days. But she was still committed to Olivia. Besides, she wanted to see how Bernadette was doing.

So Daphne stopped by Bernie's Blooms before going home, but the shop, though opened, looked deserted. Daphne called out, finally discovering Olivia in a dark corner of the back room—sobbing.

"What's wrong?" Daphne asked with concern. "Is the baby okay?"

"Yes, she's fine." Olivia sniffed. "At least I hope she is. Jeff is watching her for a couple of hours this afternoon." She reached for a Kleenex, blowing loudly.

"Then why are you crying?" Daphne put her arm around Olivia. "What happened?"

"Nothing—nothing really." Olivia started to cry again.

"Something must've happened." Daphne handed her another tissue. "You're a mess."

"Are there any customers out there?" Olivia asked.

"Not when I came in. Want me to check?"

"Please. I'll try to pull myself together."

Daphne went out and, seeing no one, flipped the WE'LL BE BACK sign over and locked the door. Whatever was wrong with Olivia might be "nothing," but she certainly wasn't ready to greet customers. Daphne got a water bottle out of the fridge and took it to Olivia, explaining that she'd temporarily closed the shop. "Tell me what's going on." She sat on a stool across from Olivia waiting.

"I don't really know. I mean, it might just be the baby blues. I've read about how women get depressed in the post-partum period, but I thought I should be past that now. Bernadette is almost six weeks old."

"Is anything else wrong in your life?"

Olivia frowned. "Well, my marriage is pretty much a shambles. Or worse."

Daphne tried to conceal her shock. Oh, she knew Olivia's marriage wasn't perfect. Not in the least. But a shambles?

"I know that Jeff loves the baby, but sometimes it seems like he's jealous of the time I spend with her. And he gets mad at me for being so tired all the time. But what can I say? It's exhausting—working, caring for an infant, doing night feedings every few hours, trying to maintain a household, cooking and cleaning and shopping and doing a ton of laundry, and—and—" Her voice cracked. "Just look at me, Daphne. I'm a mess. I haven't showered in several days. I haven't washed my hair in nearly a week. I feel like such a loser. Why is this so hard? What is wrong with me?" She started to sob again.

"You're just overwhelmed," Daphne said as she gathered Olivia in her arms. "You've got too much on your plate, Olivia. Most women take six weeks of maternity leave. You pretty much came right back to work."

"I—I know, but I need to keep this shop out of the red and I—I can't afford to—"

"Can't Jeff help out more? I mean at home. Surely he knows how to do laundry or cook a meal or do the grocery shopping."

"If I ask him to help me, he acts resentful. He reminds me that it was my idea to have a baby—and how I told him I could handle it." She wiped her nose. "And it's true. I used to brag about how I could do it all, have it all—and now I don't want it." She broke into fresh sobs, and the only thing Daphne could think of was to hug her again—and to just let her cry it out.

After a few minutes, Olivia started to gather herself back together. "I'm sorry for dumping on you like that." She went over to the deep flower arranging sink and splashed water on her face.

"What are friends for?" Daphne handed her some paper towels.

As Olivia blotted her face, taking some sips of the water that Daphne had brought for her, Daphne tried to think. "You need a break," she finally said. "And I'm going to give it to you."

"What do you mean?"

"I mean I'm going to keep Bernadette for you. I know you're still nursing her, but she takes formula too doesn't she? And you have that pump, right?"

Olivia just nodded.

"I'll keep Bernadette overnight. But only if you promise to go home and take a nice long bath. And then you and Jeff have to have a nice dinner. Go out or order in. No cooking. And then you'll get a good night sleep and we'll see how you feel tomorrow."

Olivia's eyes grew large. "You'd do that for me?"

"Of course I would."

"But Bernadette wakes up every two to three hours at night."

"No problem. I'm a light sleeper."

"And sometimes she's fussy about taking the formula. I mean, she will, but it's not her first preference."

"Well, she'll just have to get used to it." Daphne smiled. "And I'll try to keep her as happy as possible. I promise."

Olivia sighed. "A real bath...a date with my husband...a night of real rest...it sounds dreamy."

Daphne held up one finger. "But you have to promise me something."

"What?"

"Without getting into a fight, try to talk to Jeff. Swallow your pride and admit that maybe you bit off more than you can chew. At least for right now, because I suspect you'll get past this and be your old energetic can-do self before long. But tell him that you need help right now. And give him some specific suggestions for ways he can help."

"Wow, that's good advice, Daphne. You seem to know a lot about this. Maybe you should become a consultant or counselor or something."

Daphne laughed, thinking about how she dished out advice on a daily basis in the *Dear Daphne* column. Not that Olivia was aware of that. "Thanks, I'll think about it."

"You really want to have Bernadette for the *whole* night?" Olivia asked in disbelief.

"That's right. And I'll stay here and keep shop while you go home and get the baby's things ready and make a list of anything you think I need to know. At five o'clock, I'll close and lock up here. Then I'll pick up Mabel from Lola's and you'll bring Bernadette to my house. Okay?"

Olivia slowly nodded. "Okay." She threw her arms around Daphne. "Thank you so much! I don't know what I'd do without you, Daphne!"

As Daphne walked Olivia to the back door, she reassured her that it would be fun to have a baby in the house. "Mabel will be over the moon," she told Olivia as she waved goodbye. She watched her tired, disheveled friend climb into her car and start the engine. Daphne didn't really know how bad it was between Olivia and Jeff, but a long bath and a good night's sleep probably wouldn't hurt anything. And if Olivia felt somewhat refreshed tomorrow, maybe she'd see her life in a whole new light.

As Daphne went back into the flower shop, she wondered about how it would feel to be in Olivia's shoes right now. She remembered the times she'd felt a little envious of Olivia's life. Besides owning her own business, Olivia was a wife and mom. The sort of life Daphne had always dreamed of. But maybe it wasn't all that she'd imagined. Maybe she was better off being the single mom of an eight-year-old girl who slept soundly at night. It certainly sounded less complicated. Maybe Daphne needed to be thankful for her personal status quo.

Chapter 11

Olivia's car was already parked in front of Daphne's house when Daphne and Mabel pulled into the driveway. Olivia waved as she hopped out of the car, hurrying back to extract the car-seat with Bernadette still buckled in it. "I better leave her car seat with you," Olivia said as she handed it over to Daphne. "In case you have an emergency and need to go somewhere in the car." Olivia made a worried frown. "Not that you'll have an emergency, right?"

"No, of course not." Daphne smiled down at the baby. "We'll be fine, won't we?"

"Can I help?" Mabel offered.

"Want to grab that diaper bag?" Olivia picked up the Moses basket that she used for the baby's bed at the flower shop.

It wasn't long until they had all the baby gear, and the baby, spread out across the living room. Olivia handed Daphne a list of instructions and proceeded to tell her a few more things.

"I think we can figure it out," Daphne told Olivia as she guided her to the front door. "And if I have any big questions, I can just call you, right?"

"Yes, of course." Olivia nodded eagerly. "I can dash over here if you need me."

"That's right," Daphne said as she opened the door. Although she had no intention of disturbing Olivia and Jeff tonight, she hoped this would reassure the new mom. "We're only five minutes away."

"Sometimes she gets a little colicky," Olivia said as she went out onto the porch. "It's all there in my note to you."

"I'm sure it is." Daphne gave her a gentle nudge. "Now keep your part of the bargain and go home and take a bath." Daphne wrinkled her nose. "Seriously, you're getting pretty gamey."

"Really?" Olivia looked worried.

Daphne laughed. "No, but go take a bath anyway. And wash your hair!"

Olivia laughed. "Thanks."

"And have a good evening with Jeff."

"What time should I get her in the morning?"

"I don't know. Maybe we should just meet up at church."

"Really?" Olivia looked slightly incredulous. "That would be awesome."

"Then let's do it."

Olivia thanked her again, then Daphne gave a final wave and slipped back into the house. She found Mabel still hovering over Bernadette, staring at her with wide-eyed interest. "I think she likes me," Mabel said.

"And why shouldn't she?" Daphne fumbled to undo the safety straps of the car-seat. "How do these work anyway?"

"I can do it," Mabel said with confidence.

"Really?"

Mabel knelt down and went to work, and within seconds the baby was free.

"How did you do that?"

"I used to have a car seat," Mabel said. "I knew how to get out of it too."

Daphne laughed as she picked up Bernadette. "You're a handy gal to have around, Miss Mabel." She sat down on the sectional, cradling the baby in her lap. "Now what do we do with you?"

"Want me to read this?" Mabel held up Olivia's list.

"Sure. Might be educational." Daphne listened as Mabel struggled to read through Olivia's instructions, helping her to pronounce some of the more difficult words. "Sounds like Bernadette won't need to eat until around eight." Daphne glanced at the clock. "That might give us time to fix our own dinner."

But as soon as Daphne moved to fix dinner, the baby started to cry and fuss. And when Mabel's efforts and antics failed to soothe the baby, Daphne took over. But it was impossible to safely fix dinner and tend the baby. Finally, Daphne decided it was a good night for a pizza delivery, and Mabel gladly agreed.

"Why does she keep crying?" Mabel asked as they waited for dinner to arrive. They were both hovering over the portable baby bed, staring at the red-faced baby.

"I don't know," Daphne admitted. "Maybe she has a wet diaper."

"Would that make her cry?" Mabel asked.

"I don't know, but it can't hurt to check." When Daphne checked, the diaper was barely damp, but she changed it anyway. "I hope this is on good enough," she said as she finished fastening it up and snapping the pink sleeper back up. She laid the baby down in the baby basket then went to wash her hands. As she dried them she noticed that it wasn't even six o'clock yet. Less than one hour caring for Bernadette, and Daphne already felt tired. How did Olivia manage?

"I found this in the diaper bag," Mabel proclaimed as Daphne returned. "Olivia's note said Bernadette can have her binkie if she's fussy."

"Good idea. And she's certainly fussy." Daphne removed the pacifier from the plastic baggie and stuck it in the baby's mouth, staring in wonder as Bernadette sucked eagerly on the magical baby tool. "It worked!"

"Yeah." Mabel looked as relieved as Daphne.

"There's the pizza." Daphne jumped up to get her purse, and soon she and Mabel were eating their pizza in the kitchen, but Daphne kept one ear tuned into the baby in the living room, worried she might start crying again. And, sure enough, Daphne had just bit into her second piece when Bernadette started wailing.

"You finish your dinner," Daphne said to Mabel as she jumped up. "And drink your milk."

Daphne hurried to see that the pacifier had slipped out, but when she attempted to "plug" it back in, Bernadette refused. She was wailing so loudly that her face was puckered and red and her arms were shaking. Fearful that something serious was wrong, Daphne picked up the baby, rocking her and trying to think of what could be the problem. Then she remembered what Olivia had said about her being colicky. What did that mean?

When Mabel eventually joined her, Daphne asked her to run to her office. "I want you to get my iPad," she said loudly to be heard over the baby. "And help me look up something." When Mabel returned, Daphne asked her to google "colicky baby," spelling it for her. Together, with Mabel screaming, they read the description of colic, but even when they were finished Daphne felt unsure as to what she should do to calm the baby.

Still looking at the iPad, Daphne noticed an interesting connection to a video. "Click that." Daphne pointed. After an ad for baby food ran, they watched a video of a woman calming a crying baby by using what she called the 4-S system.

"Are you going to do that?" Mabel asked after the video ended.

"Can't hurt to try it," Daphne said, trying to remember the steps that all started with the letter S. "Swaddle, suck, sway and—what was the other thing?"

"Shush," Mabel provided. "You're supposed to go sh-sh-sh,"

she demonstrated.

"Right. Can you bring me that pink baby blanket from the bed? And the pacifier."

Mabel brought back the objects and, after a couple of tries, Daphne got the screaming baby wrapped fairly snugly in the stretchy blanket. "There's the swaddling." Now she tried to get Bernadette to latch onto the pacifier, and finally she began swaying her back and forth like the woman in the video, and together she and Mabel said, "Sh-sh-sh-sh…" over and over.

After about five minutes, it felt like the baby was calming down a bit, but as soon as Daphne slowed down the swaying, she started to wail again. So it was for the next hour, she and Mabel used the 4-S system to keep Bernadette quiet. As tiring as it was to perform this strange procedure, it was worth the effort to maintain some peace in the house. As she was swaying the baby, she reminded Mabel that this was room cleaning night and, for a change, Mabel did not protest or procrastinate. In fact, she looked relieved to go.

While Mabel was upstairs, Daphne continued swaying and shushing, hoping her arms wouldn't give out and wondering how long she would need to do this. What if the baby cried all night long? Would she be forced to call poor Olivia and ask for help?

Mabel returned, dressed neatly in her pajamas. She asked if they could watch a video, and Daphne gladly agreed. Any distraction sounded welcome right now. But after half an hour, Bernadette refused her binkie and began screaming again. This time it smelled like a diaper was to blame and, leaving Mabel to the video, Daphne managed to clean up the screaming baby, which was no small feat. And when she finished, Daphne decided that perhaps the baby was hungry. After all, it was nearly eight.

Setting the baby down and turning up the TV so Mabel could hear above the crying, Daphne hurried to warm up a bottle. According to Olivia, this was done by simply putting one of the prepared baby bottles into a bowl of very hot tap water for five minutes. It felt like a very long five minutes, but eventually the formula was warm and, to Daphne's relief, the baby seemed eager to eat and quieted down a bit.

But after just a few seconds, Bernadette threw her head back and started screaming so loudly that Mabel came to see what was wrong. "I thought she was hungry," Daphne explained. "And she seemed to want the bottle. But then she started to scream."

Mabel took the bottle from Daphne, attempting to put it in the baby's mouth, and the same thing happened again. Now Mabel peered closely at the nipple on the bottle. "Does this even have a hole in it?"

Daphne squinted to see better. "You know, I don't see a hole either."

Mabel turned the bottle upside down, shaking it to see if any formula would come out, but none did. Daphne asked her to fetch her sewing basket and, using a new needle, she punctured a hole in the nipple then offered the bottle to the screaming baby one more time. It took a bit of coaxing, but finally the baby latched on and began to suck.

Daphne let out a relieved sigh and thanked Mabel for her help. "In fact, you've been so helpful that you can stay up past your bedtime," Daphne offered.

"That's okay," Mabel said as she turned off the TV.

Daphne chuckled. "I don't blame you."

"And it's okay if you can't tuck me in or read *Little House on the Prairie* tonight. I'm pretty tired anyway." Mabel leaned over to kiss Daphne on the cheek.

"You're an angel, sweetie." Daphne kissed her back. "Thanks for helping with the baby. Don't know what I'd have done without you."

Mabel stroked Bernadette's smooth golden head. "I

remember when I thought I wanted a baby too, but now I don't know for sure."

Daphne laughed. "Well, babies aren't always this fussy. And look at her now, she seems totally fine."

"I guess." Mabel backed up cautiously. "And I'll remember to say my prayers," she promised as she headed for the stairs. "And I'll ask God to help Bernadette to not be such a crybaby too."

"Thanks," Daphne called after her. "I love you, Mabel."

"I love you too, Mom!" She eagerly scampered up the stairs. Clearly, she was glad to get away from the possibility of any more crying jags.

And perhaps it was Mabel's prayers or the 4-S system or simply that the colicky period was over for the night, but Bernadette seemed to settle down some. And after another diaper change and some burping and rocking, she eventually fell asleep, and Daphne gently placed her in her little bed, carrying it to her bedroom where Daphne started to get ready for bed as well.

Daphne went to bed earlier than usual, but she felt more tired than usual—not to mention a little nervous as to what a night with Bernadette might entail. Sure enough, it seemed she had barely gone to sleep when the baby began to cry again. But it was actually eleven o'clock, and since Olivia had said it was okay to feed her about every three hours, Daphne prepared another bottle. And this time she checked to be sure the nipple had a hole in it!

It was nearly midnight by the time Daphne had the baby fed and changed and got both of them back to bed again. And then at 2:30, she went through the whole process again. And once again a little before six.

By the time Daphne had the baby and Mabel ready for church, she felt utterly exhausted. Although she'd managed to grab a shower, she'd been unable to do her hair, which was curling and frizzing like a circus clown. But she didn't really care about her appearance. Mostly she just wanted to hand off Bernadette to her parents.

With Mabel's help, Daphne managed to get the baby stuff loaded and Bernadette safely buckled in the car-seat, and into the backseat of her car. And finally, in the church parking lot, Daphne spotted Olivia and Jeff driving up and, although Daphne tried to act laid back and as if it had been no big deal to baby-sit Bernadette, she did not offer to do it again. She wasn't sure that she would ever offer to do that again. Well, maybe that wasn't fair. Perhaps after Bernadette was well beyond the colicky stage. And potty-trained.

As they went inside, Daphne remembered what Mabel had said last night—about how she'd wanted a baby but wasn't so sure anymore. Daphne knew just exactly what Mabel meant by that. And as she wrapped an arm around Mabel, giving her a squeeze as she walked her to her second grade Sunday school class, Daphne couldn't help but think that her life was absolutely perfect just as it was. And she was truly grateful!

Chapter 12

It felt good to be back in their old routine when Mabel returned to school on Monday after spring break. Especially after their unexpected adventures in babysitting. Daphne couldn't remember the last time she'd enjoyed such a good night's sleep as she did on Sunday night.

But when she went to her office to work on the *Dear Daphne* column, she spent a couple minutes simply staring at the calendar. The end of March was not too far off now. And that was unnerving. She knew her new agent should receive the signed contract today, but how long would it realistically take Marta to get a genuine offer on Daphne's book? Although Daphne was no expert on the book publishing industry, she had been reading a number of writers' magazines and online blogs. She knew that rejections were far more common than genuine offers. She knew it was foolish to get her hopes up too high. Really, she should prepare herself for the worst.

And yet Marta's email had sounded so optimistic. Daphne pulled it up on her laptop and read it again. It was so positive and encouraging. Really, what would it hurt to get her hopes up, just a bit? Wasn't she due for a lucky break? Besides, she realized as she turned on her computer, Aunt Dee had made a very comfortable living with her writing. She'd supported herself and some of her family members as a single woman. Why couldn't Daphne, her namesake, do the same?

Still, after Daphne finished answering letters for the advice column—several of which needed severe reality checks—she knew that it was probably unrealistic to think she could sell a novel in less than two months. Talk about putting all her eggs into one basket. Daphne needed some kind of serious financial backup plan. A way to support herself and Mabel.

Spotting the local newspaper on top of a stack of junk mail from last week, she suddenly remembered that she used to write for *The New York Times*. Okay, maybe she'd only been a wedding reporter, but it was, after all, the *Times*. She picked up *The Apple Seed* and skimmed over the front page of the small biweekly paper. The writing was okay but certainly not stellar. She even found two typos on the front page.

She went back to her computer and pulled up her old résumé, which was quite dated. But after about an hour of tweaking, she thought it looked rather impressive. Well, for a small town paper like *The Apple Seed* anyway. And it was worth a try. She would see if they were interested in freelance writers. Or perhaps even a position as a staff writer. What could it hurt?

Since it wasn't quite one and the sun had finally come out, Daphne decided to walk to town. But first she cleaned up and, although she still had on jeans, she topped it with a tailored blazer from her New York days. Then, holding her head high, she walked into the small newspaper office.

"Can I help you?" a gray-haired woman at the front desk asked with moderate interest.

"I'd like to speak to the managing editor." Daphne smiled politely.

"You got a complaint about the paper?" The woman pointed to a wooden box on the desk that said SUGGESTIONS in all cap letters. "Put it there."

"No, nothing like that."

"You want to tell us about typos you found?" She peered above her reading glasses with a bored expression.

"No. Although I did find some typos." Daphne smiled bigger, deciding to take the friendliest route. "I'm Daphne Ballinger. I grew up in this town and moved back here almost a year ago."

"Oh?" The woman softened. "Are you related to Dee Ballinger? And Don Ballinger?"

"Yes. Don is my father. And Dee was my great aunt." Daphne didn't want to explain that Dee was actually her grandmother. That was a complicated story that she usually reserved.

"Well, Dee was a fine woman." She slowly stood and extended her hand. "I'm Marion Boswell." Her smile faded. "And I happen to be the one responsible for the typos. Besides running the reception desk and managing the classifieds, I'm the proofer too." She sighed. "Sorry to say, a lot slips by me."

"Proofing is hard work." Daphne fingered the envelope holding her résumé. "Even though I used to work for *The New York Times*, I'm not that great at it myself, but fortunately I was followed by a small pool of proofreaders. But I'm sure a small town paper doesn't have the budget to hire multiple proofers."

"You got that right. Now what can I do for you?"

"I had hoped to speak to your managing editor." Daphne felt silly to be so nervous—it wasn't like she was sixteen and applying for her first job.

"Stan is in his office. Probably done with his lunch by now. Go ahead and go back. Hopefully the old bear won't growl at you. He was in a mood this morning."

"Do you want to let him know I'm—"

"Nah, we're not much into protocol here." She pointed across a room where several desks sat unoccupied. "You can't miss it. Black door. Says Managing Editor on it."

Unsure as to if she really wanted to crash in on this "old bear" unannounced, Daphne considered simply leaving her envelope with Marion, except that the desk phone was ringing and it sounded like Marion had put on her Classifieds editor hat and was now taking down information for an upcoming garage sale. And so Daphne proceeded across the vacated newsroom, tapping tentatively on the managing editor's door and preparing herself to meet the old bear.

"Come in at your own risk!" a deep voice growled.

Imagining a grisly looking old codger puffing on a stinky cigar as he finished off a smelly tuna sandwich, Daphne barely opened the door. "Sorry to disturb you," she called in cautiously, "but Marion said to come on through."

"I said *come in,*" he yelled in a grouchy tone.

She pushed the door fully open and was surprised to see a youngish man glaring up at her from a cluttered desk. "Excuse me for—"

"Who *are* you?" he demanded, running his fingers through short curly hair that was the color of straw—as if it had been chemically bleached. "*What do you want?*"

Caught off guard, Daphne tried to gather her thoughts. "I'm Daphne Ballinger," she said quickly, holding up her manila envelope. "I used to write for *The New York Times,* but I moved to Appleton recently and, well, I wondered if you might have a position open. Or even some freelance work."

"The big city journalist thinks the small town paper will be ever so grateful to give her a job—maybe some lovely package with benefits and—"

"No, of course not," she said quickly. "I know *The Apple Seed* is—"

"*The Apple Seed* is getting pretty seedy," he interrupted. "FYI, our circulation is lower than ever. Ad space is not selling worth beans. This year's budget is already shot, and it's not even April yet. I recently laid off most of my staff writers. So, don't take it personally, but I can't offer a job to anyone. Not even a janitor, which means I've been taking out the trash and cleaning the toilets myself."

"I'm sorry." She clutched her envelope to her chest, backing out of his office. "Sorry for your troubles and sorry to take your time."

"Wait!" He held up his hand, exposing a tattoo on his wrist. "What for?"

"I'm sorry." He stood, shoving his hands into his torn jeans pockets. "My bad. Excuse my lack of manners. I shouldn't have chewed your head off like that."

"It's okay. I can see you're under a lot of stress."

"You can say that again." He approached her, sticking out his hand to shake hers. "I'm Stan Abernathy, and my mama didn't raise me up to be this rude."

"I understand." She firmly shook his hand. "I'm sorry to have troubled you."

"What was your name again?"

"Daphne Ballinger."

"Well, sorry I can't offer you a job, but welcome to Appleton."

She quickly explained that she grew up here and had moved back nearly a year ago. "I thought I may make a living selling my novel, but I realize that's a bit unrealistic."

He laughed. "Yeah, I'd have to agree with that. I have two unpublished novels of my own gathering dust."

"Oh." Now she felt stupid.

"Sorry, there I go again." He shook his head as he removed a phone from the pocket of his wrinkled plaid flannel shirt. "Blame it on low blood sugar. I didn't know it was so late. I get pretty gnarly when I miss lunch."

"I understand completely," she told him. "I can be like that too."

"You had your lunch yet?"

"No, but—"

"Well, how about we get something to eat? And then you can tell me what it feels like to work for a paper like the *Times*.

Maybe you've got some great connections there. Somebody who'd like to give *me* a job." He threw up his hands. "Then I can sell this dump."

"How did you get this, uh, newspaper in the first place?" she asked as they exited the building through a backdoor.

"Inherited it from my grandpa on my mom's side. I thought it was pretty cool at first, but the charm has definitely worn off." He told her about how he used to visit Appleton in the summertime. "I thought the newspaper was the greatest thing since video games." He looked both ways before they hurried across the street. "I couldn't believe it when Grandpa Johnson left it to me. But I didn't realize it was already going into debt. When I found out, I thought maybe I could rescue it. But that's not really happening."

As they walked into Midge's Diner together, Daphne felt Ricardo eying them with open curiosity as he said hello. "I guess it makes sense that you two should meet," Ricardo said as he set two waters on their table. "Newspaper people." He winked at Daphne.

"Yeah, she'd give up *The New York Times* to work for *The Apple Seed*," Stan said ironically.

"I thought she already gave up the *Times*," Ricardo told him.

"Well, maybe she's reconsidering that now," Stan retorted. "I sure would if I got the chance."

After they placed their orders, Stan asked Daphne why she'd returned to Appleton. She explained about Aunt Dee's death and how she felt pulled back into small town life. "But now I have a daughter to support—so I need to generate some income."

"You mean besides royalties on your bestseller novel?"

She grimaced.

"Sorry to tease you." His blue eyes looked sincerely apologetic. "Like I said, I know how it goes. Anyway, you said you have a daughter and it sounded almost as if you'd just acquired her. What's up with that?"

"That's not far from the truth." She explained about Mabel, and he just nodded.

"Well, I wish I could offer you a job, Daphne, but it's just not happening. If things continue like they're going, *The Apple Seed* will be history by next fall."

"I'm sorry to hear the newspaper is in such bad shape. I always looked forward to reading it on Tuesdays and Fridays."

"Yeah, I'm thinking about taking it to a weekly paper. How does Wednesday sound?"

"Okay." She nodded. "That might save some money."

"Maybe." He frowned. "But unless I figure out some new tricks, how to compete with the internet, or sell more ad space, or something...Appleton will lose its local newspaper."

"But there are so many new businesses in town," she pointed out. "I'm surprised they're not buying ad space."

"My last advertising man said it was hopeless."

"Is your ad space very expensive?"

"Not really."

"I'm friends with several business owners," she said, "and I've never seen them have ads in the paper. And yet it seems like it would be good business. And it's deductible."

"Yep." Stan moved his elbows off the table as Ricardo arrived with their order.

"What about you, Ricardo?" she asked pertinently. "Why don't you run an ad in the paper? Are you just cheap?"

He laughed. "I don't know. Never really thought about it before."

"Didn't Herb ever hit you up for ad space?" Stan asked.

"Not that I recall." Ricardo set a bowl of soup in front of him.

"You're kidding me." Stan frowned.

"Come to think of it, I wouldn't mind running an ad now and then. I could offer a special on my slow nights, you know?"

"Or what about putting your menu specialties in the paper?"

Daphne suggested. "Like meatloaf Monday or taco Tuesday. I sometimes forget."

"Hey, that's a great idea." Ricardo nodded.

"And what about a coupon?" Daphne said eagerly. "Like a free drink with a meal."

"Sure, I could do that. Especially during slow months like in the wintertime." Ricardo pointed to Daphne. "Maybe you should hire her to sell ad space."

Daphne laughed nervously as Ricardo returned to the kitchen. "I'm not a salesman."

"And I can't afford to hire anyone," Stan said glumly.

An idea came to her. "What if I worked on commission?"

"Commission?" He nodded with interest. "How would that work?"

She shrugged. "I'm not even sure. But maybe I could just try to generate some advertisements for you. In an effort to keep the paper in business. You could pay me what you think it's worth."

"Seriously?" He studied her. "You'd do that?"

"For a while, I might. And maybe if it went well, you'd consider giving me an editorial job." She tipped her head to one side. "I've noticed your paper doesn't have an advice column."

"You want to write an advice column?" He looked skeptical. "Let me guess, we'd call it *Dear Daphne*." He laughed. "For starters, I'd get sued by the syndication folks."

"You misunderstood me."

"Well, as you probably guessed, I can't afford a column like *Dear Daphne*."

"I figured as much."

"So, tell me, what are you suggesting?" he asked with curiosity.

"What if I could get that for you? For free?"

"The real *Dear Daphne* column for free?"

She nodded.

"Okay, you seemed like a sensible person when you were talking about selling ad space, but now I'm not so sure." He took a big bite of his burger and chewed.

"You didn't answer my question," she persisted. "What if I could get that column for free? Would that help you at all?"

"Of course it would help. Any other rabbits you could pull from your hat?" He shook some ketchup onto his fries.

"Can I trust you?" She lowered her voice, knowing this was thin ice. "I mean, I realize I don't really know you."

He shrugged. "My friends think I'm pretty trustworthy. I've never been arrested or anything."

"Well, I can get that column for your newspaper, but only if you promise to keep my involvement private."

"Hey, if you can get me that column, mum's the word." He held up his hand. "Boy Scouts' honor. And I used to be a scout, so I take that pledge seriously."

She smiled. This guy, with his fuzzy bleached hair, tattoos, and rumpled clothes, was certainly a character, but he seemed to be on the level. And if she could help him to keep the newspaper going, she was more than willing. She knew this was something that Aunt Dee would approve of. And who knew where it might lead?

Chapter 13

As Daphne was walking through town, she passed by the real estate office where her stepmother worked. Seeing Karen in the lobby, Daphne waved. Then Karen came out to say hello. "Good news," she told Daphne as she put on her sunglasses. "I just got a full cash offer on Jake McPheeters' house."

"Really?" Daphne wasn't so sure this was good news.

"I just told Jake we can close by the end of the week." Karen beamed at her.

"Well, congratulations." Daphne feigned enthusiasm. "Was Jake pleased?"

"He sounded relieved. I guess his studio apartment isn't cutting it when Jenna comes to visit. He can start doing some serious house shopping down there now." She fished her car keys out of her bag. "I see you're on foot. Need a lift anywhere?"

Daphne glanced at her watch, realizing her lunch with Stan had lasted longer than expected. "Actually, if you're going by the grade school, it's nearly time to meet Mabel."

Karen nodded to her bright yellow Mustang. "Hop in."

As Karen drove, she asked about Daphne and Mabel's trip to Florida.

"Mabel said it was the best vacation ever." Daphne chuckled. "But then she tends to have a lot of best and greatest moments."

"Considering everything, I'm guessing it's true. And Disney World—what a treat for Mabel. Jake mentioned meeting you gals down there. Sounds like you had fun." She pulled up to the school just as the kids started streaming out. "Here you go."

"Thanks, Karen."

"And Don wants to have you and Mabel over sometime this week. He's been cleaning up the patio and barbecue, acting like summer is right around the corner."

Daphne laughed. "Well, this sunny weather gives one hope. Tell Dad to give me a call." She thanked Karen as she got out of the car, waving to Mable, who was coming out of the school with Lola. Daphne knew she was probably overprotective in her habit of walking Mabel to and from school, but it was something that they both enjoyed, and she just wasn't ready to give it up.

"Hi, Mom," Mabel called out as the two girls ran to her. "Can Lola come to my house to play?"

"It's okay with me, but we'll have to get permission." Daphne pulled out her phone, hitting speed dial for Becca's number, then handing the phone to Lola. It was quickly settled, and the three of them headed for home, but Mabel and Lola, excited to play, ran on ahead, leaving Daphne to walk by herself.

As Daphne strolled along the sunny sidewalk, she felt an unexpected wave of sadness washing over her. She knew it wasn't from Mabel and Lola running ahead. And it couldn't be from the weather, because it was gorgeous out. And it wasn't even from her initial disappointment about not being considered for a paying job at the newspaper.

Her sadness was the direct result of Karen's "good news." Jake's house was sold. He was buying a new home in Miami.

It sounded so final...like the end of an era. And, sure, she'd felt resolved to this before...before their trip to Orlando. But being there last week, watching the fireworks with him, well, it had warmed her heart and reignited her hope. And now it was dashed.

Just move on, she told herself. Put one foot in front of the other and move forward. And, as she walked, she silently prayed that God would bless Jake and Jenna down in Florida. *And help me to let them go,* she added as she turned up to her house. She reminded herself that she had something to focus her energy on. And, although it would be volunteer work to begin with, it could develop into a paying job eventually. She would roll up her sleeves and do whatever she could to help preserve Appleton's only local news source.

Hearing the girls' voices upstairs, Daphne headed straight for her office, making a to-do list. For starters, she would ensure that the *Dear Daphne* column became a regular contribution to *The Apple Seed.* Besides that, she would start contacting local businesses about purchasing ad space, offering them tempting ideas in the way of coupons or promotions. And then, she decided, she would start submitting articles of local interest—for free. If Stan liked them and included them, and if the circulation picked up, they could discuss a salary later. In the meantime, it would be fun to have something to throw herself into...and a good distraction for her aching heart.

Later in the week, as Daphne was working on an article that she thought would interest Stan, she was surprised to see Spencer parking in front of her house. She hadn't seen him since their last critique group, and the next one wasn't scheduled for a couple more weeks. He got out of his car and glanced all around, almost as if he felt nervous. Then he straightened his jacket and, with something in his hand, walked up to her house.

She hurried to get the door, warmly greeting him. "Hey, Spencer, what brings you to my neck of the woods?" She welcomed him into the foyer.

His smile looked nervous. "I, uh, I just read this book, Daphne, and I felt like it was something you'd really want to read." He held up the hardback.

"What is it?" She peered at the unfamiliar title.

"It just came out," he explained. "It's a novel and, well, it kind of reminded me of your novel. I thought you might want to see it."

She thanked him. "I have coffee that's not too stale," she offered.

But Spencer just shook his head, looking down at his feet in a self-conscious way. "Thanks, but I should get back to work. I just had to do some errands in town and thought I'd stop by here too." He gave her an uneasy smile. "Didn't want to interrupt your work."

"Well, thank you for this." She held up the book and smiled brightly at him. "Have a good day."

"You too." He waved as he hurried out the door. Then, as his car pulled away, she noticed Sabrina coming across the street.

Daphne called out hello, extending the same offer of coffee.

"That would be lovely," Sabrina said as she came inside. "I was just on my way over to say 'hey' when I noticed Spencer was here." She gave Daphne a curious look. "What was that about?"

"He wanted to give me this." Daphne set the novel on the foyer table.

"Well, that must've just been an excuse," Sabrina said as they went into the kitchen. "I'll bet he's interested in you and too shy to say it."

"Oh, I don't know." Daphne emptied the coffee pot into a pair of cups.

"Don't be too sure. I got a very definite feeling at our last critique group. Remember how complimentary he was about what you read?"

"I guess so." Daphne sat down across from Sabrina.

"And so I sort of kept an eye on him, and I could tell he was watching you pretty closely. Like he was liking what he saw." Sabrina winked.

"That's because Spencer and I are friends," Daphne reminded her. "Remember, I told you about how we decided that we weren't dating material last fall. We decided to be writing friends—and nothing more."

"Sometimes friends can grow into something more," Sabrina said hopefully. "Some of the best marriages start with good friendships."

"Yes, I'm sure that's true. But don't you think there should be some chemistry too? Some electricity? Some fireworks?" Daphne immediately regretted that last metaphor. Fortunately, Sabrina didn't connect it to Jake.

"But how can you experience chemistry if you're holding someone at arms' length?" Sabrina persisted. "Don't you have to at least give them a chance?"

Daphne sighed. "I don't know. But I hardly think that Spencer is interested in me like that anyway, Sabrina."

"Then why did he make a special trip here? Just to give you a book? He could've simply emailed you about it. Or he could've brought it to our next critique group."

Daphne smiled at her eager friend. "Sabrina, I appreciate how concerned you are about my romantic life—rather, my non-romantic life—but I think you need to do what I'm doing."

"What's that?" Sabrina frowned. "Nothing?"

"I'm letting it go. If it's meant to be, it will be." To distract her, Daphne told Sabrina about her encounter with the managing editor of the local paper and how she was trying to help him save the paper. "It's just volunteer work now, but if some advertising kicks in and subscriptions pick up, it could turn into a real job in time."

"I think I met the editor at a Christmas party," Sabrina said suddenly. "Isn't *he* single?"

"I really couldn't say." Daphne wasn't about to admit that she had noticed he wasn't wearing a wedding ring, or that her general impression was that he was single. She didn't want to give Sabrina any ammo.

"I remember now. His name is Sam, right?"

"Stan. Stan Abernathy."

"Yeah, Stan. He was kind of a grungy character with funny hair and tattoos. Rather unkempt as I recall. Although I'm sure he'd be plenty attractive if you could clean him up some." She giggled.

"Maybe he's happy as is," Daphne said wryly.

"It's been a few months," Sabrina continued, "but I recall he was bummed because his girlfriend had left him. I think they'd been living together." Her brow creased. "He's probably not really your type, Daphne, but you never know."

Daphne couldn't help but laugh. "Honestly, Sabrina, if a man is breathing and single you immediately start to match me up with him. I'm surprised you haven't visited the nursing home to line up some ninety-year-old bachelor for a blind date."

"Not a bad idea," Sabrina teased. "Maybe an Alzheimer's patient. Make it easier to trick him into tying the knot."

"Thanks a lot." Daphne scowled.

"I'm sorry," Sabrina said contritely. "Anyway, I do hope your volunteer work for the newspaper pays off. I think it's very noble that you want to help keep *The Apple Seed* alive. I know how much I enjoy our little paper. You let me know if I can be any help."

"You know, Sabrina, you would be a natural sales person. You're so cheerful and positive and engaging." Daphne explained her plan to contact the local businesses to purchase ad space. "I already started making a list of possible clients and promotional suggestions."

"I'd be happy to go talk to them," Sabrina said brightly. "Just tell me what to do." So Daphne took Sabrina to her office, and before long the two of them concocted a real plan for how Sabrina could start acquiring customers.

As Daphne walked her out, Sabrina pointed to the novel still on the foyer table. "Just for the record, I still think Spencer is interested in you, Daphne. But he's just too shy to say so."

Daphne sighed as she closed the door behind Sabrina. Would she never give up on trying to marry Daphne off? Daphne picked up the novel and took it to her office, where she skimmed the first couple of pages. But not feeling compelled to read it right now, she laid it on her to-be-read pile and returned to her computer. It was possible that Sabrina was right about Spencer. Giving her that book might've been his way of showing he was interested in her. And that was sweet. But was she interested in him? Not very.

Instead of returning to her half-written article, Daphne saw that she had a new email—from Jenna—and decided to open it up.

Hey Daphne and Mabel.

I promised to write, so here goes. I'm actually in journalism class, but since the teacher isn't even here and I don't even have an assignment, I thought I'd send you a quick note. I'm sorry to say I don't like my new school. I know it's only my first week and, according to Dad, too soon to pass judgment, but most of the kids here aren't anything like the kids in Appleton. These kids are total snobs. Everything here is about money, the right clothes, and cool cars. But I did meet a couple of kids who are really nice. Cooper and Venus. I've been eating lunch with them every

day. They're not the kind of kids my mom would
like, but they accept me for who I am. That's good.
  Love,
  Jenna

Daphne felt sad for Jenna, but she agreed with Jake. Jenna just needed to give it more time. Anyway, Daphne decided to answer the email immediately. Hopefully Jenna was still in class and would read it and feel encouraged.

Dear Jenna,
  I'm so glad to hear from you and I'll share it with
Mabel when she gets home. I'm sorry you don't like
your new school. But maybe it will grow on you.
That's great you're taking journalism. You're such
a good writer! I'm doing some writing for The Apple
Seed *right now. And I'm so glad you made some good*
friends. Cooper and Venus sound nice. I hope that
things get better soon. Keep us informed.
  Love,
  Daphne

As she hit send, Daphne sighed. How hard it must be to be uprooted from her high school and good friends. But hopefully it would get easier. And it sounded like she was communicating with Jake about it. That was good. Of course, thinking about this...and thinking about Jake...well, that made Daphne feel even sadder.

Chapter 14

Daphne could hardly bear to tear the March page of her office calendar off. How was it possible that it was now April? She reached for a black marker pen and crossed of April 1. Not that the day was totally over yet, but since it was four in the afternoon, it was more than half gone. The daily countdown to May 16th, the same day Aunt Dee had passed away last year and the day that would mark the end of Daphne's one year deadline to get married this year, was officially begun.

"Forty-five days," Daphne said aloud. It sounded utterly hopeless. But, she reminded herself, it was *not* impossible. After all, all things were possible with God. Still, it would take a miracle.

Determined not to dwell on this, Daphne turned on her computer. To her delight, Stan had liked her article and printed it in last Friday's paper. And she was working on another for next week's edition. Not only that, but Stan had been pleased with the plan that Daphne and Sabrina had put together for selling ad space. After only one week, Sabrina had acquired seven new advertising accounts for the paper. Of course, they were mostly from friends' businesses, including Midge's Diner, Bernie's Blooms, The Apple Basket, The Chic Boutique and so on. But clients were clients, and Stan was not complaining one bit.

Instead of continuing with her article, Daphne opened an email from Jenna. They had already exchanged several. Until Jenna finally asked Daphne if they could communicate, sometimes, without Mabel reading what Jenna wrote. This was mostly because Jenna needed someone "safe" to talk to. She wanted to say things to Daphne that might not be appropriate for Mabel to read.

> *Hey Daphne,*
> *Thanks for your last post. Okay, I hear what you're saying and I know I need to respect my mom, but let me tell you it is not easy. She is so freaking down on my friends. When she says Cooper and Venus are "poor white trash," I want to scream. And I know that it's not that great that Cooper and Venus smoke and stuff. But it does not make them "bad" people. But my mom acts like they're criminals. She thinks that just because I'm friends with them I'll start smoking too. And that is so ridiculous. Except that the more she talks like that, the more I consider it. Maybe I will start smoking and stuff. Just to teach her a lesson. I know you won't judge me for this, Daphne. And I know you won't tell my mom either. I just need someone I can vent to. Thanks for listening.*
> *Love,*
> *Jenna*

Without thinking too hard, Daphne started to hammer back a response to Jenna. She didn't want to step on Jenna's toes, but she did want to say a few things—in the spirit of love and truth.

> *Dear Jenna,*
> *Although I agree with you that it's wrong for*

anyone to judge your friends by how they look or even the fact that they smoke, I can understand your mom's concern. Now, please don't get mad at me for saying this, but your mom loves you, Jenna. And she's probably afraid that something bad is going to happen to you. I know that Cooper and Venus have been good friends to you. But I hope that you're making other good friends too. And that you're getting involved in some school activities. You're such a smart and talented girl—and such a gifted writer. As a fellow writer, I have high hopes for you. How is your journalism class going? Any potential friends in there? And, please know, you can tell me anything. But in return, you have to allow me to express my true thoughts to you as well. Okay?
    Love,
    Daphne

Daphne was just sending that message when she saw Becca's car pulling up. It had been Becca's turn to take the girls to ballet lessons this afternoon. Daphne waved out the window, watching as Mabel hopped out of the backseat. Still wearing her tutu and carrying her shoe bag, she ran up to the house. It was at moments like this that Daphne sometimes felt like pinching herself. She and Mabel had such a full and happy life. If only it could go on like this for always.

"Mom!" Mabel called out as she ran through the house. "I gotta tell you something."

Daphne went out to meet her, exchanging a greeting and hug. "What is it?" she asked as she set the ballet shoe bag in the front closet.

"Our dance recital is on June third," she exclaimed as she handed a costume order form to Daphne. "We're doing *Alice in Wonderland* and our class is going to be the dancing flowers.

I get to be a violet so that means my tutu will be purple—my favorite color, can you believe it? Lola is a daffodil so she'll be yellow. Isn't it really, really exciting?"

Daphne nodded as she glanced at the order form. "Really exciting."

"You have to write that and make a check and get it back to Miss Kristy next week or we might not get our costumes in time."

"How about if I drop it off by the dance studio next time I'm driving that way?"

"That's even better." Mabel hugged her again. "This will be my first dance recital."

"I'm so happy for you." Daphne turned to someone knocking at the door.

"Auntie Sabrina," Mabel said with enthusiasm. "I'll let her in." She dashed to the door and started telling Sabrina about the dance recital. "And you'll come watch me, won't you?"

"Of course I will." Sabrina leaned over and kissed Mabel's cheek. "I wouldn't miss it." Sabrina approached Daphne with the biggest smile ever. It had to be about more than just Mabel's dance recital.

"You look very happy," Daphne told her.

"I'm deliriously happy."

"What's dull-eerily, huh?" Mabel asked Sabrina.

"I'm very, very happy," Sabrina told her. "Ricardo asked me to marry him."

Mabel's eyes grew wide. "Are you going to be a bride?"

"That's right, honey. Can you believe it? Old Auntie Sabrina—a bride!"

"Congratulations." Daphne hugged her. "Or maybe that's wrong. I don't think you're supposed to congratulate the bride. But I'm so happy for you."

"Of course, I want you to be in my wedding." Sabrina told Daphne. "Will you be my maid of honor?"

"Certainly," Daphne confirmed. "I'd love to. Thanks!"

"Can I be in your wedding too?" Mabel asked with excitement. "I'm going to have a purple tutu for my dance recital, I could wear it."

"I absolutely want you in my wedding too, Mabel. Will you be my flower girl?"

"Yes, yes, yes!" Mabel was jumping from one foot to the other.

"And your tutu will probably be very pretty, but I want to get you a special dress for the wedding. Okay?"

Mabel nodded eagerly. "Okay!"

"And Tootsie will be the ring bearer," Sabrina told Mabel. "But you'll have to help him with it. Can you do that?"

"Yes! Yes! Yes!"

"I want to hear all about everything," Daphne told Sabrina. "How did it happen? When did it happen?"

Sabrina told them both about how Ricardo invited her to have lunch with him. "I thought he just meant at the diner, but when I met him there, he put me in his car and drove us to the top of Rawlins Bluff." She sighed dreamily. "It's so beautiful up there. And it was a perfect day for a picnic."

"Ricardo took you for a picnic?" Mabel asked.

"Yes, he did, angel. And when we got up there, he had already set up a little table and two chairs. He even had a tablecloth and a bouquet of flowers on the table. And he had this basket of really good food. Well, I was just stunned."

"That's so romantic," Daphne told her.

"So we sat there in the grandeur of nature, enjoying each other and this scrumptious lunch and then Ricardo brought out a luscious dessert—my favorite—strawberry cheesecake. He set the cheesecake on the table, and there in the center of it was something sparkly." She held out her hand to show them an engagement ring. Although it wasn't huge and flashy, which Daphne thought was a good thing, it was very pretty.

"Beautiful," Daphne told her.

"And Ricardo got down on one knee and asked me to marry him." Sabrina's eyes were teary now. "Of course, I said yes!" She hugged them both again. "I think I'm the happiest girl in the whole, wide world."

As they continued to talk, Mabel drifted off to play, and Daphne tried to continue looking and sounding interested, but the more Sabrina talked, the harder it became.

"I'm sorry," Sabrina finally said. "I'm just rambling on and on." She put a hand on Daphne's arm. "I hope I'm not making you feel bad." She peered into Daphne's eyes. "I mean, I know that you're the one who really needs to get herself married, but I figured you'd still be happy for me."

"I'm thrilled for you, Sabrina." Daphne forced her brightest smile. "I really am." She glanced at the clock. "It's just that I should probably start dinner. Mabel had ballet today and she always is ravenous after—"

"Oh, yeah, of course. I totally lost track of the time." Sabrina stood. "I was just so excited, I couldn't wait to tell you the good news."

"I'm so glad you did. And I'm so happy for you." She walked Sabrina to the front door. "I'm happy for both of you. You guys are perfect together."

"And do you know what today is?" Sabrina asked as they went out to the porch.

"April first?" Daphne offered.

"April Fool's Day." Sabrina laughed. "And for a moment, I thought Ricardo was pulling a joke on me." She gazed down at her new engagement ring. "But this is not a joke."

"No," Daphne agreed, "it's no joke." She watched as Sabrina trotted happily across the street. And although it was true Daphne was very happy for Sabrina and Ricardo...at the same time she felt a distinct letdown. As much as she didn't want to feel the slightest smidgeon of jealousy, she still wondered—*why couldn't it be her?*

For the next couple of days, whenever Sabrina's path crossed Daphne's, the main topic of conversation seemed to always be the engagement, until Daphne finally started to cringe when she spied Sabrina coming her way. It wasn't that she wasn't happy for her friend. And it wasn't exactly jealousy. But it was discouraging. As if Sabrina's upcoming wedding, scheduled for next fall, was like a bright beacon, spotlighting the fact that May was hurtling toward her like a freight-train, and Daphne was still single.

So it was that after Mabel left for school and Daphne spied Sabrina coming out her front door—Daphne ducked out the backdoor and hurried down the alley. Headed for town, Daphne decided to get herself a coffee.

As she went into the Red River Coffee Company, she remembered the last time she'd met Jake here—and how he'd told her he was moving to Miami and given her the business card of his associate. It wasn't a happy memory, but it reminded her that she still hadn't contacted Mr. Thornton. With her May deadline quickly approaching, she should probably make an appointment.

Taking her latte to a table in back, Daphne thought about her meeting with Mr. Thornton. She could just imagine him dourly shaking his head as he grimly informed her that because she had failed to meet Aunt Dee's one stipulation— to get married—the two cats, Lucy and Ethel, would be well cared for, and The Cat House, their new home, would receive a windfall of an inheritance. And Daphne would be on her own. End of story.

"Hello?"

"Huh?" Daphne looked up to see Spencer gazing down at her with curiosity.

"You look pretty glum," he said with his typical nervous smile. "I don't expect you want company, but I thought I'd say hi."

"Please, sit down," she said eagerly.

"Really? You don't want to be alone?"

She forced a smile. "I thought I wanted to be alone. But then I, well, I wasn't enjoying it so much. Please, join me."

"Okay." He brightened as he sat across from her. "How are you doing?"

"To be honest?" She grimaced. "I've been better."

"Is something wrong?"

She shrugged. "Nothing I can do anything about. Just life."

His brow creased. "Did you read the book I brought by?"

"I'm sorry," she said with realization. "I've been so busy lately. I haven't really had the chance."

"Oh, that's okay." He seemed slightly relieved. "So have you been doing much writing lately?"

She told him about trying to help the newspaper by contributing free stories.

"I guess I should be reading it more closely," he said. "I'll go back and read your articles now."

"And if you ever feel like donating a story, I'm sure Stan would appreciate it."

"I'll keep that in mind."

"Something you can add to your bio," she said absently.

"You really do seem down, Daphne." He peered at her with genuine concern. "I'm a good listener if you want to talk."

She considered spilling her whole story to him but then knew she couldn't. "I guess I was just feeling lonely." She explained about Ricardo and Sabrina.

"I heard about that."

"And I'm really happy for both of them. But sometimes it's hard hearing Sabrina going on and on about it. You know?" She told him about sneaking out the backdoor this morning.

Spencer laughed. "That's understandable. It's kind of like being a writer and hearing that a friend has contracted a book with a big New York house. That happened to me back in college, with a friend who'd written a memoir that hadn't even seemed that good. But I had to act like I was thrilled for him. The truth was, I felt secretly jealous."

"Yes," she agreed. "That would be similar."

"Speaking of book contracts, have you heard anything from your agent?"

"Just that she's submitting it to a number of houses. And she's feeling very hopeful." Daphne's spirits lifted slightly. "I'm grateful for just that."

"Well, you're a really good writer," he assured her. "You deserve to be published."

"Thanks."

They talked about books and writing, and before she knew it nearly two hours had passed. "I need to go," she announced after she checked her phone. "I promised to meet with the managing editor at eleven, to go over some things. But it was really fun bumping into you like this."

He nodded as they stood. "Maybe we should do it on purpose next time."

She smiled. "That would be nice."

"And unless I see you sooner, I'll see you at critique group next week," he told her. "That's at your house, right?"

She confirmed this, but as she walked home, she considered his words about getting together again. Was Spencer asking her on a date? Or did he just want to chat about writing and books—with a friend? It was probably the latter. And the truth was that was all she really wanted too. A book friend. What was wrong with that?

Chapter 15

The next morning, a letter for the advice column reminded Daphne of her coffee "date" with Spencer. As she vaguely considered her answer, she wondered if perhaps she'd been too hasty about him. Perhaps she had dismissed him too easily. What if she had missed something? After all, he had all the ingredients for a good friend. Lots of people married their best friends—many remained happily married into their twilight years. Meanwhile she knew couples who fell madly in love, got married, and then got divorced. Seriously, what did she really know about any of this romance, love, and marriage business? And what qualified her to answer letters like this?

> *Dear Daphne,*
>
> *My best friend is a guy. We've been best friends since seventh grade, and in college, we made an agreement that if neither of us was married when we turned thirty, we'd tie the knot. Okay, we saw this in a movie, but it sounded like a good idea at the time. But we're both turning thirty this year and neither of us are married. My friend recently sent me an email, expressing serious interest in getting married. As much as I want to be married, I'm not*

sure I want to marry him. But then, I really do enjoy him. I like being with him. At the same time, I don't want to sacrifice our friendship if it doesn't work out. What should I do?
Befuddled in Brooklyn

Daphne stared at the blank computer screen waiting for her response. What should she tell this woman? How could she guide poor Befuddled? How could she keep her from making a regrettable mistake? Oh, it wasn't that Daphne believed that readers took her advice column too seriously. Certainly, she hoped they didn't. Even so, she liked to give the best advice possible. Even when it was difficult.

Dear Befuddled,
Your question isn't easily answered. But you probably knew that already. As you must know, many people do marry their best friends—and many of them enjoy wonderful, long-lasting relationships too. But to marry someone simply because "in college you made an agreement," sounds a bit reckless to me. While a good solid marriage should be built on a good solid friendship, I'm not sure that a good solid friendship is always the key to a good solid marriage. You need to search your heart—ask yourself if this guy is the one you want to commit the rest of your life to (for better or for worse, richer or poorer, in sickness and health). If you can honestly answer yes, then you should marry him. Otherwise, keep him as your friend and see what else life has in store for you.
Daphne

On Friday night, Daphne agreed to baby-sit for Olivia again.

But only after Olivia said it was just for a couple of hours, and only after she assured Daphne that Bernadette was over her colicky spell now. "They say it usually tapers off after six weeks," Olivia explained as she dropped the baby off. "She's been much better all week."

Mabel's reservations about babysitting were similar to Daphne's, but after the first hour, she began to actually enjoy playing with the baby and trying to make her smile. By the time Olivia and Jeff picked Bernadette up, Daphne and Mabel were almost sad to see her go.

"That was a piece of cake," Daphne told Olivia. "Feel free to ask again—anytime."

"I'd ask you to baby-sit next for me on Saturday night," Olivia said as she buckled the baby into the car-seat, "but I know you'll want to go to the wedding too."

"Wedding?" Daphne thought of Sabrina's plans, but that was still many months away.

"Mick and Julianne's wedding," Olivia reminded her.

"Oh, yeah, that's right." Daphne walked them to the door.

"Do I get to go to the wedding too?" Mabel asked after they were gone.

"I don't know, sweetie," Daphne said apologetically. She knew Mick's wedding celebration would be more adult-oriented. "It's going to be a pretty late night. I might need to find a babysitter for you too."

"I wish Jenna could come," Mabel said wistfully.

"You and me both." Daphne thought hard. "But how about Mattie? She's Jenna's best friend, and I think she baby-sits sometimes too."

"Yes," Mabel agreed. "Mattie will be fine."

As Daphne looked for Mattie's number, she explained how the girl was actually a cousin. "Not a close cousin," Daphne told her. "But her great grandpa was my grandma's brother."

"So she's my cousin too?"

Daphne just nodded as Mattie answered her phone, and soon it was settled. Mattie would baby-sit Mabel next Saturday night. Of course, Daphne wasn't even sure she wanted to go to the wedding—by herself. Originally it was agreed that she and Sabrina would go together. But with Sabrina going with Ricardo, that was out. Did Daphne really want to go stag?

Sabrina caught Daphne at home the next morning. "Daphne Ballinger, have you been avoiding me?" she asked pointedly as she followed Daphne into the kitchen.

"Avoiding you?" Daphne asked innocently. "Why would I avoid you?" She handed her a cup of coffee with a bright smile. "You know I love you, Sabrina. I've just had a really busy week. I'm sure you have too."

"You can say that again." Sabrina flopped a thick magazine onto the kitchen table. "Do you realize that December is only nine months away?"

"I hadn't really done the math on it." Daphne carried her own coffee mug to the table and sat down. "But it's not like you and Ricardo *have* to get married in December."

"But I've always wanted to get married in December," Sabrina told her. "I remember when I was little girl and my mama talking about how special it was to be a December bride. She thought that was so romantic. And my other wedding was in Vegas. In July. And not very memorable. Kind of like my marriage."

"Vegas must be hot in July."

"That's for sure. But I hope there'll be snow on the ground for my wedding. And I want holly and evergreen garlands and poinsettias and we'll have hot cocoa and candy canes at the reception. And well, you know, the works."

Daphne nodded. She did know. Sabrina had reiterated her December wedding plans more than once. "But if December is coming too quickly, you could always wait until next year." Daphne figured Sabrina would balk at this idea.

"That's too long for an engagement." Sabrina opened the bridal magazine, flipping to a page marked with a neon post-it, pointing to a pale pink gown that looked straight out of *Gone with the Wind*. "Well, that's, uh, interesting," Daphne said cautiously. "Would that be your bridal gown?"

"Oh, no. My bridal gown will be white velvet. This is a bridesmaid gown," Sabrina clarified. "Of course, I wouldn't want it in pink. I'd really like a scarlet red, but I'm not sure how your hair would look with it, although I've heard that redheads can wear red, as long as it's the right shade of red. I think red would look real Christmassy. Especially with all the greens around."

Daphne cringed to imagine that gown in scarlet. She'd probably look like Mrs. Santa on a bad hair day. Daphne leaned back in the kitchen chair, averting her eyes from that horrible gown as she sipped her coffee. Why was it that brides always insisted on dressing their bridesmaids in such hideous costumes? Was it to make the bride look better? To seek revenge for the gowns she might've been forced to wear for previous weddings? But what had Daphne done to deserve such treatment?

"I, uh, I wonder what Julianne's bridesmaids will wear at her wedding?" Daphne felt certain it wouldn't be anything like the big antebellum gown.

"I can't wait to see." Sabrina closed her magazine. "Julianne has such great taste. It'll probably be a gorgeous wedding. I told Ricardo I'll be taking notes." She giggled. "Well, not literally. But I'll be paying close attention."

Daphne tried not to glaze over as Sabrina went on and on about weddings and what she felt made them good or bad. She had obviously given it considerable thought. But how anyone could get so caught up in planning a one day event was a mystery to Daphne. Even if she were fortunate to have a wedding someday, she didn't think she would become obsessive about it. Not that she needed to concern herself.

"I'm sorry," Sabrina said abruptly. "I must be boring you."

"What?" Daphne blinked, sitting up straighter, trying to appear attentive.

Sabrina leaned forward, peering curiously at her. "I'm sorry. I realize my wedding plans are probably a little difficult for you to hear. I mean, in light of your own circumstances."

"My own circumstances?" For some reason this terminology irritated Daphne.

"Well, you know. We so wanted you to be engaged by now. But unfortunately that just hasn't happened." Sabrina fiddled with the edge of the magazine. "Maybe it's unkind for me to expect that you'd enjoy planning my special day with me. Although I must say, if the roles were reversed, I would be thrilled to help you."

"I'm sorry, Sabrina. And, no, you're not being unkind," Daphne assured her. "But I guess I'm just not that into all the wedding stuff."

"But didn't you used to cover the weddings for *The New York Times*?"

"Maybe that's the problem. I got so inundated with weddings that I just quit caring about them in general."

"So if you were getting married, would you have a wedding?"

Daphne sighed. "I honestly don't know. I mean, Olivia made me promise her that she could plan my wedding if I ever made it to the altar."

"I'd want to help you too," Sabrina protested. "Don't leave me out of the fun."

"Thanks, but you don't need to be concerned. Just focus on your own big day with Ricardo." Daphne smiled. "You know you're getting one of the best men in Appleton."

Sabrina beamed at her. "I know." But then her smile faded. "I remember when you told me how you had a crush on Ricardo as a teenager. And for a while I really thought that you two would get together."

Daphne laughed. "You and my dad. He was trying to push poor Ricardo at me when I first moved back here."

"I still remember seeing you two dancing together at the street fair last fall. I never told you this, but I felt seriously envious because I really liked Ricardo. When I saw you two together, it was like watching a scene out of *I Love Lucy*. You guys looked so perfect together that I honestly thought you'd end up married."

Daphne chuckled to think of this. "Just like Ricky and Lucy?"

Sabrina nodded soberly.

"Don't forget that they got divorced."

"That's true. But I still can't believe Ricardo didn't go after you."

"Ricardo is a great guy," Daphne admitted. "But I could never imagine myself married to him. I really do prefer him as a friend—and as my dear friend's husband."

"So that old crush? You don't still feel like that sometimes?" Sabrina still looked unconvinced. "I mean, I never would've gotten over it myself."

"I got over Ricardo way back when," Daphne assured her. "And I'm sure you're right, Sabrina, you should *never* get over him."

Sabrina's smile returned. "Oh, I won't. I know I won't."

Later that morning, Daphne was doing some damage control in the yard. A few plants had gotten bitten by some of the low temperatures last winter, and after she removed them, she realized she needed some new plants to put in their places. And so she called The Garden Guy Nursery, although with Mick and Julianne's wedding just days away, she wasn't entirely sure they'd be open. But Julianne answered cheerfully.

"I'm surprised that you guys are open," Daphne told her. "I thought you might be buried in wedding preparations right now. You're really doing business this week?"

"You bet. Spring is our busy season. We're open all week. Well, until Friday anyway. And we won't reopen for a week, when we get back from our honeymoon in Kauai."

"You don't sound very stressed out." Daphne asked how the wedding preparations were coming.

"Everything seems to be falling into place," Julianne said. "But I've tried to keep it simple. I'm using plants and flowers from our own nursery. And I don't go in for all the bells and whistles that some brides insist on. I'm pretty low key."

"I think you sound very sensible." Daphne wanted to add that Julianne could give Sabrina lessons.

"Well, you know Mick. He didn't want a big fancy wedding. He said if it wasn't going to be fun, he wasn't going to come." She laughed. "And we've got a great blue grass band coming for the reception. And, oh yeah, Mick's 'mate' Collin is here. That was a surprise. But as a matter of fact, he asked about you, Daphne."

Daphne cringed to remember how glad she'd been to say goodbye to the slightly arrogant Australian. "Well, tell Collin hello for me," she said crisply. And changing the subject, she explained her need for some new plants. With Julianne's help they decided on some hardy shrubs that Julianne promised would make it through the coldest Appleton winters. "We just got them in from a nursery up north. They're low and evergreen and spread horizontally."

"That sounds perfect."

"And Mick's doing a few deliveries this afternoon," Julianne told her. "We could throw them in if you want."

"Thanks, that'd be great. And I'm looking forward to

Saturday."

As Daphne put her phone away, she remembered the first time she'd met Mick. She chuckled to recall her embarrassment at being discovered by the handsome Aussie "gardener"—she'd only had on a flimsy nightgown at the time. Although Mick had taken it in stride. Then she'd been surprised to learn how close Mick had been with Aunt Dee. So close that she'd even wondered if Mick had been Aunt Dee's secret pick for a husband for Daphne.

As much as Daphne liked Mick, he really wasn't her type. Or so she had told herself back then. Although sometimes she wondered. Why had she been so quick to pass up opportunities with guys like Mick and Ricardo? Had she even really given them a chance?

Once again, she started running through the guys that had shown interest in her this past year. It wasn't exactly a short list either. But with each one, she had arrived at a place where she knew they were not "the one." But now she felt unsure. Just how had she known this?

Of course, the answer was fairly obvious. In fact, there had been one common denominator in almost all these relationships. One piece of the puzzle that always helped her put the kaput on getting more involved. That common denominator was Jake. But admitting this to herself was not the least bit reassuring. Especially now that Jake was out of the picture.

As she weeded a flower bed, she tried to wrap her head around this past year. Was it really true that her feelings for Jake had made her burn each bridge between her and every available bachelor in Appleton? And if she had done that, where had it gotten her? Still single, about to lose all of Aunt Dee's estate, and unemployed. Really? She threw down her spade and stood up straight. Was it possible that she had been a complete fool? And what about Jake's role in all this? He was supposed to be her legal counsel...and yet he'd allowed her to get swept away by his charms...and ruined her chances of marrying anyone before her year ended next month. Was it possible he'd done it on purpose? What if he, as the attorney, had something to gain? Oh, she knew that was perfectly ridiculous. And equally ridiculous to be angry at Jake. But she just couldn't help herself.

Chapter 16

She was still fuming when Mick arrived with the evergreen shrubs. "Sorry I can't help you plant them," he said as he set them alongside the driveway. "But I've got more deliveries to make."

"That's okay." She smiled. "I've got the holes all ready for them anyway. I just appreciate you bringing them by. Thanks."

He pulled a twig from her hair. "Looks like you've been working hard."

"Polishing up my gardening skills." She held up a hand to show him her dirty fingernails. "See?"

"Impressive." He grinned. "But you might consider some gardening gloves. Julianne swears by them."

"Smart girl." She nodded. "Are you ready for your big day?"

He shrugged. "I reckon I am. Still can't believe she talked me into it."

"Julianne is a great girl, Mick."

He laughed. "Yeah, I know. I'm a lucky bloke."

"And you love her, don't you?"

"Yeah, sure. But just because you love someone doesn't mean you have to marry them."

Daphne considered this. "But don't you want to marry her?"

He rubbed his chin. "I thought I did. But Collin's been here this week. Talking about how he loves being a bachelor and how he never plans to marry again. Makes a bloke think, you know?"

"Oh, that Collin." She waved her hand dismissively. "If you ask me, Collin has some growing up to do. No woman in her right mind would want to marry him anyway. Not if he's still drinking like a fish and treating females like dogs."

"You sound like Julianne." Mick threw back his head and laughed. "I reckon you got him pegged just about right."

"Well, you don't have to tell him I said that." She gave him a sheepish smile.

"Collin was asking about you. I think he's looking forward to dancing with you at the wedding."

She rolled her eyes. "I suppose it wouldn't kill me to dance with him. But just one dance!"

"I'll be sure to let him know." Mick chuckled. "You know, Daphne, you remind me of Dee in a lot of ways."

"Well, we were related, after all."

"Yeah, but maybe living in her house this past year has made the old girl rub off on you. Or maybe it's the dirty fingernails." He pointed to her hands. "But you really do remind me of her."

Daphne smiled. "Thanks. I will take that as a compliment."

"And, sure, she was a lot older, but I gotta say that woman had spunk. And seems to me you're getting pretty spunky too, Daph." He grinned as he opened the cab of his truck. "And it looks good on you."

As he climbed into his truck, she asked if he planned to come to their critique group tomorrow night. "I know you must be pretty busy. I'll understand if you can't make it."

"Yeah, I'll have to take a pass this month. But tell the others hey for me, and that I'm looking forward to seeing them all on Saturday night." He held up a finger. *"Be there or be square—* that's what Julianne keeps telling everyone."

She waved as he backed out of her driveway. But as she

picked up a potted shrub, carrying it to the side yard, she was still wondering at Mick's words. Really, did she have spunk? She wished it were true. So many times it felt like she passively sat back, watching life passing her by, waiting for something to happen. That wasn't what a spunky woman would do. Suddenly Daphne was sick of being a wallflower. No more sitting on the sidelines for her. Maybe she did have spunk after all!

After several hours of working in the yard, Daphne took a quick shower then, with her hair still damp, went to her computer to read her email. She was pleased to see that Jenna had written again, but to her dismay Jenna sounded more jaded and cynical than ever. Daphne wasn't sure if it was the influence of her new friends Cooper and Venus, or if it was related to Jenna's mom. Gwen would never be a candidate for Mother of the Year, but Daphne felt that surely she loved her only daughter. How could she not?

Reading Jenna's words about her mom's selfishness and their many disagreements was concerning. In her last email, Daphne had suggested that Jenna should open up about these things to her dad. But Jenna sounded worried. At first it seemed like she didn't want to trouble him, but as Daphne read between the lines, she could hear Jenna's insecurity. Jenna didn't want to rock Jake's boat by letting him see that his sweet, smart, darling daughter, was on the verge of making some questionable choices.

Daphne felt torn. As Jenna's confidante, she wanted to respect the girl's privacy. But as a caring adult who didn't want to see Jenna's life turned into a train-wreck, Daphne felt like she needed to become an informant. Yet she knew that could backfire. Not only on her relationship with Jenna. But Jake might resent this intrusion as well. What parent wants to be told by an outsider that he was blowing it? And in Daphne's opinion, Jake was blowing it.

From what she could tell, Jake was so caught up in his attempt to help Jenna fall in love with Florida that he wasn't really listening to her. He wasn't asking her the right kind of questions. And he was allowing her to slip through his fingers. At least that's how it seemed to Daphne.

Seeing it was nearly time to get Mabel from school, Daphne shot off a quick response to Jenna, encouraging her to believe and respect herself—and not to lower her standards in order to impress her friends. Daphne also tried to convince her to be more honest with her dad. And she said a silent prayer for Jenna as she hit send.

Since today was a ballet day and Daphne's turn to take both Lola and Mabel to their lesson, she drove to school, taking her turn in the drive through to pick up the girls.

"I love riding in Bonnie," Lola said with enthusiasm as the girls buckled up in the backseat.

"Me too," Mabel chirped. "And when it gets warmer, Mom is going to put her top down."

"Bonnie is the most beautiful car in the world," Lola declared. "My mom says so too."

"Tell your mom thank you," Daphne told her. As she drove through town, Daphne felt a wave a sadness rush through her. Bonnie, the classic 1955 Corvette that had belonged to Aunt Dee, was part of the estate. In just over a month, Bonnie, like everything else, would no longer be part of Daphne and Mabel's lives. In fact, unless summer came early, it was unlikely that they would drive Bonnie around with the top down and the wind blowing through their hair like Daphne had promised Mabel. Perhaps it was time to start warning Mabel of this possibility. But not today.

Daphne parked and walked the girls into the dance studio, helping them to get into their tights and tutus and shoes before she took a chair with the other moms who liked to watch while they waited. Normally, Daphne loved this time. It made her feel like a "real" mom. Not that she wasn't a real mom, but something about sitting with these women, exchanging brief bits of conversation, well, it was rather reassuring.

But as she sat there today, Daphne did not feel reassured. In fact, she felt rather agitated. And she knew that these emotions were related to Jake. So much so that it felt as if her irritation at him was growing by the minute. As if she might actually explode from it.

She knew it had started when she'd first realized that Jake was the common denominator in all her failed romances. Okay, maybe that was an exaggeration, but not by much. Hadn't Jake encouraged her to send her old boyfriend Ryan Holloway packing last summer? And for good reason too—Ryan was a selfish jerk and a cad. But Jake had also helped her to realize that marrying Mabel's Uncle Daniel was a mistake. And maybe it would've been. But was it Jake's place to point this out to her? Why did it seem that every time she got involved with a man, Jake would show up and pull the plug on it for her? Oh, she knew that wasn't exactly fair or even true, but it was how she felt!

Finally, tired of stewing over Jake's involvement in her love life, if she could even call it that, Daphne remembered Jenna's last post. Pulling it up on her phone, Daphne reread it, cringing to imagine sweet Jenna with a cigarette hanging out of her mouth, which was just one of the new vices she admitted to trying. *Partly to get back at Mom*, she wrote. *Partly because I want my friends to accept me.*

Daphne wanted to write Jenna again, pointing out that polluting her own lungs and endangering her own health was not a good way to punish a parent. She also wanted to write that friends should accept you for who you are, not for what you do or don't do. Not that Jenna would be inclined to listen to Daphne preaching at her. Instead she decided to tip off Jake. But worried that one of the moms might read over her shoulder and recognize Jake's name, Daphne took her phone out to her car to write a very heartfelt message.

Dear Jake,

I hope you don't find this email intrusive, but I have been in contact with Jenna during the past couple of weeks, and I have some cause for alarm. But before you read on, please, agree with me that you will not reveal your source of information on this. Jenna trusts me and tells me things that she doesn't feel you or Gwen can handle.

Jenna's new friends Cooper and Venus are a bit rougher than her old friends in Appleton. They smoke cigarettes at school. They also drink alcohol. And occasionally they smoke marijuana. I hope you are sitting down now. Jenna had confided to me that she has been tempted to do some experimenting on her own. She says it's partly because she wants to and partly because she's so angry at Gwen for moving her to Miami.

I've tried to counsel her to make better decisions and to talk to you about what's going on, but she is reluctant. I think she's afraid to spoil her image as "Daddy's good little girl." But Jenna is a good girl. She's a smart girl. And I hate seeing her going down this road. I'm praying that you will spend some time with her. I hope you won't lecture her or come down hard on her, but just listen to her. She deserves to be heard.

Daphne

As Daphne got out of the car, she heard her phone buzzing

to announce a new email. It seemed impossible that Jake could've responded so quickly, but out of curiosity she checked to see. To her pleased surprise the post was from her agent, Marta Stein. Hopefully it was good news. With a happily racing heart, Daphne stepped into the foyer to read her email.

> *Dear Daphne,*
>
> *As I told you a couple of weeks ago, I've sent your book proposal to several acquisition editors that I felt would be interested. I have just heard back from the first one. It is not good news. Although the editor concedes that you're an adept writer, he has questioned the content of your story. Apparently there is a recently released novel, climbing the bestsellers' list, that is strikingly similar to your book. So similar that this editor actually used the word 'plagiarism.' Although I cannot believe that you would attempt such a thing, it begs the question: Is your book an original work? You signed a legally binding contract with me stating this was original. And if your book is original, I need to know if you read this other book and, if so, were you influenced by its content? I'm reading that book right now. It's called 'After the Fair' and is published by—*

Daphne stopped reading. That was the title of the book that Spencer had dropped by her house last week—the book that he had encouraged her to read. Was *this* why? Did Spencer suspect her of plagiarism too? She felt shocked and sickened. How could this happen?

The little girls were streaming out of their class so it was too late to attempt an intelligent answer to Marta's prickly questions, and typing out *NOOOO* just didn't seem appropriate. Distracted with helping Mabel and Lola into their street shoes and jackets, Daphne knew this news from her agent would have to wait. But plagiarism? *Really?*

As she drove home, Daphne felt a deep sadness enveloping her. As if all her dreams were vanishing before her very eyes. Going up in nasty black puffs of smoke. And there seemed to be nothing she could do about it. As the girls chatted happily in the backseat, Daphne struggled to hold back her tears. She couldn't let them see she was upset. She would have to save her emotions for later—in the privacy of her own room after Mabel was tucked into bed. In the meantime, she needed to be steady and strong and dependable. She needed to be a mom.

Chapter 17

Feeling slightly robotic, Daphne went through the paces of fixing dinner, cleaning it up, and helping Mabel with her homework, but instead of playing a game like Mabel wanted, Daphne suggested they watch a DVD until bedtime. "And you can pick it." Naturally, Mabel didn't protest. At bedtime, still wearing her mechanical mom smile, Daphne tucked Mabel in, read from *Little House*, and listened to her prayers. But after Mabel said *amen* she reached for Daphne's hand, looking up at her with big brown eyes. "I know you're sad, Mom. Did I do something bad?"

Daphne leaned down to hug her. "No, darling, you have done nothing bad. You are the rightest, brightest, bestest part of my whole life." She kissed her cheek. "I love you to the moon and back, and I promise I will be back to my old self tomorrow." She kissed her again then turned off the light. And as she went downstairs, Daphne was determined to keep that promise. Tomorrow. Tonight, she needed a good hard cry. But not until she was certain that Mabel was soundly sleeping.

After her cry, Daphne kept herself up until the wee hours of the morning. Reading and skimming the novel that Spencer had given her, the similarities between her novel and this one did seem uncanny. But there were many differences too. By the time she finished the book, she knew that it would be up to her to prove her innocence. Thanks to her computer, her critique group, and several other friends who knew about her novel, it shouldn't be too difficult to do. The fact that she had to do it was irksome, but the truth was it was no one's fault. Just one of those things.

As promised, Daphne was pretty much her usual self in the morning. At least she made a sincere effort, keeping her voice cheery and animated until she waved goodbye to Mabel at the school. On her way back home, Daphne still felt troubled by her agent's accusation. Or perhaps it was the editor who'd accused her. Whatever the case, it was all very disturbing and she planned to address it.

But since she was hosting critique group tonight, Daphne didn't have time to do more than send Marta a quick post to confirm her innocence along with the promise that she could prove it too. After that, she turned off her computer and went to work thoroughly cleaning her house and baking ginger cookies. She didn't check her email until the afternoon and although Marta's response was somewhat encouraging, she still sounded slightly doubtful about the chances of selling a manuscript that was so similar to this new bestseller.

Determined not to obsess over this bad news, Daphne decided to spend some time outside in the sunshine, working on her yard and cutting some flowers to arrange for tonight's little gathering. She was looking forward to being with her writer friends and hoped to garner some sympathy and support from the diverse group.

As she was carrying her spring bouquet up to the house, Sabrina called from across the street, hurrying over to join Daphne on the porch. "Ooh, isn't that pretty." Sabrina pointed to the tulips, pansies and hyacinths in the canning jar.

"I wanted something cheerful for critique group. You are coming, aren't you?" She explained that Mick would be absent.

"We're definitely coming," Sabrina confirmed. "I have a brand new chapter to read. It's only four pages, but I think it's pretty good. And Ricardo has been making real good progress on his cookbook too. We'll both be there with bells on."

Daphne suddenly realized that she would have nothing new to read to the group tonight, but maybe it didn't matter. She sighed deeply as she toyed with the blooms in the jar. "Well, I should probably keep moving. Still have a few things to get done before I pick up Mabel."

"You seem a little down." Sabrina placed a hand on Daphne's forearm. "I sure hope I didn't offend you the other day. Going on about the wedding and my silly worries about you still being smitten with Ricardo." Sabrina laughed. "That just shows how insecure I must be deep down. I told Ricardo about what I said to you and he told me that was crazy."

"What was crazy?"

"The idea of you and him as a couple." She chuckled. "He assured me that you are not his type."

"Oh."

"I mean Ricardo really likes you, Daph. As a friend. But he never had any romantic inclinations." Sabrina smiled. "That was reassuring to hear."

"I'm sure it was."

"And Ricardo told me that I should lighten up on all my wedding talk when I'm around you. He said I was probably making you feel bad." She looked sympathetic. "And I'm sure he's right. I was being insensitive. I just assumed that you'd be as excited about it as I was. I'll try to control myself better, keep a lid on things...and be more thoughtful about how you might be feeling."

This made Daphne felt guilty—like she'd kicked a dog or dumped a barrel of ice water on Sabrina's wedding parade.

"You don't have to do that, Sabrina. Just keep being yourself—I like you just as you are. But maybe you could keep in mind that I'm not really that into weddings. So don't take it personally if I don't get all excited about a dress or something."

Sabrina hugged her. "See, that's just one more reason I love you, Daphne. You're so smart and understanding."

"I love you too."

"See you tonight," Sabrina chirped as she trotted back toward her house.

As much as Daphne loved Sabrina, and she did, she still felt a little aggravated about what she'd said about Ricardo. Plus the fact that he and Sabrina were discussing Daphne like that. Oh, she knew it was how couples should be—open and honest about things—but the comment about Daphne not being his type stung a little.

She knew she was probably reading too much into it, but as she went inside, she couldn't help but feel a bit like a castoff. Not that Ricardo had cast her off. That was silly. But the idea that he'd never had any interest in her at all—well, that sort of hurt. And she knew it was ridiculous to feel hurt. Was she really that thin-skinned?

As she put the flowers into a vase, Daphne thought about Sabrina and Ricardo. In some ways they were an odd pair. Sabrina was bubbly and outspoken whereas Ricardo was more quiet and serious. Sabrina was short and blonde, Ricardo was tall and dark. Really, they were opposites in almost every way. But then, didn't opposites attract sometimes? The important thing was that they were happy. And Daphne was happy for them. Wasn't she?

But if she was really happy for them, why did she feel so agitated every time Sabrina mentioned their wedding? Maybe it had been a mistake for Daphne to agree to be Sabrina's maid of honor. Didn't that suggest that Daphne would be enthused about the wedding—and all the plans preceding it? Yet if

Daphne were being completely honest, she would tell Sabrina that she didn't want to be involved in the planning part of it. In fact, she might not want any part of it.

As Daphne set the vase of flowers on the table in the foyer, she wondered if she was simply jealous of Sabrina. That might be why she felt so antagonistic about the wedding plans. What if the roles were reversed, like Sabrina had suggested the other day? Not just in that Daphne was about to be a bride...but what if they were completely reversed?

What if Ricardo had asked Daphne to marry him? And what if she had accepted? Daphne had dismissed this completely before, but in the back of her mind she knew that Ricardo was really quite a catch. Her dad had really pushed her toward Ricardo last summer. And it was true that Daphne had nurtured quite a crush on him in high school. What if things had gone differently and she was planning a wedding with him now?

Suddenly she remembered an unanswered *Dear Daphne* letter. She still had a couple that she'd meant to finish by the end of the week, which was tomorrow. So she hurried into her office and turned on her computer. She had just enough time to knock them out before picking up Mabel at school. She opened the first letter and, upon reading it, remembered why it had felt familiar before. Certainly it was different...and yet there was something that made her feel uncomfortable...made her feel that she needed to address something in herself too.

Dear Daphne,

I've read your column for years, but never thought that I'd actually write to you. But I'm so enraged at my ex-best friend that I don't know what else to do. You see, I'd been with this guy "Max" for the past several years. Admittedly, it was kind of an off-and-on again relationship and we fought a lot. And I broke up with him about every two months.

But my best friend "Sally" knew that I loved him and hoped to marry him someday. So the last time I broke up with him, Max told me that was it and we were never getting back together and, okay, I guess he meant it, but I've said the same thing before and taken it back later. But less than two months after we broke up, Sally started dating Max! I was furious and told her that she needed to choose between Max and me. Well, she chose Max, and now I'm done with her. But I feel like a two-time loser now. I lost my boyfriend and my best friend, and I'm so depressed I don't know what to do. Help me, please!

Double-crossed in Detroit

Dear Double-crossed,

You sound very frustrated—and understandably so. But as much as it feels like your ex-boyfriend and ex-best friend double-crossed you, I can't help but think you played a very significant role. According to your letter, you are the one who consistently broke up with Max. That tells me that you knew he wasn't really the one for you. Otherwise, you wouldn't have broken up. And I can only assume that something with that relationship was fundamentally wrong. Why else would you keep breaking up? So you need to let Max go. And if you can't forgive your ex-best friend, you might need to let her go as well. And remember that sometimes we think we want something just because someone else has it—that could be the situation with your friend and Max. You don't really want to be with him, but it irks you to see your friend with him. I encourage you to consider forgiving both of them. It might be the best way for you to have a fresh start in your own life. Because it

sounds to me like that's what you need. Learn from
what happened and move forward.
   Daphne

Daphne wasn't completely satisfied with her response letter and wondered if she'd have to revise it tomorrow. But one part of it stuck with her. Sometimes she *did* want what someone else had—or at least she thought she did. She remembered how she'd felt a little envious of Olivia's "perfect" life. Until she kept Bernadette overnight. That was an eye-opener. But lately, watching Sabrina happily concocting wedding plans with Ricardo, Daphne had tried not to feel like it was a case of insult to injury. Not only did Daphne not have a man in her life, she might end up losing everything as a result. And Sabrina knew that!

Even so, Daphne knew she needed to get over it and move on. And, like she'd advised Double-crossed, perhaps Daphne needed to forgive Sabrina too. Not that Sabrina had done anything wrong to her. But Daphne needed to forgive the fact that Sabrina's life was on a better track than Daphne's. Or at least it appeared to be. And so that's what she did.

And once Daphne acknowledged this perceived discrepancy, at least to herself, it was easier to let it go. Easier to feel honestly happy for Sabrina and Ricardo. And easier to trust God for whatever was ahead.

It hadn't escaped Daphne's radar that she had heard nothing back from either Jenna or Jake. And in some ways this was a relief. She had enough on her plate right now. And maybe no news was good news. Perhaps Jake and Jenna were talking and resolving some of these simmering issues.

It wasn't until she was getting Mabel set up with some projects to occupy her during critique group that Daphne gave them a real second thought. And only because her phone buzzed with a text message from Jake. Unfortunately it was rather abrupt and filled with irritation.

Am with Jenna now. Not going well. Thanks for interfering.

She reread the message, trying to determine if she misunderstood, but the meaning seemed clear. Jake resented her intrusion. Well, fine, she thought as she turned off her phone, just shoot the messenger. Fortunately, she didn't have time to nurture her hurt feelings because someone was at the door.

"Remember to finish your homework," Daphne reminded Mabel, "before you do this." She pointed to the new activity book that Mabel had been looking forward to.

"I know," Mabel said as she sat hunkered over her desk, pencil in hand. "And I'll get on my pajamas and brush my teeth first."

"That's right." Daphne kissed her forehead.

"And I'll put myself to bed at eight o'clock."

"And I'll pop up to tell you goodnight."

Daphne hurried downstairs to see that Sabrina and Ricardo were the first to arrive. "I'm so glad you let yourselves in," she said as she hugged them both, taking their coats and feeling genuinely glad to see them both.

"Something smells good." Sabrina sniffed.

"I made ginger cookies," Daphne told them. "The chewy kind, topped with cream cheese frosting."

"Sounds yummy," Ricardo told her.

"Help yourselves," Daphne hung up their coats. "And there's hot water for tea and a fresh pot of decaf." The doorbell rang and she excused herself to answer it.

"Hi Wally." Daphne smiled as she opened the door wide. "Come on in." She took his coat and directed him toward the cookies in the kitchen then waved to Spencer who was coming up the walk. Going out to the porch, she talked quietly to him, quickly explaining about her agent's email and the plagiarism accusation. "Is that why you gave me that book?"

He gave her a sheepish smile. "I was a little worried about it."

"Did you think I stole my story?" She peered curiously at his face.

His brows arched. "No, of course not, Daphne. I know you've been working on that novel for a long time. I've heard you reading chapters since last year. The book I gave you only came out a few weeks ago. As far as I can see, there's no way you could've gotten a hold of his story." He tilted his head to one side with a crooked grin. "Well, unless you're some kind of high level hacker with a criminal mind and you got into his computer and read it."

"Yeah, right. Because I'm so techie." She rolled her eyes.

"I was kidding."

"I know." She opened the front door, leading him inside. "I'm not sure I want to tell the others about it." She reached for his jacket.

"Why not?"

"I don't know...it's a little embarrassing."

"It shouldn't be, Daphne. Two intelligent writers coming up with similar stories. I'm sure it's happened before."

Although she felt comforted, she wasn't so sure. But now the others were gathering with their cookies and drinks. She pointed Spencer to the refreshments, and before long they were starting to read. Daphne made sure that everyone would go before her. Not that she brought anything to read, but she was trying to decide whether or not to share her interesting experience with her agent.

Finally, after she'd told Mabel goodnight, it was her turn. "I don't have anything new to read," she began slowly, "but I do have a writing related story to share. Maybe it's a cautionary tale." She glanced at Spencer, and he gave her an encouraging nod. "Or maybe it will simply be entertaining." Now she told them about the alarming email from her agent and how she'd felt blindsided by it. "I was completely devastated at first, but I'm slowly working my way through the mess. It helps to talk about it."

"So your agent is going to drop you now?" Wally said rather abruptly, making her flash back to when he'd been a rather stern high school English teacher.

"Oh, no, I don't think so." Daphne tried not to take offense.

"But can you publish your book if someone already has a book just like it out there?" Sabrina asked with concern.

"How similar are the two books?" Ricardo asked curiously.

"I just read *After the Fair.*" Daphne tossed a graceful glance to Spencer. "And while there were some striking similarities, they are two completely different books. I'm certain of it."

"But why would you be accused of plagiarism?" Wally asked. "Wouldn't there have to be exact sections of text involved? As if you directly copied? I remember catching my students in plagiarizing. I didn't take it lightly either."

"The word plagiarism was *used,*" Daphne said defensively. "But it's not as if anyone is taking legal action against me." She wasn't sure if she was just being overly sensitive, but comments like these—from her writer friends—weren't helpful. And suddenly it seemed they were all kicking it around, everyone with a different opinion.

"Hold on there," Spencer interrupted them. "Daphne can easily prove that she has been working on her novel for some time. Almost a year, right?" He directed this to Daphne.

"That's right," she said. "And I actually outlined it a long time ago. Back when I was working at the *Times.*"

"Exactly." He nodded. "So, for starters she has evidence inside her computer." He explained how easy it would be for an expert to go into her hard drive and show when she'd written various sections and, since he was a software designer, they listened respectfully to his expertise. "But besides that, what seems an unfortunate situation could actually help Daphne to sell her book. There might be a silver lining to this black cloud."

"How's that?" Wally asked.

"Publishers are interested in contracting books that are similar to titles that have done well." Now Spencer told them about an online article he'd just read. "*After the Fair* is already on the bestsellers' list. So the fact that Daphne has a novel similar to a bestseller should get her some attention. And not just because of the plagiarism claim."

"And my agent said that the editor who mentioned plagiarism works for the same house that published *After the Fair*," Daphne said.

"So he's already got a dog in the fight," Sabrina declared.

"But there are other publishers," Spencer added.

"So maybe this will all end happily," Sabrina said hopefully.

They all kicked it around some more, but eventually they wound down and, since it was late, started to leave. "And I almost forgot," Daphne said as they were standing in the foyer, getting on coats. "Mick said to tell you guys 'hey' and that he's looking forward to seeing everyone at his wedding on Saturday."

Daphne really wanted to hold Spencer back from the others in order to thank him for his encouraging words tonight. They really meant a lot to her, but he was caught up in answering one of Wally's computer questions as they went outside, so she knew it would have to wait. But she really did feel grateful for his input. It was reassuring to know that he hadn't given her that book because he questioned her. It was more because he was looking out for her. In fact, it was really sweet. It reminded her of some of the things Jake had done for her during the past year. But thinking of Jake filled her with a mixture of angst and irritation. Had he really accused her of interfering? *Really?*

Chapter 18

On Friday morning, after getting Mabel to school, Daphne finally had time to think about Jake's abrupt text from last night. She still hadn't responded to it and wasn't even sure that she wanted to. As she walked away from the school, she pulled out her phone and read the text again, just to make sure she'd understood it correctly. But it seemed crystal clear. Jake thought she had interfered. And maybe she had, but it had only been out of concern for Jenna. If Jake couldn't see that, he was not the man she had thought he was. And that was disturbing.

She considered emailing Jenna again, just to see how things were going, but seeing herself as the *interference*, she decided not to. They needed to resolve their own problems—and she needed to stick to administering advice in the anonymous format of *Dear Daphne*. Lesson learned.

Perhaps it was her general irritation at Jake—or perhaps it was crossing another day off of her April calendar and seeing it was half over with—that made her dig the dog-eared business card from the bottom of her purse. *Warren Thornton, Attorney at Law.* Somehow this no-nonsense business card did not conjure up a friendly image. But he was the one in charge of Aunt Dee's estate now, and it was probably high time Daphne had a conversation with him.

To her surprise, he sounded quite warm on the phone. "Why don't you come on down here and talk to me," he said casually. "I'll have Judy put on a fresh pot of coffee for you."

"Right now?"

"No time like the present."

And so, instead of turning on her computer, Daphne headed for town, and before long she was sitting in a dark paneled office with a man about her dad's age sitting behind a huge desk, peering at her with a concerned expression. "I've been looking forward to meeting you, Miss Ballinger. I was getting ready to give you a call."

"You can call me Daphne."

"Only if you call me Warren." He smiled as he reached for his coffee mug. "I was friends with your Aunt Dee—rather, your grandmother. I always respected her. I didn't know anything about her secret life as a romance writer and advice columnist, but she was a fine woman. Smart woman."

"I agree."

He peered curiously at her over his coffee mug. "And she set you up with quite a challenge, Daphne. How do you feel about that?"

"How do I feel?" Daphne set her coffee mug on the side table and considered this. "How do I feel?"

Warren chuckled. "It's a very unusual will."

"I'll say." And like a bottle that had popped its cork, she started pouring out her frustrations, telling him about how many men she had dated, how many men she had sent packing, and how now that there was only about a month left before her year was up, she felt like a complete failure.

He nodded with what seemed compassion. "When I read the conditions of Dee's will, I was a little perplexed. Although I think I understand her motives. She had lived alone for so long and didn't want to see you repeat the pattern. But I was worried that she'd set you up to fail too."

"I *know!*" she exclaimed. "It's like the pressure is too much."

"So how is it looking?"

"Not good."

"No prospects?"

She shook her head no.

"What do you intend to do if you aren't married a month from now?"

"Move out. Find a job."

"And Jake told me you have a child to support now too."

"That's right." She brightened. "Mabel. And even if we have to live in a tiny apartment and adapt our lifestyle drastically, we'll be okay." She explained about her agent and her book, as well as the volunteering she was doing at the local paper. "But what I'm really wondering about is whether I can continue writing the Dear Daphne column. I know that had a one year expiration date too."

He made a note. "I can contact the syndication for you about that."

"Thank you. That could make a big difference for us."

He laid down his pen, studying her closely. "So I'm curious, Daphne, have you considered marrying someone just for the sake of gaining your inheritance?"

She nodded sheepishly. "I hate to admit it, but yes, I have considered it. Of course, I always talk myself out of it. Not only does it feel disingenuous, and a bad way to start a marriage, it would be a horrible example for Mabel."

His mouth twisted to one side. "Yes, that's a good point."

"But as the May deadline draws closer, and I think about how I'm going to support Mabel, well, I just don't know what's right anymore. It's one thing to be honorable, but what if that makes you homeless? Sometimes I try to imagine what Aunt Dee would say to me. If she saw my situation, would she want to revise her stipulations?"

"That's a good question. Unfortunately, we'll never know the answer."

"The truth is I was actually considering a mock marriage—just this morning." She couldn't believe she'd just confessed that, but felt almost relieved to have the words out in the open. And she hoped he'd respect her client privileges.

His pale brows arched. "Have anyone specific in mind?"

"Sort of." She shrugged to remember her thoughts about Spencer last night and again today. She had actually wondered if there was enough time to get to know him better...and if he was a guy that she could "settle" for. Because it would be settling. She knew for a fact that she was not in love with him. But maybe being in love was overrated.

"Is he a good man? This guy you're considering?"

"I think he is. And I do like him as a friend. We dated once, but we both decided we'd rather just remain friends."

"A friend can make a good spouse."

"I know." She slowly nodded, wondering if this would be true with Spencer.

"I wish I had some magic answer to give you, Daphne. Some way to get you out of the conditions of this will. But it's tight. Jake and I talked about it extensively. It's rock solid."

"I know. And I wouldn't want to contest it anyway. I want to respect Aunt Dee's wishes. She wanted me to get married... and chances are I won't be. At least not within her timeframe." Daphne felt a lump in her throat. "I wish she hadn't been so specific about the one year thing. I might've had a chance if I had more time." But even as she said this, she wasn't so sure. In some ways another year of what she'd just been through sounded torturous. It wouldn't be worth it.

"Well, maybe your novel will sell," he said hopefully.

"Maybe." She could tell they were done now. "Thanks for listening."

"And don't forget, you still have almost a month, Daphne."

He stood, reaching to shake her hand. "Miracles still happen sometimes."

She forced a smile. "That's what it will take."

"Well, keep me informed. If you don't marry, we'll need to wrap up the estate by the end of May. That won't give you a lot of time to figure things out."

She promised to do that, but as she was leaving, she realized what he was saying. She needed to start looking for a place for her and Mabel to live. She needed to start making a real plan. As she walked down Main Street, she stopped by the newspaper office to say hi to Stan, asking him how business was going. Of course, she wanted him to tell her that circulation and advertising had improved so much that he could offer her a real job, but since he did not say this, she picked up a paper from the free pile and continued on her way.

She caught sight of Olivia outside, wearing a baby-pack as she watered the flowerboxes. "How's it going?" Daphne asked quietly, peeking at the sleeping baby snuggled in the front pack.

"Pretty good. Bernadette only needed to eat once last night. Do you know how nice that was?"

"I can imagine." Daphne smiled to remember her sleep-interrupted night with Bernadette.

"Where you been?"

"Talking to an attorney."

Olivia's brows arched. "Anything serious?"

"No, just some things related to Aunt Dee's estate."

"Oh." Olivia still looked curious. "Isn't it all settled by now? I mean she's been gone almost a year."

Daphne had never told Olivia about the strange will and suddenly realized that come the end of May, when she was moving out, she'd have a lot of explaining to do. "Oh, it's just some loose ends," she said lightly. "No big deal. But I might need to find a job. Let me know if you hear of anyone who's hiring."

"I'd hire you," Olivia said eagerly. "But we've already talked about that. Unfortunately, I can't pay much."

"Well, I might have to take you up on that offer," Daphne told her.

"I'd love to have you work here again." Olivia smiled wistfully. "You know my offer's always good."

Daphne thanked her and, although she knew it would be fun to work there, she just didn't think she could make enough to support herself and Mabel. Still, she reminded herself, it would be better than nothing. And considering the balance in her checking account, she could be down to nothing in just a few months without any income. Perhaps the prudent thing would be to go to work for Olivia immediately. Just to provide a little more cushion for them. In fact, Daphne decided, starting next week, that is just what she would do. She would tell Olivia she wanted to work at Bernie's Blooms and was ready to start whenever Olivia wanted her.

As Daphne slowly walked home, she wondered how it would feel to move out of the neighborhood that she'd loved since childhood. Aunt Dee's sweet old Victorian house had always felt like home to Daphne. And even more so after Daphne had fixed up and repaired the old place last summer. As it came into view, she felt a twisting inside of her. One month from now, it would no longer be home.

She looked at the pretty yard, with all the spring flowers blooming profusely. And in the backyard, it was already time to start planting produce. Not that she would do that now. As she went into the house, she looked at everything—as if trying to soak it all in—knowing that in time, it would simply be a memory. Hopefully Mabel would understand. And at least they would have each other.

"Why did you do this to me?" she said aloud as she walked through the dining room, running her fingers down the smooth surface of the table. "I know you loved me, Aunt Dee, but why did you set me up like this? All or nothing? A formula to fail?

Why?"

She stood there just waiting and listening, as if she expected her aunt to speak to her, but all she heard was the twittering of birds through the opened kitchen window. One more thing she would miss when they were gone. Ethel and Lucy, probably drawn by the sound of her voice, rubbed themselves around her ankles. Almost as if to comfort her.

"And you girls," Daphne said in a voice choked with emotion, "I hope you'll be happy at The Cat House. Mabel and I will come visit you there." She knelt down to pet them. "You should be treated like queens. In fact, you will practically own the place." A hot tear trickled down her cheek to think that these two old cats, as much as she loved them, seemed to have meant more to Aunt Dee than she did. And it hurt.

Chapter 19

On Saturday, with Lola and Mabel playing dress-up, Daphne sat down to answer one last letter in order to finish next week's column. She really didn't feel like giving anyone advice today. In fact, if anyone needed advice, it was probably her. As badly as she tried to keep a stiff upper lip and act like her life was on track, she felt more lost with each passing day.

She'd even spoken to Pastor Andrew yesterday afternoon when she'd bumped into him in front of The Apple Basket. She hadn't gone into all the details, like her need to land a husband in a few weeks, but she did tell him that she was looking for a job and that she and Mabel would need to find a new place to live by the end of May. "It sounds like you're on a faith walk," he told her. "I'll be preaching about that on Sunday." She promised to be there, and he promised to keep her and Mabel in his prayers.

Daphne stared at the letter on her screen, feeling almost at a loss for how to answer. And yet this woman sounded so desperate, she needed a good answer. And Daphne needed to keep giving this column her best efforts. One of her last hopes for maintaining their livelihood was that the syndication manager would be pleased with Daphne's year worth of contributions and choose to let her continue with it.

Daphne knew that the syndicate could pick anyone they wanted to write the column. Aunt Dee's control over the column she'd begun so many decades ago would be terminated on the one year anniversary of her death. But maybe it would be for the best if Daphne was replaced. There had to be hundreds of writers more qualified than she was, millions who could give advice on romance and love. She was a farce and a phony, and she knew it. Even so, she needed to answer this letter.

Dear Daphne,

I am extremely shy and very quiet, but have been secretly in love with a coworker I'll call John for the past four years. Each day I go to work hoping that I'll see him—even if just for a minute or two. I dream about him at night and fantasize about him in the daytime. Although John's always polite and friendly to me, we've never exchanged more than a couple of sentences at a time, and only in passing. I believe it's because, like me, he is very shy, but I keep hoping that one day we will both get over our reserve and have a real conversation and begin a relationship. Unfortunately I might not get the chance because another coworker that I'll call Gertrude has set her sights on John. Gertrude isn't the least bit shy and dresses in a very flashy way (to get male attention). John seems to like it when she flirts with him, but I really don't think she's his type. I am tempted to change my image and act like Gertrude in order to get John's attention, but I know that would probably be wrong. Please, give me some advice. I can't bear to see John end up with someone like Gertrude!

Hopeless in Hanford

Dear Hopeless,

You seem to have reached a crossroads in your life. You describe yourself as shy and quiet, but that image is not working too well for you. It's not helping you to make any progress with a man you are attracted to. But are you really certain that you want to make drastic changes to your appearance? Just to get John's attention? Let's consider the middle ground.

What if you changed your inward image first? Can you look inside yourself and see your fine qualities? I'm guessing that you are hard-working, conscientious, thoughtful, dependable, loyal, etc.. Before you can expect someone to appreciate you for who you are, you need to appreciate yourself. After that, you might consider brightening up your outward image. But only if it makes you feel good and builds up your confidence.

Finally, I encourage you to make a real effort to connect with John. Why not go out on a limb here? Can you invite him to get coffee with you? Or to take a walk? Or to see a movie? There is nothing wrong with a woman making the first move. So ask yourself, what is stopping you? And if you really want a chance with John, I say go for it. And even if it doesn't turn out as you hope, at least you would have tried and won't have regrets for that. And who knows, John might've had his eye on you all this time, but was too shy to say anything.

Daphne

Daphne saved her document and put it with the other letters, sending the whole works to the syndication manager. But as she went offline, she wondered if she needed to take her own advice. Maybe she should go out on a limb. Spencer, like John, was rather shy and reserved. For that matter, so was she. But during the past week, she had seen him in a different sort of light. He had proven himself a valuable friend. But was there more to him than that?

What if she took a risk and asked him out on a date? Would he balk at the idea? Remind her of their agreement to simply be friends? Or would he be mildly interested? She had no idea. And the truth was, deep in her heart, she knew that she would not do this. As desperate as her situation seemed—and according to the black slashes across the days in April it was truly dire—she was still not willing to compromise her values or integrity in order to keep a house. No matter how lovely and beloved the house was. Not for a house and a car and a significant bank account either. Daphne could not be bought. She turned off the computer with a sense of finality. And that was that.

As she closed the door to her office, Daphne knew that Aunt Dee had never meant to lure Daphne into anything less than a deeply satisfying life with someone she loved. Aunt Dee would not want Daphne to resign herself to a mediocre marriage in order to attain material wealth. As far as Daphne was concerned, she was done looking for Mr. Right. And she knew that Aunt Dee would be proud of her for it. Even if she and Mabel were poor as church mice. God would take care of them.

"Hello?" Sabrina's voice trilled through the house. "Anybody home?"

"I'm here," Daphne called out as she came around the corner.

"Forgive me for bursting in like this," Sabrina said. "But I just got an irrepressible urge to play fairy godmother."

Daphne frowned. "For Mabel? She and Lola are playing—"

"No, for you, silly." Sabrina frowned at Daphne's old sweatshirt and jeans.

"What for?" Daphne asked.

"We're going to get you all dolled up for Mick and Julianne's wedding tonight."

"But I—"

"Come on, darling." Sabrina pushed Daphne toward her bedroom. "You get in there and take a good shower and scrub your face and wash your hair, and I'll be back in a jiff with my hot rollers and a few other goodies."

"But—"

"No buts about it." Sabrina waved a finger under her nose. "Did Cinderella argue with her fairy godmother?"

"No but—"

"I warned you." Sabrina narrowed her eyes. "Don't make me get tough."

The idea of Sabrina getting tough and strong-arming Daphne was comical. And so Daphne simply nodded and smiled. "I was about to take a shower anyway," she said nonchalantly. "All I ask is you don't give me big hair."

Sabrina laughed. "I know you like soft, natural-looking waves, darling. Trust me. I won't give you helmet head or make you look like you're in a beauty contest."

As Daphne took a shower, she wondered why she even cared about her appearance. Or maybe she didn't care, and that was exactly why Sabrina insisted on intervening. The truth was Daphne didn't feel like there'd be anyone at the wedding she wanted to impress. Certainly not Collin. She shuddered to remember her last date with him. What a nightmare that had been. One dance, at the most, was all he would get out of her tonight.

Sabrina was in her element as she gave Daphne a facial and rolled her hair in hot rollers. Of course, Mabel and Lola, still dressed like princesses, had to come see what was happening. The two girls enjoyed a good laugh at Daphne's expense.

"Why is Mom's face green?" Mabel asked with a concerned

expression.

Since Daphne couldn't talk very well through the clay masque, Sabrina explained about the facial. "It will make her skin look radiant when we're done."

"You look like an alien," Lola told Daphne.

Daphne tried not to laugh, waving the girls away.

Sabrina finished her fairy godmother magic before five o'clock, and Daphne had to admit that she felt much prettier as she thanked Sabrina. "Do you have enough time to doll up yourself now?"

Sabrina waved her hand. "I got the works yesterday. Hair, face, nails. All I need is to put on my dancing dress." She grinned. "Speaking of dresses, what are you wearing?" Sabrina went over to Daphne's closet, making herself at home.

"I haven't really decided."

"How about this?" Sabrina pulled out a pretty sundress that she'd helped Daphne shop for last summer.

"I don't think that's warm enough." Daphne reached past her to remove her favorite go-to dress, a classic design in a nice sage green. "I was thinking this."

"No, no, that's too conservative." Sabrina put the dress back. "You need to be more flamboyant."

"Why?"

Sabrina gave her a sly look, as if she was holding back on something.

"What's up?" Daphne demanded.

"Well, I heard that Julianne's older brother is in the wedding, and from what I hear, he's not only very good looking and single, but he's pretty well off too."

"So?"

"So, you might get to rub elbows with him, Daphne. Don't you want to look hot? To catch his eye?" Sabrina pulled out a coral colored dress. "This is pretty."

"Olivia talked me into that last summer." Daphne held up

the silky dress, looking into the mirror. "But I'm not sure I want to—"

"It looks stunning," Sabrina assured her. "And that skirt would be great for dancing." Sabrina was going through Daphne's shoes too. Finally she emerged with a pair of chocolate brown sandals with lots of straps. "And these would be nice with it."

Daphne nodded. "I guess so." She went over to the large bureau, picking up a string of pearls that had been Aunt Dee's. "I get to pick out my accessories though."

Sabrina nodded. "Pearls will look perfect."

After Sabrina left, Daphne wasn't so sure. Did she really want to go stag to a wedding wearing a flashy coral dress? Wouldn't it be better to just blend in with the walls? But there wasn't time to think about that since she'd promised to drop Lola home while she picked up Mattie to baby-sit.

By the time they got back and Daphne ran Mattie through the paces and got the pizza ordered, she barely had time to get dressed. And so she decided to just go with it and wear the coral silk. Maybe it would be dark in the barn and she wouldn't look too bright.

"Wowie-wow-wow," Mabel exclaimed when Daphne stepped out, fully dressed. "You look beautiful, Mom."

"You really do," Mattie confirmed.

Daphne thanked them both as she put a crocheted shawl over her shoulders. She patted the little beaded evening bag that had once belonged to Aunt Dee. "I've got my phone, Mattie. You call me if you need to."

"Don't worry." Mattie smiled with confidence. "We'll be fine."

"And you make yourself comfy in the guest room," Daphne reminded her. The plan was for Mattie to spend the night so that Daphne didn't have to wake up Mabel to take the sitter home.

Daphne kissed Mabel's cheek then wiped the coral lipstick mark off with her finger. "I know that you'll mind Mattie and be a good girl."

"Yep. I will."

Daphne tried not to feel sorry for herself as she got into her car. After all, she was a big girl. Why shouldn't she be able to go to a wedding by herself? What was the big deal? She felt an unexpected tinge of sadness as she considered that this was Mick's wedding. Despite her previous certainty that he was not The One and would never be The One, Daphne had always liked Mick. He'd been a good friend to Aunt Dee and a good friend to her. And she knew he would make a good husband for Julianne.

Still, as she followed the train of cars going onto Mick's property, the same property that once belonged to her grandparents—thanks to Aunt Dee's generosity—she felt a bit lonely and conspicuously single. From what she could see the other cars had couples. Some had two couples.

She put on her *Dear Daphne* hat, telling herself not to be silly and that only very insecure people needed to line up a date to attend a wedding. But as she parked and got out of her car, she spotted Spencer's little hybrid car pulling in. She watched as he parked nearby. Staying by her car, she pretended to check her phone, but knew she was simply waiting for him. She glanced around with a nonchalant expression, telling herself that this was as much for him as it was for her. There was nothing wrong with friendly companionship. And that's all this was. Nothing more. In fact, she would make that clear to him right from the start. No room for confusion or complications.

Chapter 20

"**G**ood evening," Daphne said warmly as she went over to where Spencer was locking his car. "Unless you have any objections, I thought maybe we could hang together tonight." She gave him an uneasy smile. "Call me pathetic, but it's hard going solo to a wedding."

He looked relieved. "I was just feeling like that myself. Thanks, Daphne, I'd love to hang with you. And may I say that you look lovely tonight?" But he frowned at her feet. "However, those high heels might be a little unstable on this uneven ground." He extended his elbow toward her. "Feel free."

"Thank you." She grinned as she slipped her hand around it. "You're a scholar and a gentleman."

"Thanks." He laughed. "No one's ever said *that* to me before."

"Well, I can't imagine why." She waved at Sabrina and Ricardo as he parked his SUV. Sabrina looked surprised but pleased as she eagerly waved. "Besides, I was hoping to talk to you," Daphne told Spencer as they approached the barn. The exterior was decorated with potted plants and flowers and lit up with strings of round white lights. Casual places to sit outside were arranged charmingly here and there, and a bonfire was already crackling with several benches set around it. All in all, it was very inviting.

"What about?"

"I wanted to thank you. First of all, for caring enough to give me that novel last week. I just wish I'd read it sooner. I wouldn't have felt so blindsided by my agent."

"I guess I should've explained it better when I dropped it by. To be honest, I felt uncomfortable bringing it to your attention. I certainly didn't want you to think I was suggesting you'd plagiarized. But I thought you'd be interested. And to be fair, I'd only heard parts of your novel. But when I read that book, well, it did feel familiar."

"Yes. But I think if you read all of my novel, you'd see the differences."

"I'd love to read the whole novel," he said.

"Really?"

"Absolutely. I'm already intrigued by it. And it would be interesting to compare it to *After the Fair*."

"Then I'll give you a copy," she assured him as they got into the line of wedding guests, waiting to sign the guestbook. "I just wish that editor had taken the time to request the whole manuscript. My agent's proposal had only contained a few sample chapters and my synopsis. So, really, the editor was jumping to conclusions."

"Or jumping to contusions as my dad used to say."

Daphne laughed. "That's about right. I also wanted to tell you how much I appreciated your support the other night at critique group. I'd been feeling pretty down, and everything you said about publishers wanting books similar to bestseller books was really encouraging."

"Well, I'd done a little research on that, and it seemed to make sense. And it was good news."

"Definitely. And I looked up the article you mentioned and sent it to my agent. Naturally, she agreed with the theory. She said that's one of the best ways to launch a new author."

As they waited to go into the barn, Daphne really studied

the attractive surroundings. Besides the pretty plants and flowers and lights, there were interesting old farm tools and utensils cleverly mixed in. Daphne knew this was Julianne's creative touch, giving the barnyard a look of rustic elegance—like something you'd see in a magazine.

Maybe not the kind of wedding magazines that Sabrina had been studying lately. And Daphne doubted that Sabrina would really want her wedding to look anything like this. Sabrina was much more formal and traditional and uptown. Where Julianne had votive candles in glass mason jars, Sabrina would have sleek tapers in sterling silver candlestick holders. Where Julianne had old-fashioned garden variety flowers casually arranged in rusty tin cans and milk bottles, Sabrina would have pristine white roses in gleaming crystal.

"Which side do you want to sit on?" Spencer quietly asked her.

"Mick's, of course," she informed him.

Before long they were seated on the groom's side of the barn, with Ricardo and Sabrina joining them in the same row. The four of them visited quietly as the small blue grass band played instrumental music and the chairs in the barn slowly filled.

The wedding was simple and sweet. Mick looked Hollywood handsome, but nontraditional in his faded blue jeans and dusty cowboy boots, topped with a black tuxedo jacket. But somehow it all worked. Instead of a large bridal party, they only had a best man, which Sabrina whispered was Julianne's older brother Marcus, and a maid of honor, Julianne's younger sister Sybil. Marcus was dressed similar to Mick, and Sybil wore a simple lace dress in a soft periwinkle blue.

As the band played a unique arrangement of "The Wedding March," everyone stood and watched as the beautiful Julianne came down the aisle. Her dress was lacey and white, but more Bohemian than traditional. And her cowgirl boots flashed out with each confident stride. Somehow it was all perfect, and Daphne couldn't help but smile as Mick's eyes lit up and he reached for Julianne's hand.

The barn grew quiet as the couple repeated their vows, and before long the brief ceremony was finished and the newlywed couple was joyfully introduced to a receptive, cheering crowd. Then Mick heartily welcomed everyone. "Come on over to the tent behind the barn—where the party continues and the wedding feast awaits!"

As Spencer escorted her out of the barn, Daphne was shocked to see Jake standing in the shadows in back. *What was he doing here?* Oh, she knew he was friends with Mick. But to come all the way from Miami for this wedding? It made no sense. She felt nervous and uneasy as they got closer to him. All she could think of was their last communication—and how he'd chided her for interfering with his family. It still stung to think of it, and she felt her cheeks warming.

To her relief, Jake didn't even notice her as he continued talking to an older man. Turning her attention away from Jake, Daphne started to chatter at Spencer, going on about what a nice wedding ceremony it had been. "I guess I'm not typical," she said as they went out, following a path that was lit with two lines of softly glowing luminaries. Very enchanting.

"I'm not much of a wedding expert," Spencer said as he gave her his arm again, "but this one seems pretty good to me."

"I've never really been into weddings myself. And I've never had one of my own." She laughed nervously. "But I do like short, simple weddings. I mean, they should be heartfelt and genuine, but I don't really see any reason to drag it out."

As they got into the reception line that led to the tent, Spencer told her about a drawn out wedding he'd attended a few years ago. "It was excruciatingly long. Even the bridal party seemed to be in pain."

Before long, they were congratulating the happy newlyweds.

"That was one of the best weddings I've been to," Daphne told Julianne. "And the decorations are beautiful."

"Mick wanted to keep everything simple. And the ceremony short and sweet."

"Well, it was simply perfect." She turned to Mick. "Congratulations."

Mick grinned as he thanked her, and then she and Spencer set off to find a table. She was glad that the seating wasn't already arranged. Sabrina and Ricardo waved them over to their table, where Wally Renwald and Ricardo's mother, Maria, were already seated. Greetings were exchanged, and Daphne tried to act perfectly natural as they all visited together. But all she could think about was the fact that Jake was here.

"I never saw a bride in cowboy boots before," Maria said. "But Julianne would look beautiful in anything."

"You won't see me wearing boots at my wedding," Sabrina said to Maria, winking at Ricardo.

"You'd look beautiful in anything too," Maria assured her. And now she began to tell them about what she'd worn for her wedding back in the early 1960s.

Sabrina nudged Daphne with her elbow. "Is that Jake?" she whispered to Daphne, averting her eyes to the entrance where Jake was just coming inside the tent.

With a placid smile pasted on, Daphne just nodded.

"Interesting."

"Are these seats taken?"

As Ricardo answered for the table, Daphne looked up to see Harrison Henshaw and an attractive brunette waiting. Ricardo waved to the vacant chairs then did some quick introductions, explaining to his mother and Wally that Harrison was the architect for the new city hall building. Harrison greeted everyone, politely treating Daphne just like the others. Not that she expected him to comment over the fact that they had dated not so very long ago. Now that would be awkward. But not as awkward as she felt just knowing that Jake was here.

As their food was served, she tried not to think about Jake, and she certainly didn't want to be caught staring at him. But every once in a while she would covertly glance his way, trying to see who he was with and where he was sitting. To her relief, he took a table on the opposite side of the tent. And, while the guests at her table ate and visited, she tried to push all thoughts of Jake into the recesses of her mind. But just beneath the surface, she felt anxious and uneasy.

On one hand, she wanted to go over and speak directly to Jake. She wanted to demand to know why he had written such a rude and heartless note to her, especially when he must've known she was only trying to help. On the other hand, she knew that a wedding was hardly the place for a confrontation and heated conversation. Besides that, she didn't enjoy conflict.

As dinner wound down, toasts were made and Mick eventually announced that the best part of the wedding was about to begin. "We got a super little band and some dandy libations over in the barn. You're all invited to dance the night away with us!"

"Let's go," Ricardo told Sabrina. And quickly their table emptied and they all followed the luminaries back to the barn where the band was already playing a lively tune. Daphne had no idea whether Spencer could even dance—or if he'd want to dance with her. She suddenly felt guilty for the way she'd entrapped him as her escort. What about her resolve to make sure he understood this was not a date?

"Please, feel free to dance with anyone you'd like," she said quietly to him. "Or not dance at all if you'd prefer. I don't want you to feel like you're stuck with me."

"If I have to be stuck, I don't mind that it's with you." He chuckled. "Would you like to dance?"

"I'd love to."

Daphne was glad to join the others on the dance floor. In

case Jake came in, it would put even more distance between them. And to her surprise, Spencer was a decent dancer. So when he asked her to dance a second time, she was relieved. This way she wouldn't be standing around twiddling her thumbs when Jake came into the barn. She just wasn't ready to face him yet. Maybe she never would be.

So it was she danced several dances with Spencer before they traded partners with Sabrina and Ricardo. Daphne liked dancing with him since he was a really good dancer. Then Collin showed up and insisted on collecting his one dance, which turned into two.

Collin was just whirling her around when she spied Jake standing by the door, looking on with a slightly perplexed expression. She suddenly remembered how Jake did not like crowds. And he wasn't a big fan of dancing either. And for some reason this made her feel sad and rather sorry for him. He did not appear to be having a good time.

As Collin spun her again, she could tell that Jake was getting ready to leave. And just like that, she knew she needed to catch him—to speak to him. Even if only briefly.

"Excuse me," she said abruptly to Collin, extracting herself from his grasp. "But if you recall I promised you just one dance." She smirked at him, and before he could protest she hurried away. Following Jake as he went outside.

"Wait," she said as she caught up with him. "I want to talk to you before you leave."

Jake looked mildly surprised. "Hello there, Daphne. I wanted to talk to you too, but you looked like the belle of the ball in there. I hated to interrupt."

She smoothed her hair and sighed. "Well, I was ready for a break."

He led her over to where the bonfire was burning brightly, waving to a nearby bench. To her relief, no one else was out here at the moment. But as she sat down, she had a flashback to a time very similar to this—in this very same place. She wondered if Jake remembered it too.

"This feels familiar," he said quietly.

"Yeah, it does."

He turned toward her with interest. "You wanted to talk to me. Go ahead. I'm listening."

She took in a deep breath. "Well, that last text message you sent me was pretty harsh," she said quickly. "The truth is, it hurt my feelings. A lot. I thought you would understand that I was only trying to help Jenna. I never meant to interfere, Jake. For you to say that—"

"Wait a minute." He held up his hands. "Sorry, but I'm lost here. What are you saying exactly?"

"That accusing me of interfering was just plain rude, Jake. I really care about Jenna. We've been communicating via email, and she's really opened up to me. She's told me all sorts of stuff—things that are concerning. And, well, I just thought you should know. But then you wrote me that text and it was kind of like being slapped in the face." She locked eyes with him. "And, well, I just wanted you to know. That's all."

Jake had already reached into his jacket pocket to remove his phone. "I am really lost here, Daphne. What you're saying makes no sense to me. I'm trying to remember exactly what I said to you. I'm sure you misunderstood."

"I'm sure it's there on your phone." She tapped his phone. "Read it for yourself."

Staring at his phone, he scrolled down then eventually read the text aloud.

"*Am with Jenna now. Not going well. Thanks for interfering.*"

"Yes," she said triumphantly. "That's it."

He looked up with wide eyes. "Oh, Daphne, I can see how that must've sounded to you. You thought I was being sarcastic, didn't you? Like *thanks a lot for sticking your nose in my business.* Right?"

She just nodded.

"What I really meant was *thanks*. I was glad that you'd jumped in like you did. As I recall, you'd apologized in your email to me, worried that you had interfered. I was saying *thanks for interfering—*as in *I really appreciate it.*" He leaned closer, peering into her eyes. "I'm so sorry."

Her hand covered her mouth. "Oh, Jake. I'm the one who should be sorry. I totally misread it. And then I misread you." She shook her head in realization. "I'm really sorry. I should've known you wouldn't say something like that."

"That's the problem with texts and emails. They can be easily misconstrued." He pocketed his phone then reached for her hand. "Please, forgive me."

"Of course. But you need to forgive me too."

Now they just sat there for a long moment, with only the sound of the music coming in the barn mixed with cheerful voices and the occasional crackle of the bonfire.

"So how is Jenna?" Daphne finally asked. "You said it wasn't going well. Did it get any better? Did you guys talk some more?"

He shrugged. "I'm still not sure what's going on with Jenna. I mean, she eventually told me all the things I'm sure she thought I wanted to hear. But it didn't sound sincere to me." He sadly shook his head. "I used to think that I'd won the teenager lottery with that girl. Never a bit of trouble. But that seems to be over now."

"I think that's due to the influence of her new friends, Jake. You must be able to see that."

"Not according to her. According to her, she's just being a normal teen. Rebelling and questioning everything and anything. It's like she resents having been such a good girl for so long. Like the world owes her this adolescent opportunity to dissent."

"She resents having been moved from her school and her

friends in Appleton, Jake. Surely you know that."

"But sometimes it seems as if she likes Miami. We've had fun exploring the beaches and surfing and stuff."

"I'm sure she loves those times with you. But I don't think she loves Miami. At least that's not what she was telling me."

Jake's brow creased as he pursed his lips. Clearly he was frustrated. And Daphne felt she was partly to blame. And so she decided to change the subject. "Why are you in Appleton anyway, Jake?"

"Oh, I had some unfinished business to attend to. The sale on my house closed and I had to sign papers this afternoon."

"I heard your house sold." She tried to hide her disappointment.

"So I still need to get some things from my house moved into a storage unit. But I cut it kind of close. Have to wrap it up before my flight tomorrow afternoon. Lots to do."

"That's not much time." She knew she should let him go, but she just couldn't say goodbye. Not yet. "So do you like living down there? I mean, if Jenna wasn't a factor, is it a place you would've wanted to move to anyway?"

He peered closely at her. "I think you already know the answer to that."

She folded her arms across her front as a shiver went through her. "The night air is getting cool," she said abruptly. "And I know you have a lot to get done. I don't want to waylay you anymore."

"Yeah." He slowly stood. "I only planned to stay long enough to see the wedding ceremony." He offered a faint smile. "It was really nice. I'm happy for both of them."

She stood too. "Then I should let you get on your way."

"And I should let you get back to your *date*." He tipped his head to the barn.

"What?"

"I couldn't help but notice you're with Spencer tonight. I

was a little surprised since I thought you'd given up on him. But, really, he's a good guy, Daphne. He'd be a good catch. And you have less than a month left."

Suddenly Daphne wanted to scream and shout and stomp her feet and throw something. *Really?* Was that how Jake felt? Like she was just looking for *anyone?* Anything warm and breathing and wearing pants? Was he actually suggesting that she should just settle for Spencer because he was a *good guy?* *Really?* Instead of throwing the hissy fit that was storming within her, Daphne narrowed her eyes at him.

"Things aren't always what they seem, Jake McPheeters. Goodnight!" And she turned on her heel to head back inside.

"Wait." He reached for her arm, gently grabbing her and turning her to look at him again. "What do you mean by *that?*"

"Just that Spencer is *not* my date. We simply happened to arrive here at the same time. And since we're writing friends and we were both alone, we decided to hang out together. That is all. *He is not my date.*"

Jake's eyes warmed. "Well, that's good to know."

Suddenly Daphne no longer felt cold. But she did feel a little flustered and slightly confused. What was going on here? And how much more could her heart take when it came to Jake? This back and forth, hot then cold, happy then sad? How much could a girl get jerked around and still land on her feet? But, as he drew her closer to him, she knew she had no choice in the matter.

As Jake pulled her into his arms, leaning in to kiss her, she knew it was useless to fight it. So she gave in completely— feeling her heart falling and tumbling, as she lost herself in the most passionate, electrifying kiss of her life. And, even if this was a one-time fluke or a moment never to be repeated again, she did not regret it. Not one bit.

Chapter 21

The amazing kiss was just ending when Daphne heard the sound of boisterous voices. She looked over to see a small crowd of happy wedding guests, including Sabrina and Ricardo, coming outside for fresh air. Suddenly she and Jake were not alone anymore.

Sabrina's brows arched as they joined Jake and Daphne by the bonfire. "So this is where you've been keeping yourselves. Spencer was just looking for you, Daphne."

"Oh." Daphne was still trying to catch her breath after that kiss. "Well, I was thinking I should get home," she said abruptly. "Mabel's with the babysitter, you know?"

Sabrina nodded with a slightly suspicious expression. "I know." She glanced over at Jake. "So, how are you doing?"

"I'm okay." He shoved his hands in his pocket, almost as if he felt guilty.

"How's Miami?" Ricardo asked him.

Daphne jumped in now, explaining how Jake had been signing real estate papers today and how he needed to get things moved into a storage unit by tomorrow.

"Yeah, my flight back to Miami departs around two tomorrow," Jake told them. "So I need to get the house emptied by eleven or so."

"You need some help?" Ricardo offered.

"Hey, that'd be great," Jake said gratefully. "I can handle the small stuff, but there are a few larger pieces that could be tricky." So they arranged to meet at his house at seven tomorrow morning. "I'll try to have the rest of it packed up by then." Jake glanced at his watch. "So I better get moving. It's going to be a long night tonight."

"And I should go too," Daphne said quickly. She turned to Sabrina. "Would you mind telling Spencer goodbye for me?"

Sabrina's eyes twinkled. "Not at all."

And so Jake and Daphne told the others goodbye and headed toward the dark area where the cars were parked. "Mind if I take your arm?" She asked a bit timidly as she tottered over the uneven ground. "These shoes aren't great for—"

"Not at all." Jake slipped an arm around her waist, pulling her closer to him.

As a thrill ran through her, Daphne wasn't sure which was more dangerous. Wobbling around on high heels or being so close to Jake that she felt dizzy.

"Do you really need to get home for the babysitter?" Jake asked as they slowly walked down the darkened driveway.

"Actually, Mattie is spending the night at my house," she confessed. "But I was ready to leave anyway."

"I think we should talk," Jake said quietly.

She nodded. "Uh-huh."

"Want to meet me for a cup of coffee?"

"But don't you need to pack? I know you've got a lot to do and not much time to do it."

"I don't care if I'm up all night, Daphne. Right now I just need to talk to you. Okay?"

So they arranged to meet at an all night café on the edge of town. As Daphne drove, she wanted to pinch herself. Was this for real? Then, as she parked and walked up to the café, she started to feel giddy. Was this really happening? Had Jake really kissed her? Had he really said they need to talk? In a serious way?

Jake was already waiting by the door for her. "By the way, I meant to tell you that you look stunning tonight, Daphne." He smiled with approval. "But in my opinion you always look beautiful. Whether you're dressed to the nines or just wearing old jeans and a paint-smeared sweatshirt."

"Really?" She looked into his deep brown eyes. "You *mean* that?"

"Absolutely. And, believe me, I've been looking for some time now." He winked as he opened the door for her.

Another warm rush of excitement rippled through her as they went inside.

"Sit where you like," a waitress called out to them.

"Thanks," Jake said. "We'll take a couple of coffees."

As she slid into a booth across from him, Daphne felt like this was a dream. A sweet, enjoyable dream that she hoped would never end.

The waitress brought their coffees, pausing to study them with interest. "You kids all dressed up with no place to go?"

Daphne laughed. "We've been at a wedding."

"Oh, well, then." She set their coffees down along with a creamer and sugar. "You're probably not interested in our French apple pie. Made fresh today."

"I never got a piece of wedding cake," Jake told Daphne.

"Oh?" Daphne didn't want to admit that she'd barely touched her own food tonight—that she'd been too nervous thinking about having a confrontation with Jake.

"Want to share a piece?" he asked her.

"Sure." She smiled.

"Can you do it à la mode?" Jake asked the waitress.

"You got it, honey."

Although the coffee tasted slightly metallic, Daphne didn't care as she slowly sipped it, gazing at Jake. This felt like a real date. A totally unexpected but real date.

"There are so many things I want to say to you, Daphne."

"Really?" She continued gazing at him, no longer worried that he would catch her staring. Taking him in and thinking she had been wrong, nearly a year ago, when she'd thought Jake, with his dark hair and dark eyes, resembled the actor Jon Hamm. The truth was that Jake was much better looking.

"What happened by the bonfire," Jake said slowly, "was real. It was not just one of those things. It was premeditated and authentic and genuine."

She just nodded.

"I wanted you to know that."

"It was authentic and genuine on my end too," she said quietly.

"I'd been wanting to kiss you like that for a long time. But I thought I'd never get the opportunity."

"I'm glad you took the opportunity."

His face lit up with a smile. "Me too."

The waitress brought a generous wedge of pie with a big scoop of ice cream on it, setting it down between them with two forks. "Bon appétit."

They thanked her and picked up their forks.

"But we still have a problem," Jake said as he forked into the pie.

"Yes, I know." She forked in as well.

He held his forkful of pie up as if to make a toast. "But here is to solving our problem, Daphne. Here's to us."

"To us." She touched her forkful of pie to his.

The pie was surprisingly good. Or maybe she was so full of happiness that a stale slice of bread would've been tasty. She didn't really care.

"Miami is a long way from Appleton," Jake said grimly.

"I know."

He peered curiously at her. "Would you and Mabel be

interested in moving down there?"

As she considered this, it felt like a teeny tiny pin prick had slipped into her fully inflated balloon, allowing a tiny hiss of air to escape. "I don't know." She set down her fork to pick up her coffee. "The truth is, I don't think it would be good for Mabel. But, selfishly, I would probably consider it—at least for a little while. But then common sense would kick into gear and I wouldn't be able to do it, Jake."

He nodded. "I knew that already."

She sighed.

"Forgive me for even asking."

She forced a smile, repressing the urge to ask him what *exactly* he was asking her. Did he simply want her to relocate down there so they could continue a romantic relationship, get better acquainted, see where it went? Or was he thinking of marriage? Of course, she hoped it was the latter. But even so... what would she say? Would she sacrifice Mabel's happiness to attain her own?

"That's just one of the many things I admire about you, Daphne."

"What's that?" Had she missed something?

"That you place Mabel's well-being above your own. You have the true mothering instinct." He frowned. "I wish I could say the same about my ex-wife."

"Oh." She nodded glumly as she forked another bite. "You know, Jake, based on what Jenna had been telling me, Gwen isn't enjoying being a mom at all."

"Tell me something I don't know." He sipped his coffee. "Gwen has never been a good mother. Oh, she's not abusive, and you can't even accuse her of neglect, although I do think she's been emotionally neglectful. But she has never put Jenna's best interests above her own. She proved this brilliantly when she moved Jenna from Appleton to Miami." He forked another bite of pie. "Gwen is, I'm sorry to say, a very selfish, self-centered, narcissistic woman."

Daphne didn't know what to say.

"And I'm not saying that out of spite," he told her. "It's just the sad truth."

"Jenna has intimated the same thing," Daphne quietly confessed. "She hasn't been feeling very respectful of Gwen. Not since the move anyway."

"Believe me, I know."

"Why can't you and Jenna move back to Appleton?" Daphne asked suddenly.

"Jenna and me? Back here? Without Gwen?" He said this as if it had never occurred to him before.

"Why can't you, Jake?"

He laid down his fork with a creased brow. "That's a very good question."

"I realize it's a custody thing," she said, "but Gwen was the one who chose to move out of the state. And you have even attempted to follow in order to be with your daughter. But Jenna is the one who's being sacrificed. I would think a judge could see that."

"Good point. Also, she's sixteen and most judges feel that's old enough to make her own decision about which parent she resides with."

"And you know Jenna would pick you."

"I think she would. But Frank is pretty wealthy. And their Miami house is pretty swanky. They live in an affluent neighborhood. She goes to one of the top schools in that area."

"But Jenna's not impressed with money. And from what I hear, she's not connecting with the affluent kids at her school anyway. So apparently Frank's fat bank account isn't making much of an impression on her. Not to mention that her new friends—although they might be sweet kids—aren't the best influence for her."

"I know."

"Jake, you're an attorney. Why don't you fight this battle for yourself? And for Jenna?" She reached over to grab his hand. "Why would you settle for a lifestyle that isn't in Jenna's best interest? Or your own?"

He let out a long sigh. "I promised Gwen—back when we divorced more than eight years ago—that I would never contest her custody of Jenna."

"Why did you promise that?" Daphne removed her hand from his. "Especially if you knew she wasn't such a great mom?"

"I felt like I had to, Daphne. I think I already told you how I'd been kind of a workaholic. In some ways I felt responsible for my marriage hitting the rocks. In her own way, Gwen had tried to make it work. And it just made sense that we could share custody. More than anything I wanted a congenial divorce. For the most part, it's been one. I paid alimony and child support and Gwen never denied me the chance to spend time with Jenna." He made a wry smile. "Although I'm sure she saw me as a free babysitter most of the time. Even now, I can tell she's relieved when I take Jenna for a weekend. More time for her and Frank alone."

"Not to mention that Jenna might be making them a little miserable by arguing about things and demanding her own way."

"Gwen has mentioned that it's been difficult."

"Maybe it's so difficult that Gwen would be glad to let you have Jenna full time now. She might welcome this time alone with Frank."

"I know what you're saying, Daphne. But you don't know Gwen. Sometimes she can be completely irrational. She just doesn't think like you or me. If I tried to get Jenna, it could blow up in my face. Gwen could turn it into a custody battle. Just for the sake of drama and a power play." He frowned. "And the last thing I want is to see this turn into an ugly court case.

That never ends well for anyone. And it seems like the kids pay the highest price."

Daphne nodded. "Yeah, you're probably right."

"I know it doesn't make complete sense."

Daphne had to agree with him. It didn't make sense at all. But at least she felt like she understood Gwen a little better now. The woman was a spoiled brat. Okay, Daphne never planned to say that to anyone, and she wished she was wrong, but it seemed to fit. Gwen wanted her way—no matter what it cost others.

"I have an idea," Daphne said suddenly.

"What?" Jake looked hopeful.

"What if you decided to move back to Appleton?"

His brow creased as if trying to follow her. "Yes?"

"Well, Gwen really likes that you're there to help with Jenna right now, doesn't she? I mean, you're around to co-parent, and you can do damage control at school, and you take Jenna away every weekend. But if you were gone, if you were back here, Gwen would be stuck on her own with Jenna and—"

"And if Jenna was acting out, the way she's been doing lately, it would drive Gwen and Frank bonkers."

Daphne nodded.

"That's not a bad idea." Jake chuckled as he reached for her hand. "You might've just solved our problem." But his smile slowly faded. "Except for one thing."

"What?"

"My house is sold. I don't even have a place to live in Appleton anymore."

Daphne considered offering to take him in, but knew that was premature. "What about an apartment?"

He nodded. "Yes, I suppose I could look around." He glanced at his watch. "Speaking of such things, I should probably get back to my house. I still have a lot of packing to do."

"Want some help?"

"Seriously?"

"I'm a pretty good packer."

"But you're wearing your pretty dress and—"

"It's okay," she assured him. "I can still pack."

He grinned. "Okay, this I gotta see." He got up, reaching for her hand and pausing to drop some cash on the table. "Time's a wasting."

Daphne wasn't sure what she'd gotten herself into as she followed Jake to his house. And she felt a little uneasy to see that it was already nearly ten o'clock. Of course, the wedding was probably still going full throttle now. Seeing that a U-Haul truck was parked in Jake's driveway, she parked on the street.

As she got out of her car she realized that, although she'd picked up Jenna here, she'd never actually been inside Jake's house. The small ranch house reminded her a little of her dad's old place, where she'd grown up. It was nice enough, but compared to Aunt Dee's beautiful Victorian, well, it was a bit on the boring side.

"It used to look better in here," Jake said apologetically as he led her inside. "But I already started packing so it's kind of messy."

Daphne laid her shawl on a chair. "Tell me what to do, Jake. Put me to work."

He frowned at her dress. "I just hate letting you ruin that beautiful dress, Daphne. And, as you'll see, my bachelor homemaking skills are a little unpolished. It's pretty dirty in places."

"Do you have something I can borrow?" she asked. "Old sweats or jeans?" She held her hand like a measuring stick between them. "You're not all that much taller than me."

He grinned as he gathered her in his arms, pulling her close to him. "But you're wearing those high heels too." He leaned in to kiss her, and suddenly her head was spinning again.

"I, uh, I thought I came here to help you pack," she said a

bit breathlessly after a couple of sustained kisses that left her seriously lightheaded.

"Yes. Sorry about that." He stepped back. "I'll go find something for you to put on, okay?"

"Great."

Before long, dressed in an old pair of blue jeans that she'd cuffed and cinched with a belt to keep them from falling off, as well as a college sweatshirt, Daphne was packing up the contents of Jake's kitchen. Meanwhile, he was working on the bathrooms.

Jake had put on some jazz music to accompany their packing and Daphne, hoping to get the entire kitchen boxed up, had lost all track of time. She was nearly done when Jake came in. "Hey, you're good," he told her.

"Thanks."

He slipped an arm around her, pulling her close again. "And you're not bad at packing either."

She laughed.

"I don't know about you, but I need something to wash down the dust." He opened the fridge. "Not much in here. Bottled water and root beer."

They both picked root beer, going into the living room for a short break.

"I've been trying to determine your style." Daphne took a swig.

"My style?"

"You know." She waved her hand over the black leather couch she was sitting on. "I can tell you like modern and traditional. But there's a few vintage things too. Then I'll run across something I can't figure out. Like those pink bowls."

He laughed. "Jenna picked out the pink bowls when she was little. For cereal and ice cream since I didn't have good bowls with the dish set I had. The vintage items are probably from my mom. Things I've been saving for Jenna. I probably should've asked you to put them in a separate box."

"I can still do that," she offered.

"Great." He patted the leather sofa. "And this was from my modern phase. I went through that shortly after my divorce. But I am probably, for the most part, traditional." He reached over to pull her closer to him, wrapping one arm around her shoulders. "I can't believe you're here with me now, Daphne."

"I know. I was feeling the same way," she confessed. She leaned into him, allowing herself to relax and feeling like everything about this was so right.

"I don't know why it took us so long." He took a sip of his soda.

"It's been a crazy year." She suppressed a yawn, realizing that she was sleepy and wondering what time it was, but not really caring.

"We still have a lot to talk about." He was playing with a strand of her hair. "Have I ever told you that I love your hair color?"

"Really?"

"It reminds me of a September sunset." He leaned over to sniff it. "Smells wonderful too."

She giggled. Then, leaning her head back into the sofa, she sighed deeply. "I'm so happy right now, Jake. I feel like this is a dream. Like I'm going to wake up and it'll all be gone—poof."

"This is not a dream," he said soothingly, still playing with her hair. "Although it will end briefly when I go back to Miami tomorrow. Not looking forward to that. But I'll be telling myself it's just temporary. I have a case down there that I need to wrap up. It's not a big case, but I believe in it. Although I could probably keep working on it here too. But there are some facts I need to gather while I'm still down there."

"What sort of case?"

"It's a wrongful death suit. An employee at a small chemical corporation died from lung cancer. But since she'd been a

smoker as a youth, the company denies any responsibility."
He explained about how a few other employees were having
health problems too, and she was really trying to listen—and
it was interesting. But as he continued talking in a low quiet
tone, Daphne felt herself slipping in and out of an amazing
dream. She did not want to wake up.

Chapter 22

Daphne woke suddenly—looking around the room and trying to get her bearings. But seeing a stack of boxes nearby reminded her. This was Jake's house. She'd been helping him. But what time was it? She leaped to her feet and dashed to the kitchen to look at the stove clock. 2:37? Could that possibly be right?

"I thought I heard footsteps," Jake said as he carried a box toward the front door. "I was just about to wake you and offer to drive you home. But you looked so peaceful and—"

"Oh, Jake." She grabbed her evening bag and shawl. "I've got to get home. What will Mattie think?"

"Hopefully she's sound asleep." He set down the box and leaned over to kiss her. "Sorry, I should've woke you, but I got busy with packing and—"

"I've got to go." She reached for the door.

"Just be safe," he said as he opened it for her. "I can drive you if you—"

"No, no, I'm fine." She forced a smile.

"Will I see you in the morning?" He walked outside with her. "Oh, that's right, this is the morning." He chuckled.

"Yes. I'll definitely be back here to help you." She unlocked her car and Jake pulled her toward him for one last kiss.

"Goodnight," he said quietly.

"Goodnight." She stared at him in wonder. "I'll see you in a few hours."

As Daphne drove across town, which was dark and quiet, she still felt like she was in a dream. Only this dream was a bit disturbing. She hated to think she'd been out this late. Leaving a teenage babysitter with Mabel for so long. It seemed irresponsible and unlike her. Oh, she knew that she'd had her phone with her. And she'd even made sure to turn it back on after the wedding. But still!

She pulled into the garage, glad that she'd left it open since the garage door hinge had recently developed a loud squeak, but not wanting to alert any of her neighbors as to her late night whereabouts, she decided to leave the door up for now. It wasn't until she was sneaking up to the house that she realized she didn't even have on shoes. Instead, she was wearing a pair of Jake's athletic socks. As well as his old jeans and sweatshirt. Fortunately no one was around to see her.

She quietly letting herself into the house, listening intently. Was Mattie awake? Would she wake up? Daphne didn't want to frighten her, but she did want to go upstairs and make sure all was well. First she grabbed her bathrobe, pulling it on over her curious outfit before she tiptoed up the stairs. Mabel's door was cracked open enough that Daphne could see that she was peacefully sleeping. The guest room door was halfway open and it appeared that Mattie was soundly asleep as well.

Feeling like she'd just dodged a bullet, Daphne slipped back downstairs and quickly got ready for bed. Of course, she was wide awake by the time her head hit the pillow. Replaying everything that had happened between her and Jake tonight, she still wanted to pinch herself. Was it really real? And would he and Jenna truly move back to Appleton like he hoped? Finally, in an effort to shut down her brain and get a few more hours of sleep, she went back to her old childhood routine, doing what Aunt Dee had taught her— counting her blessings in alphabetical order.

When Daphne woke up, it was to the sound of giggling female voices. And according to her alarm clock it was nearly eight. She grabbed up her bathrobe and hurried out to see what was going on.

"There she is," Sabrina said with an amused smile. "Sleeping beauty."

"Good morning," Daphne told her.

"You slept in late," Mabel said with curious interest.

"That's because she had a late night," Sabrina explained.

"I already fixed Mabel and me some breakfast," Mattie told Daphne. "But if you don't mind, I think I'll head home now."

"Do you need me to drive—"

"It's okay. I can walk," Mattie offered. "You know how close my house is."

Daphne ran to get her purse, generously paying Mattie and thanking her for doing such a great job.

"Anytime," Mattie said happily as she pocketed the cash. "Mabel's easy to baby-sit."

"I started a pot of coffee," Sabrina said after Mattie left. "It should be ready." But she turned to Mabel now. "Hey, darling, could you do me a great big favor?"

"What?" Mabel asked eagerly.

Sabrina explained that Tootsie was lonely. "If you could just take him for a little walk around the neighborhood, I would be so grateful. And I'll gladly pay you."

"You don't have to pay me, Aunt Sabrina." Mabel was already getting her jacket. "I want to take Tootsie for a walk."

"I need a couple minutes to get dressed," Daphne told Sabrina.

"I'll pour the coffee," Sabrina said.

Daphne rushed to her room, but felt slightly shocked to see Jake's rumpled clothes on her bedroom floor. Reminding herself that she'd simply borrowed them, she tossed the garments into her closet then quickly pulled on her own jeans and sweatshirt, hurrying back out to the kitchen where Sabrina was sitting at the kitchen table with an expression that was a mixture of smugness and curiosity.

"Tell me everything," Sabrina said as Daphne sat down.

"Everything?" Daphne took a sip of coffee.

"I know you didn't come home after you left the wedding. Or if you did come home, you must've left again. Because Ricardo brought me home pretty late. Close to midnight." She sighed happily. "It was such a wonderful, magical evening."

"I know." Daphne sighed too.

Sabrina's brows arched with interest. "How so?"

"Oh...the wedding, of course." Daphne smirked. "Wasn't it beautiful the way Julianne had it all set up?"

"You know that's not what I meant." Sabrina set her cup down with a clunk. "I want to know where you were last night, Daphne Ballinger. I was worried about you. Your garage door was wide open and your car was not in it."

Daphne just nodded, picking up a blueberry muffin from the plate on the table. "Did you make these?" she asked Sabrina.

"Yes. But back to where you were." Sabrina tipped her head to one side. "Where were you?"

"Jake and I decided to meet for coffee after we left the wedding."

"You left the wedding before nine o'clock. Don't tell me you were having coffee until after one in the morning."

"You watched my empty garage until one AM?"

"That's right. And I tried texting you too. But did you answer?"

"I guess I didn't hear the buzz. You could've just called me."

"Trust me, I was about to, but I sort of figured you were with Jake. And I didn't really want to interrupt anything. But I told myself that if you weren't home by two, I would call you. But then I fell asleep." Sabrina shook her head. "Honestly, Daphne, I even considered calling the police. But then I woke up around three and your car was there."

"I'm so sorry to have worried you, Sabrina. I never meant to stay that long, but I fell asleep."

"*Over coffee?*" Sabrina looked skeptical.

Daphne knew she had to tell Sabrina the whole story. Anyway, most of it. She wasn't sure she was ready to divulge everything just yet. So she explained about helping Jake pack, how they'd taken a break, and how she'd fallen asleep.

"Just like that old song?" Sabrina started to sing. "Wake up, little Daphne, wake up!"

Daphne pointed at the kitchen clock. "And I promised Jake I'd come back this morning to help him pack." She stood up. "I need to get Mabel and get over there."

"Want me to watch Mabel for you?" Sabrina offered.

"Would you mind?"

"Not at all. And Ricardo is probably there by now too. He was going to help Jake load the heavy stuff."

As Daphne got her car keys, she wondered if Jake would really even need her help after all. He'd looked like he was nearly done when she'd left him last night. But she didn't care—she just wanted to see him before he left. She thanked Sabrina. "And I shouldn't be gone long. Jake has to head for the airport around eleven."

"And when you get back you can fill me in on the real story," Sabrina said as she accompanied Daphne outside. "With all the details."

Daphne waved a dismissive hand, but she had a feeling that Sabrina would worm it all out of her. If Sabrina ever needed a new career, she should consider detective work. As Daphne drove toward Jake's house, she wished she'd taken more time to fix herself up a little. But then she remembered what Jake had said last night. He thought she was beautiful—whether dressed up for a wedding or wearing her grungiest clothes. She loved that!

As she parked her car, Ricardo and Jake were carrying the leather couch out to the U-Haul truck. Staying out of their way, she watched with amusement as they tried to fit it into the half-filled truck. "Why don't you set it on end?" she suggested. And so they did—and it fit.

"Just in time to rescue us," Jake said as he came over to hug her. "Thanks!"

"Tell me what you want me to do," she said.

"I think most of the small stuff is packed now," Jake told her as they went back inside. "But there's still the front coat closet, which is a mess, if you want to tackle it." He picked up a bag sitting next to the front door. "But this is yours. You might want to put it in your car so it doesn't get lost in the shuffle."

She peeked inside to see her coral silk dress from last night. "Oh, yeah!" She nodded in embarrassment. "I'll put this away." As she hurried the bag out to the car, she remembered how she'd left Aunt Dee's pearls on the bathroom counter, hoping Jake had put them in the bag too. But a quick check reassured her that not only had he packed everything, he'd carefully wrapped the pearls in tissue and inserted them in a Ziploc bag as well. So thoughtful.

While Ricardo and Jake loaded a few more furniture pieces before heading to the storage unit, Daphne started in on the coat closet. Like with everything else, she tried to sort as she boxed things up, carefully labeling the contents on the outside of the cartons. But this closet was definitely a mishmash. Winter coats, sports shoes, tennis rackets, a bowling ball, several umbrellas, golf clubs, and numerous other miscellaneous items.

Since the guys were still gone by the time she finished, she decided to do a quick check around the rest of the house to see if anything had been overlooked. She discovered one missed cupboard in the laundry room, which she quickly emptied. But after that, it seemed that everything was boxed up and ready to go. And she got the broom and started to sweep. The house obviously needed a good cleaning, but as far as she could tell, the cleaning supplies had been packed too.

After the guys came back, she helped them load the boxes in the truck until there was nothing but Jake's packed bags and dust and debris left in the house. Jake reached for the broom still in her hands. "I'll take that." He grinned. "I appreciate the effort, but I've got a cleaning crew scheduled to come in here tomorrow."

"Oh, that's good." She dusted her hands on her jeans. "I guess this is it then."

"Ricardo and I need to take this last load," Jake told her. "But I'd like to see you before I leave. Can I pop by your house for a few minutes?" He looked down at his grubby clothes. "Maybe clean up a bit before I head for the airport?"

"Of course," she said eagerly. "Do you think you'd have time for a quick bite of lunch before you go? I could throw something together and—"

"That'd be fabulous, Daphne. Thanks."

As she drove home, she tried to think of something easy and good to fix for lunch, but all she could think about was Jake. She hadn't dreamt last night after all. She hurried into the house to discover Sabrina and Mabel engrossed in a coloring book that they'd brought home from Disney World.

"Jake is stopping by for a quick lunch before he goes to the airport," Daphne called to them as she headed to the kitchen, doing a fast search of her refrigerator and pantry.

"What are you fixing?" Sabrina asked.

Daphne frowned. "I really need to get groceries."

"Well, I just happen to have a chicken that I was planning to make into chicken salad today."

"That sounds good."

"How about I go whip that up." Sabrina looked in the fruit bin of the fridge. "You could make a little fruit salad."

"Good idea."

Sabrina pointed at the ginger cookies left over from critique group. "And there's your dessert."

Daphne laughed. "What would I do without you?"

"I'll be back in a jiff with the chicken salad." Sabrina pointed to Daphne's grubby outfit. "That might even give you some time to clean up your act."

Daphne shrugged. "Jake said he thinks I'm beautiful—even like this."

"Well, that man is a keeper."

Even so, after she got the fruit salad thrown together, Daphne knew she needed to clean up a little. She finished just in time to hear Mabel welcoming Jake into the house.

"Come on in, Jake," Mabel said in a hospitable way. "Mom's in her room. I don't think she's sleeping. But she did sleep pretty late this morning."

"She did, did she?" Jake chuckled.

"Here I am," Daphne said as she emerged. "Wide awake, thank you very much." She tousled Mabel's hair.

Jake held up his carry-on bag. "Mind if I utilize a bathroom to clean up a little?"

Daphne pointed him to the hall bath upstairs. "It's roomier," she explained. "Make yourself at home."

As he went up, she explained to Mabel about how he had to pack up his house and was catching a flight back to Miami.

"I wish him and Jenna could move back here," Mabel said glumly.

"I do too." Daphne nodded, determined not to spill any beans about Jake's tentative plan to get Jenna back to Appleton.

"Sabrina told me to tell you that she put something in the kitchen for you," Mabel announced. "And she asked if I could come over to her house. We're going to look at flower girl dresses. Can I please go, Mom?"

Daphne grinned, knowing that Sabrina had more on her mind than flower girl dresses. "Of course you can."

"She asked if I can have lunch with her, too." Mabel looked hopeful. "Can I, please?"

"*May* I?" Daphne corrected her then smiled. "Sure. Tell Auntie Sabrina thanks."

Daphne went to the kitchen to discover that Sabrina hadn't only whipped up some chicken salad, she'd made it into sandwiches too. As Daphne set up their lunch, she wished that it didn't have to be such a quick one. But she knew Jake needed to be on the road soon if he wanted to make his flight.

"This looks fantastic," Jake said as he sat across from her at the kitchen table. He looked all around with appreciation. "You know I'd been missing this place down in Miami."

"Really? You missed my kitchen?"

"I missed the whole house." He nodded. "As much as I was missing Appleton." He reached for her hand. "But not as much as I missed you."

She smiled happily.

"Do you mind if I ask a blessing?"

"Not at all."

As Jake said a simple prayer, Daphne felt like this was one of those moments—the kind that one never forgets, the kind that would flash back in years to come. As he said amen, she felt almost completely and perfectly happy. Except for the part that he would soon be leaving.

"You know, I had imagined getting together with you on this trip," Jake said as they ate. "I'd actually envisioned myself finding you at the wedding, taking you by the hand to the dance floor, and waltzing away with you." He chuckled. "Even though I'm a lousy dancer. But it seemed to work in my head."

"I wouldn't have minded if you'd stepped on my toes a few times," she confessed. "It would've been worth it."

"That probably would've happened too. But my vision of a romantic dance floor scene went up in smoke when I saw you dancing with all those other guys. First it was Spencer—and I have to admit you two looked good together. Then Ricardo, whose dancing skills put most males to shame. Although I wasn't that worried since he's engaged. Then that Australian guy stepped in. Well, that got my blood to boiling a little. But I figured you were just being polite...especially since you were there as Spencer's date."

"And you were all wrong."

He smiled. "Thankfully."

"But what if I hadn't come after you?" she asked with concern. "What if I hadn't ended my dance with Collin and followed you out?"

"That's a very good question."

"So you're glad I chased you down?"

"Of course I'm glad." A shadow washed over his countenance.

"Is something wrong?"

"No, not really."

"What is it then?"

"I was just thinking about your questions. What if you hadn't come after me?"

"You would've left Appleton and never thought of me again?"

He somberly shook his head. "No, I would keep thinking about you. But I would do some rationalizing, Daphne. Like I've done in the past."

"What kind of rationalizing?"

"Oh, you know, that it's not meant to be...that the odds are stacked against us...there's the thing with Gwen and Jenna. And then there's a little something you said once...something that comes back to haunt me quite regularly."

"What?" she asked eagerly. "What did I say?"

"We were talking about the kind of men you'd consider

marrying...it was last summer and I hadn't known you for long...but you mentioned you would prefer not to marry someone who'd been divorced. And, believe me, I understand that. Broken marriages come with their own problems."

"Oh, but I was probably talking about Ryan then. Remember him pressuring me to marry him last summer? And it was complicated because I'd really thought I was in love with him back in New York. But then I hadn't known he'd been married at the time. But even when he told me they were divorced—or nearly divorced—well, I knew I didn't want to marry him. Period. And I probably just used the divorced thing as an excuse."

"So you don't think of me like that? Damaged goods?"

She couldn't help but laugh. "No, Jake, I have never thought of you as damaged goods."

"Or that I brought along baggage?" He studied her closely.

"Well, I did notice your carry-on going with you upstairs. Don't forget it by the way."

He chuckled. "It's sitting by your front door." He glanced at his watch as he chewed his last bite of sandwich. "And as much as I hate to leave you, I'm already cutting it close." He pushed his chair back and stood.

"I know." She reached for the plate of cookies. "How about I put some of these in a baggie for you?" She stood too, just looking at him.

"You're an angel." He set down the cookie plate and pulled her close. "Somehow I'm going to leave Miami and get back here to you, Daphne." He kissed her, sending shivers of pleasure up and down her spine. "It might not be as easy as we hope, but it will be worth it." He pushed a strand of hair from her forehead. "Can you be patient and wait for me?"

"Of course." She resisted the urge to point to the calendar on the fridge, reminding him of her mid-May deadline. She knew that he was aware of it.

"Thanks for everything. I'll call you later." He kissed her again and then, with his baggie of ginger cookies tucked into his carry-on, he hurried out to his rental car, waving to her as he drove away. She stood there watching, filled with a strange mixture of joy and sadness. Joy for what had happened between them, sadness to say goodbye. But mostly it was joy. Just plain old joy.

Chapter 23

After Daphne went back into the house, she felt so excited that she couldn't help but dance her way into the kitchen. She was still dancing when Sabrina showed up, asking Daphne to tell all.

"Where's Mabel?" Daphne asked, looking over Sabrina's shoulder.

"Lola came by after we finished lunch. The girls just took off on their skateboards."

Sabrina helped herself to a ginger cookie. "Still taste good after several days. You'll have to give me your recipe." She nodded to the tea kettle on the stove. "Is that hot?"

"Want some tea with your cookie?" Daphne offered.

"Yes, I do," Sabrina declared.

"How about if we have tea and cookies out on the porch? That way we can wave at the skater girls as they pass by."

"Perfect." Sabrina picked up the plate of cookies and Daphne tossed some tea into the teapot.

Soon they were comfortably settled on the wicker chairs on the porch and Daphne, trying to contain her excitement, informed Sabrina of the blossoming romance between her and Jake.

"I just knew it," Sabrina said triumphantly. "So exciting."

"I suppose the relationship has been blossoming for a while," Daphne admitted. "But so many times it got nipped in the bud."

"I know." Sabrina nodded. "Ricardo and I were just talking about that. He has high hopes for you and Jake." She giggled. "But he's also got some concerns."

"Concerns?"

"Well, I promised I wouldn't say anything." Sabrina took a sip of tea.

"What do you mean?"

"Oh, I assured him it was probably nothing."

"What was probably nothing?"

Sabrina waved her hand nonchalantly. "Nothing."

"What are you talking about?" Daphne demanded. "Surely you didn't tell Ricardo about me coming home so late last night, did you?"

"I didn't need to. Ricardo discovered your clothes in Jake's bathroom this morning."

Daphne slapped her hand over her mouth. "Oh, no."

"Don't worry, honey. I told him it was probably perfectly innocent." She peered curiously at Daphne. "It is, isn't it?"

"Of course it is." Daphne explained about borrowing old clothes to help pack. "It was pretty dirty, and my silk dress would've been ruined."

"I figured it was something like that."

"Oh, dear." Daphne shook her head. "I hate thinking that Ricardo found that...or thought that."

"I think it just caught him off guard, Daph. He didn't know what to think."

"Well, please, straighten him out."

"Don't worry. I will." Sabrina looked intently at Daphne. "So did Jake ask you?"

"Ask me?"

"You know, did he get down on one knee? Did he propose?"

"No, of course not. I mean this is all happening so fast

anyway. It was like going from zero to sixty."

"Yes, but you made it to sixty, right?"

"Well, I don't know. I mean, how do you define sixty?" Daphne felt her cheeks growing warm. "I mean, honestly Sabrina, all we did was talk and, well, kiss."

Sabrina laughed. "Well, that is progress. But when you talked, did he mention marriage at all?"

"Marriage?" Daphne tried to think if the word had actually come up.

"You know, where you put on the white dress and walk down the aisle?" Sabrina teased. "You do have a deadline, you know."

"Believe me, I know."

"So...did Jake *mention* marriage? Did he hint at it at all?"

"Not exactly. I mean, it seemed like we were talking all around it. We were talking about him and Jenna moving back here. We talked about us, our relationship. We talked about my previous aversion to divorced men, but he had misunderstood me. He thought it was related to him. But it wasn't."

"So you didn't actually talk about tying the knot?" Sabrina looked disappointed.

"Not specifically."

"Oh." Sabrina looked perplexed.

"Everything is happening so fast," Daphne told her. "It's not like we can rush it."

"I know, I know." Sabrina nodded.

"And I'm really happy." Daphne offered a big smile. "I really am."

Sabrina brightened. "That's wonderful. I'm happy for you." Now she frowned slightly. "What about the word 'love'—was that mentioned?"

Daphne thought hard. "Well, maybe not specifically. But I could feel it in the air. I really could."

"I'm sure you could. But we really need something more

concrete, Daphne."

"Like *I love you* written in stone," Daphne said wryly.

Sabrina's eyes lit up. "Now that would be something, wouldn't it?"

"Maybe...but something was definitely going on between us." Daphne could hear the defensiveness rising in her voice. "I could feel it deep inside of me, Sabrina. It was real. And I know Jake felt it too. We moved forward. We stepped into a *real* relationship. I know we did."

"That's great. But you need to move fast. The clock is ticking."

Daphne just nodded, waving as the little skateboarders came rolling down the sidewalk. She knew the clock was ticking. But for the first time in nearly a year, she wasn't sure she cared. Even if Jake didn't propose marriage in time, as long as he eventually proposed, she didn't really care.

As promised, Jake called Daphne when he got to Miami on Sunday evening. The conversation was warm and intimate, but the word "love" was not mentioned. Nor was the word "marriage." But Daphne told herself that didn't matter as she set down her phone. Her relationship with Jake could not be ruled by the calendar. It needed to blossom and grow without pressure. And, although she continued using a black felt pen to ex out the passing days in April, she remembered Jake's words. She needed to be patient. She needed to wait for him. And that's what she planned to do. She would keep her spirits up and hope for the best.

But as the week wore on, Daphne's spirits began to sag a bit. It started with another rejection from her agent. Marta tried to make it sound like it didn't matter, pointing out that this particular publisher was having financial struggles anyway, but Daphne couldn't help but feel saddened by the news.

"I just want to feel like I'm financially independent," Daphne confided to Sabrina on Wednesday morning as they both collected their mail.

"Well, you would be financially independent if you married Jake," Sabrina pointed out.

"Doesn't that sound a little incongruous?" Daphne shook her head at the irony. "That I have to marry to attain independence?"

"It is a bit odd." Sabrina wrinkled her nose. "But then I remember my mama telling me that if I married the right man, I could live life on my own terms."

"What does that mean exactly?"

"Oh, I think my mama thought it meant I'd be taken care of," Sabrina admitted. "And in my mama's world, that was a good thing. Unfortunately, Edward could provide financially for me, but that was all he could provide. Well, you know about all that."

"Well, even if I should marry Jake—and I really do hope that he asks me—I still want to bring something to the table."

Sabrina waved her hand to the house behind Daphne. "You'd bring all this."

"Only if we're married in time."

"So has Jake called you?"

Daphne nodded as she leaned down to pull a weed that was sneaking in between the crack in the sidewalk. "He calls every evening. After Mabel's gone to bed."

"And you don't talk about your future? About the possibility of marriage?" Sabrina persisted. "The subject just never comes up?"

"Mostly we've been talking about the situation with Gwen and Jenna." Daphne had already told Sabrina about the plan to get Gwen to release custody of Jenna. "It sounds like Gwen got pretty stressed out last weekend when Jake was gone. Apparently Jenna was really pushing Gwen's buttons. On

Saturday Jenna wanted to go to a party with her friends and Gwen put her foot down. So Jenna threw a real fit."

"Good for Jenna." Sabrina laughed.

"Well, I don't know." Daphne frowned. "I mean I sort of respect Gwen for not letting Jenna go to that party."

"I wonder how long it'll take for Gwen to crack." Sabrina flipped through a magazine in her pile of mail.

"Well, Jake told Gwen that he would be unavailable to have Jenna this upcoming weekend," Daphne explained. "And he really does need to work on a big case. Especially if he comes back to Appleton like he wants. But I guess Gwen threw a big fit. She and Frank had already made a reservation to go to the Keys for the weekend. She even threatened to leave Jenna home alone."

"Would that be considered neglect?" Sabrina asked.

"I don't really know. I mean, Jenna is sixteen."

"Yeah, but left on her own for a whole weekend. That seems irresponsible."

"Speaking of irresponsible, I need to get to work."

"You're really getting a lot of hours at Bernie's, aren't you?"

"Just twenty hours a week. But that's plenty."

"But you told Olivia you can't work next Tuesday morning, right?"

"I have next Tuesday off," Daphne assured her. "I'll be all ready to go wedding dress shopping with you."

"It's not exactly shopping," Sabrina explained. "It's a trunk show."

"So they pull the dresses out of a trunk?"

"No, that's just an expression."

Daphne forced an interested look as she endured the explanation, then excused herself to go to work.

While working at Bernie's Blooms, Daphne had to be grateful for the distraction of keeping shop and helping customers. It was better than sitting in her office feeling sorry for herself for getting her second rejection. Besides that, she reminded herself, she was in a relationship with Jake. That was plenty to be happy for. And if that wasn't enough, she had Mabel too. What more could she ask of life?

But that evening, after she'd tucked Mabel in bed, Daphne felt uneasy when her phone didn't jingle. Usually Jake called before nine. But nine came and went. And then ten turned into eleven...and Daphne knew that he wasn't calling. Not only that, but it seemed too late to call him. She considered sending a text, but remembered their track record with texts... and decided not to.

Besides, she decided as she got into bed, she didn't want to come across as pathetically insecure. Or controlling. Or pushy. If Jake wanted to call her, he knew her number. And even if he hadn't actually said the words yet, she knew that he loved her. At least, she was fairly sure. And she was absolutely certain that she loved him. Not that she'd said as much yet either. Maybe she should be the one to break the ice. Or not.

To Daphne's relief, Jake called on Thursday, apologizing profusely for missing the previous night. "I was buried in research and lost track of the time." He let out a weary sigh. "I really need a legal assistant to help me wade through all this."

"I wish I could help you."

"I'm sure you could. If you were here."

"Or if you were here," she said wistfully.

"Speaking of that, I've already started looking into rentals in Appleton. Unfortunately, there's not much out there. I thought a little house would be nice, but that's sure not happening. I found a couple of apartments, but they're not on the side of town where I'd want to raise a teenage daughter."

"I know which ones you mean," she admitted. "I looked at those myself."

"You did? Why?"

She cleared her throat. "Well, mid-May is coming up. I have to plan for my future—and Mabel's." Now she told him about working at Bernie's Blooms. "But what I really want is to get hired at the newspaper. I've been doing a lot of free work for Stan Abernathy. But the paper's barely hanging on." Finally, she told him about her recent book rejection and how the one editor practically accused her of plagiarism. "But Spencer has read both books now and he can see that mine's different."

"I'd like to read your novel too," Jake said in a tired sounding voice. "Can you send me an electronic copy?"

"Do you really have time?"

"I'd make time for that."

"I'll send you one before I go to bed."

"Speaking of bed, I promised myself to get some sleep tonight." He made the sound of a yawn. "I was up until four in the morning yesterday. Then I had to be up for an appointment at nine."

"You go to bed," she insisted. "Get your beauty sleep."

"Yeah, I need it." He chuckled. "But you sure don't."

"Goodnight, Jake."

"Goodnight, Daphne."

As she set her phone down, Daphne wondered how long it would take them to say those three little words. Perhaps she should bravely go there first. Or not.

Even though Jake had sounded exhausted, she didn't feel sleepy. And since she'd been thinking about Jenna this week... and praying for her...she decided to send her a quick email. She picked up her iPad and quickly typed one out.

> *Dear Jenna,*
> *I know it's late, but I wanted to touch base with you. I know you're going through some hard stuff. And I'm worried that I've alienated you by sounding*

too much like a mom and not enough like a friend. But it's only because I love you and I believe in you and I want to see you living your very best life.

So if I've offended you or intruded, I hope you'll forgive me. And if you need to talk, I hope you'll ask. In the meantime, Mabel sends you her love. And so do I. You are a very special girl!
Daphne

She hit send then set her iPad down to get ready for bed. And by the time she finished washing her face and brushing her teeth, she heard a ping announcing she had an email. She opened it up to see that Jenna had already written a response.

Dear Daphne,

I'm not mad at you. I've just been really busy. Sorry not to write. Mom's been acting like Cruella de Vil. Well, she's not actually killed any innocent puppies. Not yet anyway. But she sure likes to stomp on my heart. I'm sorry, but I really do hate her, Daphne. Please, don't tell anyone I said this. I don't like Frank much either. And Dad is acting all weird too. Being really distant. Seriously, I'm starting to feel like everyone is abandoning me. But at least I have my friends. And I'm glad that I have you to talk to. Thanks for writing to me tonight. I was feeling down.
Jenna

Daphne wrote a quick response to Jenna's note, reassuring Jenna that she was here and ready to listen, and that she could be trusted. She expressed sympathy and reminded Jenna that she was not alone, and that lots of people loved her—including Mabel and Daphne. She wanted to tell Jenna that Jake was busy with a big case right now, but realized that she'd have to explain how she knew this—and just didn't feel ready to go there yet. Better to just be Jenna's friend for now. Let the future take care of itself.

Chapter 24

On Friday afternoon, as Daphne walked Mabel home from school, she decided that being a single working mother was not that easy. Not that she had expected a walk in the park. After all, she'd been raised by her own widowed dad. And even though Dad had received help from Aunt Dee, he had complained occasionally that single parenting was a hard row to hoe. Consequently, Daphne had always done her part, cleaning and cooking, trying to compensate for the lack of a mom in the home. So, really, she wasn't unaccustomed to hard work. Maybe she just needed to pace herself.

And working at Bernie's Blooms was for the most part pleasant. Customers were usually congenial. The surroundings were pretty. And she appreciated getting hours that were compatible with Mabel's school day. But by the end of the week, especially after spending the past couple days organizing the backroom, Daphne felt worn out.

At least they had the weekend ahead of them now. She was looking forward to kicking back and, hopefully, a couple of good long conversations with Jake. And perhaps by Monday she'd be fresh and ready to return to work again. But as they were walking, she got a text from Olivia that she wished she could just ignore. She let out a loud sigh, causing Mabel to look at her with curiosity.

"What's wrong?"

Daphne held up her phone. "Olivia wants to know if we can keep Bernadette on Saturday night."

Mabel looked slightly concerned. "For the whole night?"

"No, just a couple of hours so that Olivia and Jeff can go out."

Mabel still looked uncertain. "Do you think she'll do that crying thing again?"

"I don't think so. Last I heard Bernadette is completely out of the colicky stage. And, remember, she was just fine the last time we watched her."

"Well...okay." Mabel nodded in agreement. "I guess we can baby-sit her then. Can we have a pizza too?"

Daphne texted back an affirmative. "Yes."

Mabel let out a cheer.

Daphne took in a deep breath as she pocketed her phone. Inhaling the fresh air, she admired the spring flowers blooming profusely in the yards along their street. "Isn't this a beautiful day?"

"Yeah!" Mabel grabbed Daphne's hand, swinging it as she hopped and skipped beside her. "Can Lola come over to play at our house? Just until dinnertime?"

"If it's okay with her mom."

Before long, Daphne was sitting on the front porch with a tall iced tea, watching contentedly as Mabel and Lola did cartwheels and somersaults in the lush green grass of their front yard. Sabrina and Tootsie came strolling down the sidewalk, looking as if they'd just been to town. Sabrina, dressed in a pink and white checked pantsuit, looked springy and fresh. And Tootsie, not to be outdone, had on a little matching vest.

"You two look festive," Daphne yelled from her porch.

"Hey, y'all," Sabrina called back. "Check out Tootsie's bowtie."

The little girls ran over to see Tootsie, begging Sabrina to take him on another walk, so they could show him off in the neighborhood. Sabrina gladly handed his leash over to Mabel. "I'd be grateful if you wore him out some. Ricardo and I are going out tonight and poor Tootsie will be home alone again."

"I can baby-sit him tonight," Mabel offered.

"Better check with your mom first."

"Okay!" Mabel and Lola took off running with Tootsie trotting between them.

"Got any more of that?" Sabrina pointed to Daphne's glass.

"Sure. Have a seat and I'll get it."

Daphne returned with an icy glass. Handing it to Sabrina, she sat down with a tired sigh. "Thank goodness it's Friday," she told Sabrina.

"You got that right. Ricardo thought he had to work at the diner tonight, so I figured I'd just go in and keep him company, but he just told me we can go out after all." She took a sip.

"Do you ever help him at the diner?"

"Oh, sure. I love playing in that fabulous kitchen of his. But I have to watch myself."

"Watch yourself?"

"Remember it's Ricardo's kitchen. He is king of that kitchen."

"What about *your* kitchen? Who reigns there?"

"Naturally, I'm queen." Sabrina chuckled. "But I let him rule in there sometimes. I'd be a fool not to. Good grief, that man can cook up a storm. But sometimes I make him step aside and put his feet up. I don't think he minds." She winked.

"You guys make such a great couple."

"Well, thank you."

"Where is he taking you tonight?"

"He wouldn't say. But you know how he likes to surprise me."

"Sounds like fun." Daphne felt a ripple of jealousy. Not exactly jealousy. Maybe it was more longing. She certainly wished no ill on Ricardo and Sabrina. But it would be so nice to be going out on a date with Jake tonight. If only he weren't so far away.

"So...what's the latest on Jake these days?"

"Oh, well, he's pretty busy. He's buried in a wrongful death lawsuit. Trying to collect testimonies to help prove that this woman—"

"No, no." Sabrina held up a hand. "I mean how's it going as far as his relocation plans? What's the timeline there? When's he coming back?"

"I, uh, I'm not really sure."

"But you guys talk every night, right?"

"Pretty much."

"And you don't talk about *that*?"

"Well, he's got a lot on his plate. Poor guy. I mean, he's barely settled in Miami, which he hates, his house here sells, and now he's got to figure out how to move back, find a new place to live. And, of course, there's the whole custody business with Gwen to work out. It's not been easy."

"But I thought Jenna was doing her part to drive Gwen and Frank nuts so they'd happily hand her over to Jake."

"Well, it's not like anyone's told Jenna to do that. It was simply that we were hoping her natural teen angst would help Gwen to adjust to the idea."

"Well, I have my own theory about Gwen."

"Really?" Daphne looked at her with interest.

"I guess it's not really my own theory. It's something I heard at my hair salon the other day. But they're usually pretty reliable resources."

"Yes...I'm sure." Daphne tried not to roll her eyes.

"Anyway, I was telling my hairdresser about our trip to Florida and that we got to spend time with Jake and Jenna. There was a woman in there who has known Gwen for years and, admittedly, this lady is kind of a gossip. But she said that

MELODY CARLSON

Gwen only kept Jenna because it allowed her to get more money out of Jake. Apparently, between her alimony and Jenna's child support, she was able to live rather comfortably."

"But Gwen is married now. No more alimony."

"Yes, but I got to thinking that she might not want to part with that child support."

"But that's for Jenna, not Gwen. Besides that, Frank is wealthy. He can easily support Gwen and Jenna."

"Sure, but like the lady at my salon pointed out, Gwen likes money. She probably enjoys getting that child support. You know, directly into her own pocket. She doesn't have to account for it to Frank. Kind of like mad money."

"Mad money?" Daphne shook her head, trying not to feel mad about what she knew was small town gossip. "Well, I honestly don't know what to think about that."

"My point is this, Daphne—if my hunch is right, *Gwen might be reluctant to part with her darling daughter.*"

Daphne ran her finger down the sweating glass as she absorbed Sabrina's insinuation. Was it possible that Gwen would hold onto Jenna just for spending money? Besides being hard to believe, it was so wrong!

"Anyway..." Sabrina swung her finger in front of Daphne's nose. "You and Jake might need to come up with a different plan. Jake's a lawyer. He should know a legal way to settle this thing."

Daphne pursed her lips, unwilling to confide to Sabrina about Jake's promise to Gwen. As much as that eight-year-old promise might ruin everything for the present, how could she fault Jake for being a man of his word? And, really, was this truly any of her business? Or Sabrina's?

By Saturday evening, Daphne questioned the sensibilities of a long distance romance. Oh, it wasn't that she minded being home with Mabel and babysitting Baby Bernadette. But it was a little difficult witnessing Sabrina and Ricardo coming and going and so obviously in love and thoroughly enjoying their engagement. Even Olivia and Jeff seemed to be enjoying a night out together. Meanwhile Daphne was changing diapers and watching *The Little Mermaid*, again, while eating pepperoni pizza.

And, really, it wouldn't be so bad if she didn't feel like her whole life was caught in a frustrating limbo that never seemed to end. It didn't help when, after baby Bernadette went home and Mabel went to bed, Daphne stayed up until eleven waiting for Jake to call.

She reconciled herself with the possibility that Jake had taken pity on Jenna and decided to spend the weekend with her after all. Because the last email Daphne had received from the displaced teenage girl had been filled with sadness and despair. Jenna was stressed about being left home alone for the entire weekend. And from what Daphne could detect, Jenna had barely made it through Friday night on her own. She'd heard strange noises in the middle of the night and worried that someone was breaking into their multi-million dollar home. The situation really aggravated Daphne, and she had wanted to express her outrage to Jake tonight. Except that he never called.

But as she felt herself drifting off to sleep, she decided this was a good thing. She would rather Jake be distracted in the parenting of Jenna than be obsessed with calling her by nine o'clock every night.

On Sunday morning, Daphne and Mabel went to church as usual. And, as usual, Daphne was encouraged by Pastor Andrew's straightforward but uplifting sermon and even took the time to tell him this afterward. "It was just what I needed to hear," she said.

"Thank you for telling me that." He looked earnestly into

her eyes. "Tell me, Daphne, how are you doing?"

She felt slightly taken aback by the intensity of his question. "Well, I guess I'm doing okay. I mean, I'm discovering that being a single mom comes with its challenges. But I think I'm adjusting."

"I know you're working at Bernie's Blooms," he said.

"Yes, and it's a great place to work." She frowned. "But I guess my personal life feels like it's sort of hanging in the balance." She stopped, knowing she'd said too much.

"Hanging in the balance?" He peered curiously at her.

"Oh, I don't know." She forced a smile. "I guess I get a little worried about the future sometimes. But that's exactly why I needed to hear your sermon today. Thank you."

"You're welcome, Daphne." He nodded. "And if you ever need to talk, I'm here. And I'm a good listener."

She considered this. "Well, I might take you up on that. Thank you."

As Daphne left to get Mabel, she wondered if it really might help her to make an appointment with Pastor Andrew. Especially if she could be sure of client/counselor privilege. Besides Sabrina, there really wasn't anyone to discuss her troubles with. And with the mid-May date quickly approaching, she just wasn't sure. What if Jake had no intention of marrying her? After all, he'd never spoken of it. Not specifically anyway. He had seemed to make some insinuations. But where did that get her? And why was he stringing her along like this? Why had he promised to call every night, but then not done it? Especially considering how he was honoring his promise to Gwen—despite how that promise felt like it was unraveling Daphne's whole life.

Daphne tried to push these thoughts away as she and Mabel walked across the parking lot to her car. "What do you want to do today?" she asked as she unlocked Bonnie.

"Can we put the top down and go for a ride?" Mabel asked

hopefully.

"That is a fabulous idea. Want to help?" And so together, they put Bonnie's top down and took the pretty car for a ride in the countryside, eventually stopping for lunch at a roadside diner that was reputed to have the best cheeseburgers for a hundred miles. Daphne wasn't sure that Ricardo would agree, but she had to admit they were surprisingly good.

After they finished and Mabel was using the restroom, Daphne's phone buzzed with a text message. Pleased to see it was from Jake, she eagerly opened up.

> *Bad news. Jenna is missing. Frank and Gwen's home was vandalized. Trying not to fear the worse, but have contacted police. Please pray.*

Daphne felt horrified as she read and re-read the message. But seeing Mabel emerging from the bathroom, she knew she had to wear a poker face. No way was she going to frighten poor Mabel with this news. But as she drove them toward home, she prayed silently. And fervently.

Chapter 25

As soon as they got home, Daphne asked Mabel if she wanted to invite Lola over to play. This was to buy some time to talk to Jake in private and find out what was going on. As soon as Lola arrived and the two girls went outside to enjoy the sunshine, Daphne called Jake's cell phone.

"I'm sorry to bother you," she said quickly. "But I'm so worried about Jenna. What's going on?"

"I don't know," he said in a voice filled with despair. "Gwen and Frank came home around noon today. Their house was totally trashed and Jenna was gone."

"Jenna's *gone*?"

"Yes. At first Gwen thought Jenna was kidnapped since she's not answering her phone or text messages."

"Do you really think she was kidnapped?"

"No. Now that I've been to their house and seen the place, I don't think she's been kidnapped. Or not exactly."

"What do you mean?"

"It looks like there was a wild drinking party there."

"Oh?"

"Like teenagers do, you know, when the parents are out of town. But usually they try to clean it up and pretend like it never happened."

"Seriously?"

"That's what it looked like to me. And Frank and Gwen felt the same way too, the more they looked around."

"But Jenna isn't there?"

"No. And Frank and Gwen now feel certain that Jenna's hiding out because she's embarrassed to show her face. They're sure she's behind it, and that she invited her hoodlum friends over for the weekend. Like a payback for being left home alone. But I can't believe Jenna would do something like that. It's not like her."

"Jenna did send me an email Saturday morning," Daphne began carefully.

"An email about *what*?" Jake asked.

"She told me that she was home alone. She'd been afraid the night before. On Friday night. She'd heard noises and thought it was an intruder and—"

"*I never heard about this!*"

"Probably because she wasn't really talking to you, Jake."

"But she told you about this, being home alone, and frightened?"

"Yes, as I mentioned, Jenna and I have been in touch."

"But you didn't tell me that Jenna was alone and scared."

"Because, by the time I heard about it, Jenna realized that it had been nothing. No intruder. She was just scared about being home alone."

"She shouldn't have been home alone."

"I agree." Daphne was trying not to feel hurt by his sharp tone. Almost as if he partially blamed her for this.

"But that doesn't explain her whereabouts now."

"There's something else, Jake."

"*What*?" he demanded. "Please, don't keep anything from me."

"Jenna mentioned that she planned to invite Venus and Cooper over last night. She didn't want to be alone."

He let out a groan. "So...do you think she really did have a wild drinking party with her friends?"

"I don't know. I mean, that just doesn't sound like Jenna to me."

"Jenna has been changing."

"I realize that. But the real Jenna wouldn't—"

"I wish you'd told me this sooner, Daphne."

"If you'd called me last night, I would've."

"The phone works both ways, you know."

"I know...but..."

"I'm sorry, Daphne. But I'm feeling pretty stressed right now. I've got a missing daughter and a mountain of work to get done."

"I understand, Jake. And after hearing about this, I do wish I'd told you sooner. But I've been a little busy too."

"Well, I better get off the phone and see if I can get a hold of those kids. Cooper and Venus. You don't by any chance have their phone numbers?"

"No."

"Last names?"

"Sorry."

"Okay. I'll let you know how it goes."

Daphne felt terrible after they said goodbye. Everything about that conversation was all wrong. But mostly she was worried about Jenna. And although she knew it was a long shot, she decided to send Jenna a text message. And she decided not to tip her hand while doing it.

Hey, Jenna. How's it going? I was worried about you spending the weekend alone. Wished Mabel and I could've popped down there to join you. Everything okay? Let me know. Love, Daphne

Within seconds Daphne's phone binged with a new text

message.

> *My life is a mess. I don't know what to do. I feel*
> *like just giving up.*

Daphne felt slightly frantic as she typed back a fast response.

> *Jenna, call your dad right now. He loves you more*
> *than anyone on earth. Call him and tell him what's*
> *going on. He will help you. I know he will. I love you,*
> *sweetie. Please, call your dad. Love, Daphne.*

As Daphne waited for a response from Jenna, she prayed. And after a few minutes, Jenna texted back, assuring Daphne that she was about to call her dad. Daphne texted her back saying that was a relief—and that she was praying for them.

On Monday morning, Daphne felt blue as she went to work at Bernie's Blooms. Her sadness was directly related to Jake's lack of communication last night. She felt sure that Jenna must've called him. But what happened after that? Had Jake had a good talk with Jenna? Had Jenna been returned to Gwen and Frank? What was going on down in Miami? And yet she didn't want to call. Despite Jake's statement that the phone worked both ways, she felt like Jake was the one who should call her back. Besides, hadn't he said he would?

Shortly before noon, Daphne heard her cell phone ringing and, hoping it was Jake, she hurried to the backroom to answer it. To her disappointment, it was Sabrina.

"Are you okay?" Sabrina asked with concern.

"I'm fine," Daphne said woodenly.

"You don't sound fine to me."

"Sorry."

"I'm concerned for you, Daphne. You don't seem like yourself. I saw you talking to Pastor Andrew yesterday. And then I noticed you pacing back and forth in your living room last night. I can tell something is wrong."

"I guess I've been a little down." Daphne heard the bell on the door jingle. "But I can't talk now. A customer just came in."

"Well, you get a lunch break, don't you?"

"Just half an hour."

"I'll be there at noon," Sabrina said briskly. "Bringing you lunch."

Daphne was about to protest, but whoever entered the shop was calling out, "Yoo-hoo!"

Daphne put on her shop smile as she wrote down the customer's order for a large flower arrangement for a fiftieth anniversary celebration later in the week. "Olivia will put it all together for you, and it will be delivered by Wednesday afternoon."

"Perfect," the elderly woman told her. "And she'll put a lot of metallic gold touches in it?"

"Yes." Daphne pointed to the order sheet. "See, I wrote *lots of metallic gold* and underlined it twice."

"Thank you." The woman smiled. "It's for my sister and brother-in-law. You know not everyone makes it to their fiftieth anniversary."

Daphne nodded. "Yes, that's quite a milestone."

At noon, Sabrina showed up with a small basket. "Lunch has arrived," she said as she flipped the CLOSED sign on the door.

"That's very sweet of you." Daphne led her to the backroom. "But it wasn't necessary."

"Well, I've been worried about you." Sabrina set the basket on the small break table, starting to unpack it. "And this morning I looked at the calendar and I felt seriously concerned. Do you realize you have only twenty days to get hitched?"

"Thanks, Sabrina, I really needed to hear that today."

"I'm sorry, darling. But it's the truth." She handed Daphne a paper plate.

"Believe me, I know how many days are left." Daphne sat down on a plastic chair.

"So what exactly is going on with you and Jake right now?" Sabrina handed Daphne a sandwich and a bag of chips.

"I, uh, I'm not really sure." Daphne sniffed the sandwich. "Egg salad?"

"Isn't that your favorite?"

Daphne shrugged. "Yeah, I guess."

"See, you are really bummed about something. Please, tell Auntie Sabrina what's up."

And so Daphne told her about Jenna being alone and the party and how Jenna was missing and how Jake had almost sounded accusatory to her.

"Oh, my." Sabrina shook her head. "No wonder you've been stressed. That's terrible. But Jenna is okay?"

Daphne told her about yesterday's conversation. "But I never really heard how it turned out. Jake told me he'd call with an update. But he didn't." Daphne felt close to tears now. "I know I could call him, but he sounded so cranky yesterday... well, I just didn't want to."

Sabrina sighed as she poured them each a cup of lemonade. "Well, I'm sure that Jake is feeling stressed too. Goodness, he's been through a lot in the last couple of months. It's probably not bringing out the best in him."

Daphne sniffed. "He did apologize. I mean, when we talked yesterday. That was before I told Jenna to call him. After that I heard nothing."

Sabrina's brow creased. "Well, maybe you should just call him."

"I know, and I would, but I also know he's buried in a tough case. I hate to disturb him. Especially if everything is fine now."

"Except that you're not fine."

Daphne made a brave smile as she took a bite. "You know, I'm feeling better now, Sabrina. Thanks for intervening." She held up the sandwich as she chewed. "And this is really good."

Sabrina chuckled. "Well, it's your recipe, silly. Remember you gave it to me last summer? But I'm glad you're feeling better. Are you still on for the trunk show tomorrow?"

Daphne really wanted to say *forget it*, but Sabrina looked so hopeful, she just couldn't. "Yeah, sure," she told her. "Olivia gave me the day off."

"Oh, goody." Sabrina's face lit up. "I can't wait."

That night, after Mabel had been tucked into bed, Daphne sat down to her computer to finish one more letter for the column. And, truthfully, to keep herself awake in the hope that Jake would call. Although she wasn't holding her breath. As hard as it was to accept—after the magical time they'd had together on the night of Mick's wedding—she was afraid that perhaps that had been it. Jake wasn't really ready for a serious relationship with her. At least not right now.

She opened and read the next letter then immediately wished that she hadn't. Mostly because it was hitting too close to home. All evening she'd been trying to concoct some honest and believable excuse for bowing out of Sabrina's trunk show excursion tomorrow. Really, the last thing Daphne wanted to do was to look at wedding gowns. But she had promised and, unlike some people who would go unmentioned, Daphne liked to keep her promises.

> *Dear Daphne,*
> *I'm getting married in a few weeks—which is totally thrilling. Except for one thing. My older sister 'Kim.' She cannot seem to get over her broken heart. After being engaged for two years, her fiancé broke*

it off in January of this year. They broke up shortly after I got engaged. And since my mom had already reserved our church—which is in high demand in June—I decided to use Mom's reservation and have my wedding then.

But as the date gets closer, my sister seems to be getting more and more nasty about it. She's always sniping at me about something. And it feels like she wants to ruin my whole wedding. I've even considered uninviting her to be my maid of honor. But I know that would break Mom's heart. Is it fair for Kim to make me miserable on my big day? What should I do?

Aggravated in Akron

Dear Aggravated,

While I can understand wanting a June wedding, I do think it was a little insensitive for you to take your sister's wedding date. It's not surprising that her nose is out of joint. Have you ever taken the time to sincerely apologize to her? And to listen to her side of her heartache? Or are you so involved in your own happiness that you've neglected your sister?

You need to tell Kim how sorry you are for her broken engagement and admit that it was thoughtless to take her wedding date without her blessing. Hopefully Kim will accept your apology and adjust her attitude. Hopefully she will want to support you on your wedding day, but you need to help her reach this place. Remember that a wedding is just one day, but sisters are sisters forever.

Daphne

On some levels, Daphne could relate to poor Kim. It wasn't

easy to stand by and watch while someone else planned their joyous event. And Daphne was well aware that some brides could become quite self-centered while planning a wedding. To be fair, Sabrina—despite her enthusiasm—had gone out of her way to be sensitive to Daphne.

So much so that Daphne suddenly felt guilty for being such a wet blanket to Sabrina at times. Really, it was time for Daphne to get over herself. She was Sabrina's maid of honor and it was time to start acting more honorable about it. And so, as Daphne got ready for bed, she was determined to be positive and helpful and excited and enthused as she went with Sabrina to look for wedding gowns tomorrow. Even if it killed her. And, really, who died from shopping for wedding dresses?

Chapter 26

With a resolve to be a supportive maid of honor, Daphne took care to put on an outfit that Sabrina would approve the next morning. A swingy floral skirt topped with a lacy shirt and a peach colored cashmere cardigan. And heels! And several minutes before they were supposed to leave, Daphne showed up on Sabrina's doorstep wearing a big smile.

"Ain't you the tom cat's kitten."

"What?"

Sabrina laughed. "That's southern for you look pretty. Thank you for making the effort, darling."

"And I know you offered to drive today," Daphne dangled her car keys, "but I also know how much you love riding in Bonnie."

Sabrina's eyes lit up. "Well, what're we waiting for?"

As Daphne drove on the highway, Sabrina happily chattered about this and that—and thankfully not just wedding stuff either. "So, I'm dying to ask," Sabrina finally said as they were coming into Fairview. "You must've heard back from Jake."

Daphne pursed her lips, trying to think of a congenial answer. "Well, no...but I've decided that no news is good news. At least regarding Jenna. I'm assuming that everything is all straightened out by now and that Jake has probably got his nose on the grindstone again."

"I'm sure you're right." Sabrina pulled out the GPS on her phone, directing Daphne to the wedding boutique.

"This looks like a nice place," Daphne said as they drove past the bridal shop.

"Oh, it is. But the reason I'm so excited about this trunk show is because of the designer. Have you heard of Clarisse Granville?"

"No." Daphne spotted a parking space on the street, maneuvering to get Bonnie into it.

"Clarisse is my favorite wedding gown designer, and I was just blown away to hear she was having a trunk show in Fairview. I figured I'd have to go to Atlanta to get a look at her gowns."

"I didn't realize that." Daphne looped the handle of her purse over her shoulder, bracing herself for a morning filled with white lace, brocade, and satin. "This should be fun."

"Oh, yeah." Sabrina nodded eagerly. "I'm happier than a hound dog with two tails."

Daphne laughed as she pushed open the door. They were instantly met with the sound of classical music, an elegant scent, and a well-dressed woman carrying a silver tray with half-filled champagne flutes. "Are you here for our special event?" she asked with arched brows.

"We certainly are." Sabrina flashed a pair of tickets in front of her.

"Welcome, ladies!" the woman held out the tray to them.

With their champagne in hand, Daphne trailed Sabrina as she began to peruse the racks of Granville gowns. And before long, with the encouragement of the saleswoman, Sabrina went into the elegant dressing room to try on her favorite gown. Although it wasn't white velvet like Sabrina had hoped for, with three-quarter length sleeves and a sweetheart neckline, it seemed appropriate for a December wedding.

Daphne found a comfortable chair near the dressing rooms, watching as other brides-to-be emerged in various gowns.

"What do you think?" Sabrina asked as she came out.

Daphne wasn't sure what to say. Petite Sabrina seemed to be nearly lost in the big white gown. "I don't know." Daphne stood, coming over to stand by Sabrina in front of the big three way mirror. "What do you think?"

"I look like the Michelin Man." Sabrina frowned.

"That is too much dress for you," the saleswoman said. "You need a more delicate dress."

"I agree," Daphne told her.

Now all three of them were looking through the racks, coming up with dresses that seemed more suitable for a petite woman.

"And what about Daphne?" Sabrina asked the saleswoman. "She's my maid of honor, and we haven't decided what she should wear. But it's a December wedding. So I was thinking about something red or green. Christmassy, you know."

"Red and green are very strong colors. And a redhead in red?" The saleswoman's brow creased.

Daphne nodded. "My concerns exactly."

"What about a pale green? Or perhaps even a deep evergreen, almost black."

Sabrina frowned. "Oh, I wouldn't want to see Daphne in black. But pale green might be nice."

"I have something." The saleswoman pointed Sabrina back toward the dressing room. "You go try those on, and I'll help Daphne. How many bridesmaids are in the wedding party?"

"Actually, it's just me," Daphne told her. "But my little girl will be the flower girl."

"Oh, that's nice." The woman removed a lacy dress from the rack. "This is celadon green."

"I really like it." Daphne couldn't believe how pretty it was—so much better than some of the bridal magazine photos

Sabrina had been showing her. She held it in front of herself. "Is it long enough?"

"It's tea length. And you're so tall that I know it will look gorgeous on you. Especially with the right shoes."

"I really do like it."

"Why don't you try it on?" The saleswoman led Daphne to another dressing room section, not as fancy as the bridal section, but much less busy.

By the time Daphne emerged in the celadon green gown, Sabrina was waiting for her. "Now that's an interesting dress." Sabrina had a slightly doubtful look.

"You don't like it?" Daphne looked at her image in the mirror next to Sabrina. She actually loved this dress. Made of intricate lace that draped nicely, it was rather simple...and yet very elegant. The lacy hemline was uneven, which added to its overall appeal.

"I do like it, Daphne, but it's not right for my wedding." She held out her arms, looking at the fluffy white satin gown she was wearing. "Neither is this."

"Okay." Daphne smiled to hide her disappointment.

Sabrina turned back to Daphne. "Don't get me wrong, that dress is gorgeous on you, Daph. But you're so tall, you look good in anything."

"Not necessarily." Daphne wanted to point out that she looked ridiculous in anything with too many ruffles or frills or bows, except that those were exactly the sorts of dresses that Sabrina adored.

"I'm hopeful about the next gown I'm trying," Sabrina said. "It's actually nothing like what I thought I wanted, but I really like it."

"Great!" Daphne forced an enthusiastic smile. "I can't wait to see it. While you change into it, I'll go get out of this."

But before Daphne removed the celadon green gown, she took one more look in the mirror. It really was perfect. At least for her. Too bad Sabrina didn't think so. But, Daphne reminded herself as she removed it, this was Sabrina's wedding. She needed to call the shots.

Daphne carried the lace gown back out, hung it on the rack where they'd found it, and then went over to wait for Sabrina. And this time, when Sabrina emerged, she really looked pretty. Like a real bride.

"Oh, Sabrina, that dress is stunning," Daphne told her.

"I don't know." Sabrina frowned. "It's rather plain, don't you think?"

"Not plain. It's classic. And it makes *you* look beautiful."

"That's right," the saleswoman confirmed. "Very classic. And you said you wanted something traditional, Sabrina."

"Yes, that's true." Sabrina studied herself in the big mirrors. The gown's bodice had the appearance of being strapless, except that there was a thin gauzy fabric above it, and the skirt was smooth yet full.

"It reminds me of Audrey Hepburn," Daphne said. "In one of your favorite movies too."

"*Sabrina?*" Sabrina's eyes lit up.

"Yes, something about this dress is like that movie."

"Really?" Sabrina looked hopefully into the mirror. "You know, I just love that movie. And I love Audrey Hepburn too."

"Well, that is definitely an Audrey Hepburn sort of gown," the saleswoman told her.

Sabrina gave the full skirt a twirl and then looked at her image again. "What about the bare arms?" Sabrina looked uncertain.

"You have lovely arms," Daphne said.

"Do you think Ricardo will like it?" Sabrina asked.

"He will love it."

"Okay." Sabrina gave the saleswoman a decisive nod. "I'll take it."

"Perfect." The woman clasped her hands. "We'll take your

measurements today, Sabrina, unless you plan to lose or gain weight, and we'll place the order as soon as possible."

"Oh, I'm sure I could afford to shed a few pounds—"

"Sabrina Fontaine," Daphne chided her. "You have a perfect figure. And I'm sure Ricardo would agree wholeheartedly."

Sabrina laughed, gently elbowing the saleswoman. "See why she's my maid of honor?"

"Speaking of that." The saleswoman led them to a nearby rack. "I think I know just the right gown for Daphne. It's not the color you want, but you can have it made in any shade you like." She went through the colorful gowns, finally removing one in a dark lavender. She held it up and, with its smooth sleeveless bodice, it was similar to Sabrina's except that the skirt was tea length.

"Ooh, that's pretty," Sabrina said. "I even like it in that color."

"That's Mabel's favorite color."

"But it's not really Christmassy."

"Oh, it could be," the saleswoman told her. "If you paired it with evergreen and white, purple can be rather festive for Christmas." She handed the dress to Daphne. "Why don't you try it while Sabrina still has on her gown? We can see how you look together?"

Before long, they were standing in front of the mirrors together and even the other customers paused to comment on how nice they looked together.

"Not like Mutt and Jeff?" Sabrina teased.

"You look beautiful," a young woman wearing a strapless white gown assured them.

"Then it's settled," Sabrina told the saleswoman. "We'll order both of these in our sizes. And we'll go with purple."

"Mabel will be thrilled," Daphne told Sabrina.

"We'll find her a pale lavender dress," Sabrina said. "And Tootsie will have a white tuxedo with a purple bowtie."

"Tootsie?" the saleswoman asked.

"That's Sabrina's Chihuahua."

The woman laughed. "After you change out of your gowns, we'll get Crystal to get your measurements."

All in all, as they were driving home from Fairview with the top of the convertible down—after a nice little lunch—Daphne had to admit that it wasn't a bad day. "That was actually rather fun," she told Sabrina as they were coming back into town. "Thanks for including me."

"Thank you for coming. And for helping me find the right gown. It really was the right one, wasn't it?"

"Absolutely, Sabrina. You looked like a million bucks. Ricardo will be blown away."

Sabrina chuckled. "Okay, you keep telling me that."

Daphne checked the time as she pulled into her driveway. She had about an hour before it was time to pick up Mabel from school. Just enough time to relax. She thanked Sabrina again and then went into the house, ready to get out of the high heels and put her feet up, but she was barely inside when her phone started to jangle.

To her pleased surprise, it was Jake. "Hello," she said pleasantly.

"Daphne," he said in a slightly somber tone. "It's good to hear your voice."

"Yours too," she said in a slightly crisp tone.

"I know, I know—I forgot to call you last night. I'm sorry, Daphne. But my life has been in crazy mode the past several days."

"I'm sorry to hear that." Her voice softened. "How is Jenna?"

"I honestly don't know."

"What do you mean? Haven't you talked to her?"

"I've talked to her. Well, according to her I've lectured her. But she is not talking to me."

"Why not?" She kicked off her shoes and sat down on the sectional.

"I think she's mad at the whole world right now."

"Oh?" Daphne leaned back, trying to imagine what Jenna might be feeling right now. "No teenager likes to be ripped away from her friends and her high school. Maybe she has a right to be a little mad."

"But to do what she did?"

"What did she do?"

"She had that horrible party at Gwen and Frank's house. Gwen is even acting like I should take some of the financial responsibility for it."

"Why?"

"Good question. Probably because it's been expensive cleaning it up and replacing damaged things."

"Oh, dear." She sighed. "But Gwen was the one to leave Jenna home alone. Doesn't she need to own that?"

"That just shows how much you don't know about Gwen."

"So is Jenna back with them?" Daphne tried to imagine what that would feel like for Jenna. The hostility must be thick in that house.

"No, she refused to go back. I can't even get her to apologize to them." He let out a long sigh. "But I'm pretty sure that Frank is pleased that she's out of their house."

"What about Gwen?"

"I don't know."

"So Jenna is with you?"

"Yes. I've been calling her zombie girl because she goes around in silence. I don't know what to do with her. It's like she's not even Jenna anymore."

Daphne felt a sad lump in her throat. "I'm so sorry, Jake." Her voice cracked with emotion. "I hate hearing that about Jenna."

"I hate saying it, but it's the truth."

"Is she going to school?"

"Yeah."

"You need to get full custody of her," Daphne said firmly.

"Jenna needs to come back to Appleton, Jake. And the sooner the better."

He didn't say anything.

"What happened on Saturday night was just the beginning," she told him. "Do you really want to let her continue down that path?"

"Of course not!"

"I don't know what to say, Jake. I've been praying for Jenna. I'll be praying even harder now."

"Thanks."

"And for you too."

"I'm sorry to sound so testy about this, Daphne. I guess I just needed to unload on someone."

"You can always unload on me."

"But I don't like to hurt you. Please, forgive me."

"You're in a tough spot. I can't imagine how frustrating it must be."

"I just want my old Jenna back."

"I know."

"Speaking of that, I should get going. I have to drive almost an hour to pick her at her school. Just one more perk in my little drama."

"Let me know if I can do anything to help. Even if you just need to vent."

"Thanks. I appreciate it."

After Daphne hung up, she did what she promised to do— she prayed for Jenna. And then she prayed for Jake. She wished there was more she could do, but then she had to laugh at that. How could she possibly do more than God? Best to leave this mess in his hands.

Chapter 27

As Daphne went through the usual afternoon and evening paces, despite the heaviness in her spirit as she thought about poor Jenna, she made sure to keep a cheerful lilt in her voice. It wasn't until she was tucking Mabel in that she mentioned that Jenna really needed their prayers.

"Is Jenna sick?" Mabel asked with concern.

"Not exactly. But she's in a hard place. We need to send her some love."

Mabel sat up. "Can I write her a letter right now?"

"Not right now since it's late. But how about if I send an email and tell her that you love her and are praying for her."

Mabel nodded eagerly. And then she closed her eyes and sincerely prayed. "Dear Father God, please tell Jenna that I love her. And please give her a great big hug...." As she continued, earnestly and with childlike faith, Daphne had to wipe a tear from her eye.

"Amen," Mabel proclaimed. "There. That should do it."

Daphne smiled. "Yes, that should do it." She leaned down to kiss her. "Goodnight, sleepyhead."

"Do you know that poem that Sabrina says when she tucks me in?"

"A poem?"

Mabel giggled. "A funny poem."

"No." Daphne shook her head. "I don't know it."

"Then I'll say it for you."

"Okay."

Mabel grinned. "*Time for bed, sleepyhead. No, no, no, said slow. Put on the pot, said Greedy Gut, we'll have a sup before we go.*"

Daphne laughed. "Very good."

"Sabrina helped me learn it one time when she babysat me."

"You'll have to teach it to me sometime." Daphne turned out the light. "Goodnight, sweetie."

Daphne chuckled to herself as she went downstairs. Mabel was such a treasure. She couldn't even imagine her life without her. As she sat down on the sofa, Ethel and Lucy came bounding in, nestling in next to her. "You girls are pretty sweet," she told them as she petted them. "But you don't really hold a candle to Mabel."

Feeling a buzzing in her pocket, she remembered that her phone was on silent mode. Reaching for it, she was surprised to see it was Jake again. Twice in one day. Hopefully it wasn't bad news.

"Hey Jake."

"Is it too early to call?" he asked eagerly. "Mabel to bed?"

"It's a perfect time to call. How are you doing?" Unless she was mistaken, he sounded much more like his old self. "And how's Jenna?"

"I'm much better, thanks. And, again, I apologize for anything stupid I might've said while I was in the grinder. You know me, Daphne, I tend to say it like it is."

"I actually like that about you."

"I'm glad."

"So, tell me, what's going on. Did Jenna come out of her zombie zone?"

"You're not going to believe it."

"Tell me everything," she said with excitement, spooking the cats as she eagerly jumped to her feet.

"Okay. Well, I've never been a very good poker player, but I decided to give it a shot today," he began.

"Poker?" Daphne was confused.

"Okay, I'll start with the beginning. After I talked to you, I picked Jenna up from school. She was still giving me the silent treatment. So as I was driving, I asked her if she wanted to move back to Appleton. To be honest, I wasn't even sure how she'd answer. For all I knew, she might be perfectly happy with her wild loser friends, you know?"

"Oh, I hope not."

"Anyway, it was the first time since this whole debacle began that I'd actually seen her eyes come back to life. As soon as I mentioned Appleton, I had her attention."

"She wants to come back?"

"Oh, yeah. So I suppose I was feeling a little desperate. And I asked her if she wanted to go back to Gwen and Frank's."

"*What?*"

"Yeah, that was her reaction too. But then I told her that I had a plan."

"A plan?"

"It was sort of forming in my head as I drove. I imagined Jenna and me playing poker with Gwen—and the way we would win would be by bluffing our hand."

"Really?" Daphne tried to imagine this.

"I told Jenna that I wanted to walk in and act like I was dropping Jenna back with them. After all, Gwen has custody. So, I was going to say, here you go. Here's your daughter. Good luck."

"Oh?" Daphne could just see Gwen's face.

"I told Jenna all she needed to do was just act natural—like she'd been doing the past couple of weeks. I assured her I'd do the rest."

"What happened?"

"First of all, Gwen was shocked to see us. And I could tell that their house was pretty much all put back together. I told her the news. And Jenna, who was dressed in this horrible looking outfit that was probably inspired by her new friends, dropped her backpack in the foyer and, giving Gwen a surly look, tromped into the kitchen where she started making herself an after school snack." He chuckled. "And doing it in a rather messy way."

"Oh, no." Daphne couldn't help but laugh.

"Well, Gwen was fit to be tied, but she was trying to control herself. So then I informed Gwen that I wouldn't be able to have Jenna on weekends anymore. I told her I was working nearly 24/7 these days, which is actually pretty much true. And then I told her that I had decided to move back to Appleton. So Gwen would be on her own with Jenna from here on out. Well, Gwen asked Jenna how she felt about that and Jenna just rolled her eyes like she didn't care."

"But she does care."

"I know that. At least I do now. I wasn't so sure this morning."

"So what did Gwen do?"

"She started to throw a little hissy fit, but when she realized it was getting her nowhere and that I was leaving, she begged me to wait. She told me that Frank wouldn't put up with it anymore. She even pretended to cry, saying that her marriage couldn't survive raising a messed up teenager."

"Oh, dear! Did Jenna hear this?"

"Yes. But I'm pretty sure she's heard things even worse than this before. She didn't even flinch. She just kept making this huge messy sandwich. Honestly, she had food spread all over the place. I almost started laughing."

"And then what?"

"Gwen begged me to take Jenna with me. But I kept playing

hard to get. Finally, I told her the only way I'd take Jenna was if we made it legal. Gwen would have to sign a document assigning Jenna's full custody over to me."

"Seriously?"

"Yep. And she agreed. And since I just happen to be an attorney, I knew just how to do it. I borrowed Frank's computer and found a website with legal forms. I printed several copies out, and Gwen and I both signed them in front of a notary at a nearby mall, and then Jenna and I went and gathered up everything she wanted from Gwen and Frank's house and now she is here with me."

"Jake, that's fantastic."

"Yeah, it was pretty cool."

"And so how is Jenna doing? Is she happy?"

"I don't know. It still feels like she's mad at me."

"Oh?"

"But I just can't help thinking it's related to her life here in Miami. Her new friends. Her new school. If she could just get back to Appleton. But I really need to wrap up this case before I leave. I'm interviewing these people in person. It could take a couple more weeks."

Daphne was in her office now, staring at the calendar where April was nearly obliterated with black exes over all but a couple of days. She barely had two weeks until Aunt Dee's mid-May deadline. Did Jake know that? Did he even care? Was it selfish for her to even be considering this now?

"Why don't you send Jenna to me?" she offered.

"To you?"

"Sure. I have plenty of room in this big old house. And Mabel loves Jenna dearly. She was even praying for her tonight."

"I don't know...."

"It makes perfect sense, Jake. Jenna can get back in her school. Back with her friends. Mattie will be so thrilled. And when you get back to Appleton and find yourself a place to live, she can join you. Really, it's the best plan."

"It does sound good. Thanks, Daphne. That's very generous of you."

"You know I love Jenna too. And I honestly think she'll return to her old self if she's back here. Like I said before, the sooner the better."

"Well, I'll talk to her about it. I don't think she's gone to bed yet."

"Good."

"You're certain about this, Daphne?"

"Absolutely certain."

"Okay. If Jenna likes this idea, I'll book her a plane ticket for as soon as possible."

"Perfect."

"Thanks, Daphne."

"You're very welcome, Jake. I'm actually really relieved to think Jenna will be back here in Appleton. It feels like she'll be safe again."

"I know."

As they were saying goodnight, Daphne was very tempted to tell Jake that she wanted him back here in Appleton too. And even more tempted to say, *I love you.* But she just wasn't quite ready. Or maybe she needed to hear it from him first.

Chapter 28

On Wednesday morning, Daphne's phone jingled as she was fixing breakfast. Pleased to see it was Jake, she answered cheerfully. "Good morning."

"It is a good morning," he responded. "Even here in Miami."

"What's up?"

"What's up is that Jenna loved the idea of returning to Appleton and staying with you. And I was able to find a seat on a plane that leaves around noon. Jenna will arrive in Fairview around eight tonight. Can you pick her up?"

"You bet. Why don't you email me the details about her flight and I'll see if Sabrina can come stay with Mabel this evening." Daphne winked at Mabel, who was all ears at the kitchen table.

"Will do. Thanks again, Daphne. You don't know how much this means to me."

"We can't wait to see Jenna," Daphne told him. "And I promise to let you know as soon as I pick her up at the airport."

Mabel was dancing around the kitchen now, singing, "Jenna's coming home! Jenna's coming home!"

After Daphne finished talking to Jake, she explained the situation to Mabel. "I would've told you sooner, but I wanted to make sure first."

Mabel hugged Daphne. "I'm as happy as a hound dog with two tails!"

Daphne laughed. "Aunt Sabrina is rubbing off on you."

As Daphne waited in baggage claim, she felt both happy and nervous. According to Jake, although Jenna was glad to return to Appleton, she was still acting different. And it sounded as if he was yet to have a really good conversation with her.

Standing by the baggage carrousel, Daphne watched hopefully for Jenna. She knew the plane had landed ten minutes ago, but so far no sign of Jenna. As Daphne remembered how Jake had described the wild drinking at Gwen and Frank's house, she felt a wave of concern. What if Jenna had really changed? What if she still wanted to play the rebel in Appleton? Jake had mentioned her weird outfits. What if she wanted to do that here? And what if she tried to have a wild party in Daphne's house? Or set a bad example for Mabel?

Had Daphne been mistaken or irresponsible to agree so readily to take Jenna into her home? After all, Daphne's first allegiance had to be with Mabel. If Jenna had truly turned into a juvenile delinquent, there would be trouble. Why hadn't Daphne considered these things before? Was it simply because she was hopelessly smitten with Jake? A man who still hadn't proclaimed his love for her, let alone mentioned marriage?

Daphne spotted Jenna, slowly making her way toward the baggage claim area. She had a backpack and a carry-on and she looked tired and bedraggled. But when she saw Daphne, her eyes lit up. In that moment, Daphne knew she had a make-or-break decision. And she made it.

Opening her arms wide, Daphne ran toward her, embracing her like her long lost child. "Oh, Jenna, I'm so glad to see you. I'm so glad you're coming to stay with us. Mabel is over the moon." She kissed Jenna's cheek then reached for her carry-on. "Let me help you."

"Thanks." Jenna gave her a shy smile. "I have a checked bag. Dad only let me check one. He's mailing the rest of my stuff to me."

"That makes sense."

Jenna spotted her bag, and Daphne took her backpack while Jenna went over to snag it. "Okay," Jenna told her. "Ready to go."

"You look tired," Daphne said as she led her outside.

"I feel tired."

"I figured you probably won't want to go to school tomorrow," Daphne said as they headed to the parking area.

"I don't know. I might want to go."

"Well, it's up to you."

As they walked, Daphne explained about her job at Bernie's Blooms. "It's only while Mabel's in school. No weekends."

"I want to get a job this summer," Jenna said as they loaded her bags into the car. "I'm so glad you still have Bonnie," she said as she got into the passenger's side.

"And I've already had the top down a few times on sunny days." Daphne started the engine, and as she navigated her way out of the terminal, neither of them spoke. But since they had an hour long drive ahead, Daphne thought this might be a good time to talk. "Jenna, I know you've had a rough go of it. And if you need to talk, well, you know that I'm here for you."

"What exactly did Dad tell you?" Jenna asked in a stony voice.

"Not much. I mean, I know about the party at your mom and Frank's house."

"Well, that wasn't my fault," Jenna said hotly.

"You mean the party wasn't your fault?" Daphne kept her tone calm and even.

"Yeah. I did invite Cooper and Venus over that night. But that was all. I never invited those other kids."

"How do you think they heard about it?"

Jenna shrugged, folding her arms across her front like she was done talking.

"Is it possible Cooper or—"

"*Venus did it.* She denied it. But I checked her phone the next day. She texted a couple of friends."

"And did those friends text some other friends?"

"Yeah. Venus told them that Frank had a bunch of beer and wine and liquor."

"I bet that disappeared fast." Daphne couldn't help but question a parent leaving a teenager alone for a weekend with that much alcohol in the house. Seemed like an invitation.

"I tried to control things," Jenna continued. "But it was impossible. And the truth is, I didn't really care. Not at first anyway. But when it started to get out of control, I got scared. I mean, they were breaking stuff and throwing it into the pool. I tried to get them to stop, but they wouldn't. I considered calling the cops, but then I'd have to explain everything. Finally I talked Cooper into driving me home with Venus. I spent the night at her place." Jenna groaned. "Talk about a messed up family. Venus's mom is a crack head. And their apartment smells like an outhouse."

"That's too bad."

"Yeah. I told Venus she should report her mom. But Venus said that would put her in a foster home. And she's already been there, done that. At least with her mom she has some control over her life."

"Poor Venus."

"Yeah." Jenna turned to look at Daphne. "See, that is what I like about you, Daphne. Instead of calling Venus a total loser—like my mom and dad do—you care about her. You feel empathy for her."

"I can't speak for your mom because I don't know her that well. But I'll bet your dad would have empathy too. Except that he's so worried about you, Jenna. His first job is to parent and protect you." Daphne remembered her concerns about Mabel just minutes ago—how she would protect her against Jenna if necessary. "I'd feel the same way about Mabel."

"Yeah. I get that. And usually, Dad's a good parent. But not lately. It's like he's completely forgotten how to listen. He was like judge and jury when he heard about Frank's house. Like he knew I'd planned this big party and personally destroyed the place. And I didn't." She let out a little sob. "I really didn't."

"I believe you, Jenna."

"Thanks."

"But you know what they say about a dark cloud having a silver lining?"

"I guess." Jenna nodded. "Like good comes out of bad."

"Well, it seems like good came out of what happened Saturday night. I know you didn't plan it that way. But I'm personally glad that you're coming home to Appleton now."

"Yeah, I am too. Maybe you're right. Maybe this is the silver lining."

"And I'm sure that, in time, you'll think of a way to explain to your mom and Frank—and your dad too—what really happened that night."

"Like they care."

"I think they do care, Jenna. And you should care too. You don't want them thinking the worst of you. They deserve to know the truth. I mean, when you're ready to tell them."

"Maybe I'll write them a letter...someday."

Daphne reached over to squeeze Jenna's hand. "I really am glad you're here, sweetie. It just seems right."

"Thanks." Jenna's voice cracked slightly. "When Dad told me I got to stay with you, I was really happy."

"Mabel and I got your room all ready for you. Of course, you can do as you like with it. But we put on fresh sheets and cleared out the closet."

"Thanks, Daphne. You're a good mom." Jenna let out a loud

sigh. "And I just want you to know that I'm still the same Jenna. Mom and Dad kept saying I changed. And I know it looked like I changed. But I'm the same on the inside."

"That's what I believed."

Daphne felt relieved to see that Jenna was up and dressed and ready for school in the morning. Mabel was so happy to see her that she didn't even want to see her leave.

"Do you need a ride?" Daphne offered as Jenna picked up her backpack. "Or should I go with you to help you enroll again?"

"No, Dad said he'll take care of it by phone. And I can walk. It's not even a mile from here. Lots better than riding the bus like I used to do. Maybe if I get a job this summer, Dad will let me get a car."

"You're old enough to have a car?" Mabel asked in awed wonder.

"Sure. I'm sixteen."

"Wow, that's cool."

Jenna laughed. "Yeah, cool. You have a good day, Mabel. I'll see you after school, okay?"

"Okay!"

Daphne watched as Jenna headed out the front door. Dressed in her blue jeans, converse tennis shoes, and a gray hoodie, she looked like her old usual self. "You can take the girl out of Appleton, but you can't take Appleton out of the girl."

"Huh?" Mabel looked up from her waffles with curiosity.

"Jenna's back," Daphne said cheerfully.

"Yes!" Mabel agreed. "Just like a big sister."

Daphne wondered about that, as she walked to work later. What would it be like to meld Jake's little family with her little family? Oh, sure, Mabel and Jenna had always gotten along nicely during short stints. But what about day in and day out? Most teenagers didn't relish the idea of noisy, nosey little step-siblings. Not that Jake was getting any closer to proposing marriage. For all Daphne knew, he just wanted to be good friends. Okay, maybe friends and something more. But what? A housemother?

Having no answer, Daphne put the question aside as she entered the flower shop. Working at Bernie's Blooms was feeling like old hat to Daphne by now. She knew the routine and no longer felt the slightest challenge there. It was just a job. And not even enough to provide a livelihood in the likely event that Daphne failed to marry within the next couple of weeks. But this was something she tried not to think about. After all, she was doing what she could. And she had no intention of strong-arming anyone, including Jake, to the altar with her.

That afternoon, as Daphne was waiting for Mabel and Lola to finish their dance lessons, her phone buzzed with a text. Hoping it might be Jake, she quickly pulled out her phone. Although it wasn't Jake, Daphne still felt excited as she read the text from her agent, Marta Stein.

> *Good news, Daphne. An acquisitions editor from Persenger House, a new imprint owned by Penguin, has asked to see your whole manuscript. He was very excited about the book. And has no concern over* After the Fair. *Onward and upward!*
> *Marta*

Daphne sent back a quick, exuberant thank-you and, eager to share the news with someone, shot a quick text to Jake. The truth was she liked having any excuse for making contact with him. And, although she hated interrupting his work, she had sent him several messages of encouragement in regard to

Jenna. She hoped that having that weight off his mind might help him with the case he was building.

And she really respected him for sticking with this case. Like he'd said, it wasn't a big case as far as potential earnings. But it could make a huge difference in the lives of the deceased woman's three surviving children, now living with a grandmother in a singlewide trailer. The more Daphne heard about this woman's story, the more she wanted Jake to do his best and win it for her.

When Jake described gathering work records, personal testimonies, lab reports, affidavits and so on, she could tell he was overwhelmed. For right now, the best gift she could give him was her patience. He did not need her to push him. And so she was determined to keep a low profile in his life. And when he didn't respond to her text about her agent's good news, she did not hold that against him.

Instead, after giving Lola and Mabel a snack, she went over to tell Sabrina the news. And her shrill cry of joy was reward enough. "I told you it was going to sell," Sabrina told her. "Just you wait—we're all going to say we knew you when. Just like your Aunt Dee." She lowered her voice. "Writing all those romance novels as Penelope Poindexter. Of course, no one got to say they knew her because she kept it such a secret." She peered at Daphne. "But you won't, will you?"

"I don't see why."

"That's right. We'll shout it from the rooftops." Sabrina pointed over to Daphne's house, where Jenna was coming home from school, looking a little tired, but at least she had a bit of spring in her step. "How's it going with our rebel girl?"

"She is not a rebel girl," Daphne corrected her. "That was a short phase that she left behind in Miami."

"Oh, good."

"I better go check on Mabel and Lola," Daphne said. "But I just wanted to share my news."

Sabrina crossed two sets of fingers. "Here's to a book contract!"

On Friday, while polishing off a bowl of clam chowder at Midge's Diner, Daphne got another good piece of news. This time it came in the form of Stan Abernathy. "Just the woman I'm looking for," Stan announced as he entered the diner.

"That sounds serious," Ricardo teased Daphne. "But watch out, I've heard that our editor is a bit of a cad." He winked at Stan.

"Thanks a lot for outing me," Stan told Ricardo as he went to Daphne's table. "Can I join you?"

"Of course." She nodded to her empty bowl. "I was just finishing." She tipped her head across the street toward the flower shop. "And I need to get back to work."

"This will just take a minute." He laid his palms on the table. "I'd like to make a proposal."

Ricardo chuckled from behind the counter. "What'd I tell you, Daphne."

"Not that kind of proposal." Stan grinned at her. "But if I was in a marrying mood, well, who knows."

"What kind of proposal?" She blotted her mouth with a paper napkin.

"I want to offer you a part-time job at the paper. It'll be a combination of staff writer and ad sales. You interested?"

Daphne considered this. Compared to Bernie's Blooms, it sounded great. Plus, she knew that she couldn't provided for herself and Mabel with just one part time, minimum wage job. "Sure," she told him.

"Great. I can't afford to put you on payroll until June. And I can't pay you much. But the upside is that I'll let you have a flex schedule and you can work from home some of the time if you want. I know you've got your little girl."

"Thank you." She beamed at him. "That's great."

He stuck out his hand. "So are you in?"

"I am." She shook his hand.

"Do I hear wedding bells?" Ricardo teased as he set iced water in front of Stan.

"Not yet," Stan told him. "But you never know."

"You guys." Daphne laid some cash on the table and stood. "I'll leave you to plan your own weddings." She laughed as she left, but as she crossed the street, she realized that in the course of just a few days, her fate seemed to have changed. Not only did she have a publisher interested in her book, she had a job lined up at the newspaper as well.

Did this mean that she was going to pass by her mid-May date as a single working mom, lose her inheritance? Maybe so. And maybe she didn't really care. Maybe it didn't really matter.

Chapter 29

Throughout the weekend, Daphne felt unexpectedly peaceful and happy. Having Jenna in her home felt so natural and normal—like it was meant to be. And so far the two girls were getting along surprisingly well. Although Daphne had to gently remind Mabel to respect Jenna's personal space a couple of times.

But now it was Sunday afternoon, and Daphne was humming contentedly to herself as she raked her freshly mown grass into a pile. She inhaled the aroma of pungent grass and sweet cherry tree blooms as the sunshine warmed her head. Other than the chirping birds, the yard and house were quiet with Mabel and Jenna out on a bike ride.

But a tap on her shoulder made Daphne stop raking and turn around. Sabrina, dressed in white Capri pants and a yellow polka-dot shirt, peered up at Daphne with a curious expression. Next to her was Tootsie, in a matching yellow t-shirt that said *hotdog* on the back, looking up with a similar expression.

"You look so happy," Sabrina said with a tilted head. "Is there something you haven't told me?"

"I don't think so." Daphne smiled. "I guess I'm just feeling good." She waved to the blue sky with a few fluffy white clouds drifting by. "Isn't it a beautiful day?"

"Yes, but there has to be more going on." Now Sabrina started grilling Daphne about Jake.

"Jake is just fine," Daphne told her, starting to rake again.

"But what on earth is going on with him?" Sabrina demanded.

"Like I told you, he's working on this wrongful death case," Daphne started to reiterate the latest things Jake had told her last night. "It's really getting interesting—"

"No, no, I don't mean that." Sabrina glanced around then lowered her voice. "You *know* what I mean."

Daphne just shrugged. "I honestly don't know, Sabrina."

"What is going on with you and Jake? Have you made any progress? Is that why you're so happy?"

"I'm happy for a lot of reasons. I'm about to have two jobs, which should be enough to support Mabel and me. I have a book being considered for publication. And I even found a little rental house that's not too far from the grade school that'll be available in June."

"So that's it?" Sabrina frowned. "You're just giving up?"

"*Que sera sera.*" She swooshed the last of the grass into the big pile.

"Really? *Que sera sera?*" Sabrina looked skeptical. "You're really okay with this? No matter which way it goes."

"I'm at peace." Daphne picked up the bucket of flowers she'd cut from the yard earlier, carrying them up to the porch where she had a vase waiting.

"You don't care how it turns out?"

Daphne shrugged as she began setting one bloom at a time into the vase. She felt like she was getting better at floral arrangements. So much so that she hoped Olivia might even let her try her hand at some at work.

"All right, Daphne, if you're okay with it, I guess I can be okay with it too." Sabrina seemed to relax a little as she leaned against the railing.

"Good." Daphne held up the vase. "How's this?"

"Very pretty." Sabrina sighed. "And really, it's probably just as well that you're resigned to your spinsterhood, especially since you only have about eleven days, not counting today, to the deadline anyway."

"Twelve." Daphne went into the house with Sabrina trailing her.

"Fine." Sabrina retorted. "*Twelve.*"

"And, don't get me wrong, I never said I plan to remain a spinster." Daphne set the vase on the marble topped table, turning it to the best angle.

"But, honestly, Daphne, don't you feel bad about losing all this?" Sabrina waved her hand around the foyer. "I mean, you'll be car-less and homeless and penniless."

Relieved that Jenna and Mabel were still gone, Daphne measured her words. "It is what it is, Sabrina. And, no, I don't really feel bad about losing all this. I mean, yes, it's inconvenient. And I do have a lot of happy childhood memories here. Adult memories too. But it's not the end of the world. Good grief, there are refugees around the globe who are truly homeless. I'll simply be between homes. And I am not penniless."

"What about Jenna when you're forced to move?" Sabrina demanded. "Will she continue to live with you?"

"I don't know. But it's okay if she needs to." Daphne considered this. "It might be a little tight. The girls would have to share a room, but I think it would—"

"Well, if it comes down to that—you and the girls will have to come stay with me."

"I couldn't do that, Sabrina. Not with you about to get married and—"

"It would only be until you get on your feet. Surely you'd find a place by December."

"Much sooner than that. Probably by June." Daphne wasn't

as certain of this as she sounded. "But that's really generous, Sabrina. Thanks."

"It's the least I can do. But once again, I have to ask—where does Jake fit into all this?"

Daphne shrugged, studying Sabrina's perplexed expression and wondering why she had such a problem letting this all go. It wasn't like it was Sabrina's inheritance about to vanish into thin air.

"Do you think that Jake is using you?" Sabrina said abruptly.

"*Using me?*" Daphne frowned. "What on earth do you mean?"

"Well, he's got you taking care of his daughter. Call me suspicious, but is it possible that he simply pretended to be interested in you, just so you'd take in Jenna for him?"

"That's ridiculous. I would've taken in Jenna anyway."

"But Jake still calls you every night?"

"He does. And lately sometimes during the day too."

"And, in all these conversations, he's never told you he loves you?"

Daphne shook her head.

"Or spoken of marriage?"

She shook it again, wishing that the conversation would end.

"Well, it's just the strangest thing."

"I don't see why." Daphne heard the sounds of voices and realized that the girls were back. "But enough talking about this now." She headed for the door, greeting them.

"Jenna took me to the library," Mabel announced. "And if you sign a paper for me, I can have my very own library card." Mabel pulled some books out of her bike basket. "And Jenna got these on her card for me."

"Those look like good books." Daphne went out on the porch to see better.

"This is *Anne of Green Gables,* and Jenna said she'd read it to me!" Mabel's eyes glowed with enthusiasm. "She said it was her favorite when she was my age."

"My dad read it to me when I was little," Jenna told Daphne.

"I always loved the Anne books too," Daphne said.

As the girls carried their books into the house, Sabrina gave Daphne one last disappointed look. "I wish there was some way to talk sense into you," she said. "I feel like a good fairy godmother would try harder."

"I appreciate your concern, but I'll be fine," Daphne reassured her. "And if you're really that worried about me, why not do like Pastor Andrew said today. Pray about it."

"Believe me, darling, I do." Sabrina made an exasperated sigh. "But maybe I need to pray harder. Or else find some new brand of fairy godmother magic. Because I'm telling you, my wand is just not cutting it."

On Tuesday morning, as she puttered around the flower shop, dusting and straightening the shelves, Daphne was trying to keep her spirits up. But it wasn't easy today. Mostly because she hadn't heard from Jake last night. The last conversation she'd had with him had been on Sunday. And it had been brief and distracted. She blamed it on his work, but just the same she couldn't help but wonder. What if Sabrina was right? Maybe Jake wasn't truly interested in her. Perhaps he simply saw her as a good temporary parent for Jenna.

As she was pondering these questions while rearranging the candle section, she was surprised to see Olivia entering the front door of the flower shop with Bernadette in her arms. "Good morning!" Olivia chirped happily. "How are you?"

"I'm fine." Daphne leaned over to coo at the baby, tickling under her chin. "But what are you doing here?"

"I have some things I need to work on," Olivia said. "And I didn't have my key handy to get into the backroom, so I just came in this way. Can you get the port-a-crib set up for Bernie?"

"Sure." Daphne hurried back to extract the folding baby bed out of a storage closet, moving it over to the spot by the flower arranging bench to set it up. Stretching the pink checked sheet over the mattress and laying a fluffy baby quilt down, it looked sweet and welcoming.

"Thanks so much," Olivia said as she laid Bernadette down on the bed.

"Do you have a lot of arrangements today?" Daphne asked, although she hadn't noticed any big orders come in.

"Not exactly. But I need to get organized for a wedding that's coming right up."

"I didn't think you had any weddings until the first weekend of June." Daphne peered up at the calendar chart.

"This one just came up yesterday afternoon." Olivia reached for a catalogue, flipping it open. "Mostly I just wanted to get out of the house. I get sort of bored at home sometimes. Just me and the baby, day in day out. Especially now that she's sleeping better at night. I have more energy. And I'm getting more efficient with my time too. I'm starting to think that keeping shop with a baby isn't such a big deal after all." Olivia continued flipping through the book.

"Well, that's nice." Daphne still thought it odd for Olivia to show up out of the blue with no forewarning.

Olivia pointed toward the shop, where the door bell was jangling. "Better get that."

As Daphne exited the backroom, she wondered if this meant that Olivia wasn't going to need her help as much now. Was Daphne's job in peril? She smoothed her work apron, preparing to assist the customer, but when she saw who it was, she stopped in her steps. "*Jake?*" She blinked in wonder. "What are you doing here?"

He gave her a slightly sheepish smile. "I'm here to see you."

"Oh, well." She smiled, holding her hands up. "Here I am."

He moved toward her, sweeping her into a big bear hug. "And just as beautiful as ever too."

She felt her heart rushing and her cheeks blushing as they embraced, and a little disappointed as he released her. "But, really, what are you doing in Appleton?" she asked again. "Last time I spoke to you, you were in Miami. You never mentioned—"

"Like I said, I came to see you."

"You came all the way from Miami to see me?" She tipped her head skeptically to one side. "What about Jenna?"

"Of course, I want to see her too. But she's in school right now." He reached his hands around her neck and, to her surprise, he was untying her apron.

"What're you doing?"

"Taking you away from here."

"But I'm working."

"No, you're not," Olivia said as she came into the shop. "You have just been given time off for good behavior. I don't expect to see you back here today. Understand?"

Daphne didn't know what to say as Jake laid her apron on the counter.

"Come on," Jake told her. "Do you need to get anything?"

"Here's your purse." Olivia pulled it out from beneath the counter.

"So you knew about this?" Daphne asked her.

Olivia just grinned as she gave her a little finger wave. "Have fun, kiddies."

"We will," Jake said with confidence as he reached for Daphne's hand, leading her outside into the sunshine. "You ready for this?"

"I'm not sure. I think I'm in shock."

"I'm sorry, Daphne. I didn't mean to catch you completely off guard. I thought you'd enjoy the surprise. Don't you want to play hooky?"

She laughed. "Well, yes, as a matter of fact I do. As long as it's with you."

He opened the passenger door to what must've been a rental car, but a pretty nice one. "Here you go, my lady."

Daphne couldn't help but giggle as she slid into the car. Was this for real?

Chapter 30

Daphne was familiar with the expression "butterflies in the stomach," but she'd never fully understood it. In fact, as a writer, she'd dismissed the metaphor as a sentimental cliché. Yet now she understood. Sitting here next to Jake, riding through the verdant spring countryside, unaware of their final destination and not caring, even listening to him describe his progress on the upcoming court case...well, it was all magical and wonderful, and she felt slightly breathless as he turned down a rural road.

"Are you hungry?" he asked.

"Oh, I don't know."

"Well, I am. I hope you are too."

She glanced at her watch. "Well, it's nearly noon. I guess I am." She peered down the unfamiliar tree-lined road. "Where are we, anyway?"

"This is Oren Creek Road."

"Oh?"

"You've never been down this road before?"

"Not that I recall. Although Aunt Dee sometimes took me for rides down roads like this. Where does it go?"

"Worried that I'm kidnapping you?"

She smiled. "Not particularly."

"This road goes to Lake Tamalik. Ever been there?"

"No, but I've heard of it. Isn't that where all the rich people go for summer vacations?"

He laughed. "Well, there are definitely some wealthy people with cabins there. But not everyone is rich."

"If memory serves, I think your family has a cabin there." Daphne suddenly remembered how Mattie had told her about it last summer. The time she'd gotten the wrong impression that Jake and Gwen were getting back together.

"My step-dad's family had one of the first cabins on the lake. My uncles built a few more cabins later on. Anyway, my step-dad left his cabin to my mom. And my mom has pretty much handed it over to me."

"Nice of her." Daphne frowned. "Is that where you're taking me? To your cabin?"

He laughed. "Well, not exactly. Not to stay anyway. I was just missing the place and thought it might be fun to take a boat ride."

"Oh, yes," she said with enthusiasm. "I'd love to see Lake Tamalik from a boat."

"Great." He turned onto a narrow dirt road. "Almost there."

When a tiny woodsy cabin came into view, Daphne leaned forward to see it better. "What a charming place," she said. "Is that it?"

"No, that's Uncle George's place." He continued down the road, turning into a driveway of a much bigger woodsy cabin. "This is it."

She looked all around as they got out, taking in the majestic pine trees and gleaming blue lake. "Wow, this is beautiful. And that air smells so good, I want to bottle it up and take it home with me."

He chuckled. "Want to look around a little?"

"You bet I do."

He walked her toward the lake, pointing out spots of

interest, including the boat dock where some of the motorboats were in dry dock, but a nice little rowboat seemed to be ready and waiting. "Is that yours too?" she asked.

"Yep." He nodded. "But how about we get a bite to eat before we take it out?"

"Is there a restaurant around here?" She looked around the shore of the lake, where cabins of varying sizes were visible.

"There is a restaurant over there." He pointed across the lake. "But they won't open until after Memorial Day. That's when it starts getting busy around here." He took her arm, leading her back toward the cabin. "But I think we can wrestle something up here."

"Really?" She imagined them munching on sardines and soda crackers, but didn't really care. As long as she was with him, it didn't matter. But as they went up the path to the cabin, she saw a deck where a couple of chairs and a table with a white table cloth seemed to be waiting. And as they got closer, she could see that the table was set with china and crystal and silver. There was even a small vase with three red roses in it.

"Very elegant." She glanced curiously at Jake. "Does your cabin always have a formal table on the deck?"

"No, I think this might be a first."

"Interesting."

He pulled out a chair for her. "Have a seat."

"Thank you." As she sat down she thought that the china looked familiar.

"I'll be back," he told her, going inside the cabin.

She ran her finger around the gold trimmed plate. "Sabrina," she said aloud. Daphne suddenly remembered helping Sabrina unpack her dishes last year. She had china identical to this.

Jake emerged with a large picnic basket. "Look what I found." He started to unload it, setting out small containers of salads and sandwiches and a large bottle of sparkling cider.

"You found that in your cabin?" Daphne sniffed the pasta

salad. "This smells and looks just like Ricardo's famous pasta salad."

"You don't say." Jake grinned as he sat down. "Mind if I ask a blessing?"

"You know I don't."

As Jake prayed, Daphne felt like the butterflies in her stomach were not only multiplying, but having a party as well. When he said amen, she could barely contain herself. "This is so amazing," she said quietly. "Being with you. Being here. It's like a dream." She looked around. "Is it a dream?"

"If it's a dream, it's a good one." He handed her the plate of sandwiches.

As she took one, she tried to imagine how Jake had managed to pull this off.

"You're being very quiet," he said as they ate.

"I'm just so awed by all this, Jake. I'm trying to figure out how you did it. How were you in Miami one day, and then you show up here the next day? And there's all this." She waved her hand.

"Just like magic." He grinned.

"Yeah." She nodded.

"The truth is, I had help."

Daphne pointed at her plate. "I thought this looked like Sabrina's china."

"Do you want me to confess, or do you want to just keep thinking I'm a magician?"

"Let's just enjoy it," she said happily. "For now."

And so they did, just chatting and joking and enjoying each other, but then as they were finishing up, Jake got more serious. "I have some things I need to confess to you, Daphne." He slowly stood

"Confess?"

"Yes. In the spirit of full disclosure. Do you mind?"

She shook her head no, bracing herself for—*what?* She had

no idea.

He took her hand. "But I'd rather make my confession out on the water, if you don't mind."

She gave him a sideways look as they went down the deck stairs. "Is that so that I can't run away? A captive audience?"

He chuckled. "Maybe so."

Before long, she was seated in the front of the boat and Jake across from her in the rear, was manning the oars, rowing them out into the center of the lake. His words about a confession were making her uneasy. What sort of confession did he have? Everything about this excursion had been so perfect and delightful, she hoped he wasn't about to pull the rug out from under her. How many times had that happened this past year?

"It's so peaceful out here," he said as he stopped rowing, letting the oars rest in their holders and dangling his hands over his knees. "I don't know how many times I've come out here just to think. And sometimes to pray."

"It's perfect for that."

"In fact, I came out here in time for sunset last night. Very pretty too."

"You were in town yesterday?"

He nodded. "So, back to my confessions." He sighed. "First of all, I need to tell you that after my marriage with Gwen fell apart, I made the decision to never marry again."

"Oh..." Daphne wasn't sure how to react.

"Unless I found the perfect woman," he added.

"Nobody's perfect," she said quietly.

He chuckled. "Well, that's true. But I guess I meant *perfect for me.*"

She nodded, afraid to say anything—afraid to break this spell.

"I knew almost from the first moment I met you that you were different, Daphne. And my next confession is that I have loved you almost from the start."

She felt her heart leaping within her. "Really?"

"Yes. But I'm not done, I have another confession."

"Okay." She held back now, despite wanting to proclaim her love for him. She wanted to hear this confession first. Just in case.

"As you know, I've known all about the details of Dee's will. Even before you knew. And I think I've told you that I actually tried to talk Dee out of it." He shook his head. "It was just so strange. I couldn't imagine how it could really work out."

"You and me both."

"So anyway, Dee insisted you were the kind of woman who would respect her conditions. And she even told me that you were the kind of woman that would be perfect for me."

"Aunt Dee said that?"

He nodded. "She did. In fact, I almost thought the whole thing with her will was a set up. As if she thought she could force the two of us together. A way to marry off her spinster niece." He laughed. "Not that you were like that. I quickly figured out that you could have your choice of men. Certainly you have, too."

"Except I didn't choose any of them."

He smiled as he reached for her hand. "So many times I wanted to just throw caution to the wind and declare my love for you, Daphne. But then something would come up. Another man. My ex-wife. You name it. It just seemed like every time we got close, the wheels would fall off. You know?"

"I know." Her eyes were locked on his, hoping the wheels weren't about to fall off again.

"So back to my confession. As much as I loved you, I was uncomfortable marrying you before your deadline."

"Really?" Now this surprised her.

"I didn't want to enter into a marriage where it could ever be misconstrued that I married you for money. Do you understand?"

She thought about this then slowly nodded. "I do understand."

"So even though it felt like we were finally moving forward with no more red lights, I was a little worried. I wanted to wait until the deadline was past. And then I was going to proclaim my undying love and ask you to marry me."

She looked longingly at him. "I don't care about the inheritance," she confessed. "I mean, sure, I'll miss some things. But they are just things. What I really care about, Jake, is you."

He gripped both her hands in his now, gazing into her eyes with an intensity that almost took her breath away. "And one final confession."

"Okay."

"I wouldn't even be here now, except that your friends rigged an intervention."

"What?" She pulled her hands away, sitting up straighter.

"Please, don't get mad, Daphne. Not at them. And not at me."

"But what are you saying, Jake? That my friends strong-armed you into *this*?"

"No. No one had to strong-arm me. They simply talked sense to me. On Sunday night, Sabrina arranged a Skype session. She invited Olivia and Ricardo to participate. And between the three of them, they talked some sense into me."

Daphne was trying to wrap her head around this.

"I told them that I planned to propose to you, but that I wanted to wait. Sabrina, without completely spilling the beans about Dee's will, insisted that it was pure selfishness on my part to wait. And, honestly, Daphne, it was like a light went on. I could see that she was right. It was just plain old selfishness for me to wait. And suddenly I realized that I needed to get up here and make things right." Jake actually got onto one knee now, kneeling awkwardly in the rowboat which was tottering from side to side. Trying to keep his balance, he reached for her hand.

"Daphne Ballinger, I love you. I have loved you almost from the moment we met. I swear to you I would never marry you for your money—and that was all that was holding me back. But I would be very happy if you would agree to become my wife. Either before your inheritance, or afterward. Whichever way you want it." He looked earnestly into her eyes, with the boat still tipping from side to side.

Daphne felt her heart doing flip-flops, but she was determined to remain calm. "Jake McPheeters," she said solemnly. "I do believe I have loved you nearly from the start too. And you were always the reason that every other relationship fizzled. No other man had a chance to steal my heart, Jake, because it already belonged to you. And, yes, I would love to become your wife." She felt a huge grin filling her face as she tried not to giggle. "And if you don't mind, I would like to be married *before* my deadline." She got more serious. "But I don't want you to think that I'm marrying you for my money. Do you believe me?"

"I absolutely believe you." Jake reached into his pocket to produce a pale blue box that looked slightly faded and old. "I'll understand if you would like something different," he said as he opened it to reveal a gorgeous diamond ring. "But this was my mom's ring. And when I told her what I planned to do, she insisted on sending it. I had her ship it next-day FedEx to Warren Thornton for me. I just picked it up on my way to the flower shop."

Daphne stared at the ring. "I love it."

"We can have the size adjusted if we need to. My mom is a petite woman."

Daphne smiled as she held out her left hand. Even though she was tall, she had slender fingers, and as Jake slipped it on, it actually fit.

"That's amazing. But then why should I be surprised?" He chuckled as he leaned forward, pulling her toward him as he gently but passionately kissed her. They lingered in the kiss for a long moment, but with the boat rocking precariously, they finally pulled apart. And then they just sat there gazing at each other in wonder.

"I can't believe this," Daphne finally said.

"I know." Jake slowly shook his head. "But I sure like it."

"There's not much time to plan a wedding," Daphne said. "You really don't mind if we do it before my deadline?"

"Not if you don't mind." Jake reached for the oars. "I know some women would throw a fit over having to plan a wedding in such a short amount of time."

Daphne laughed. "Yes, I know a few of them myself."

"Although I'm not sure you need to be concerned about that." Jake began to row them back toward the dock.

"Really?" Daphne studied him. "Did you want to elope?"

He laughed. "Well, no, not really. I mean, I wouldn't want a big fancy wedding. But I would like to have our family and friends around. Wouldn't you?"

"Absolutely." She nodded eagerly. "But why did you say I shouldn't be concerned? Do you realize it's only a week and a half to the deadline?"

"Well, according to Sabrina and Olivia, they have already started to plan our wedding."

"Of course, they have." Daphne laughed.

"Do you think they can pull it off?" Jake lined the boat up with the dock, getting out and tying a line.

"I wouldn't be a bit surprised." She held onto his hand as he helped her out of the boat. And there with the dock swaying gently beneath them, he took her in his arms once again and this time they kissed without the fear of falling overboard.

Chapter 31

Both Mabel and Jenna were delighted to hear the news when they got home from school that afternoon. And neither of them seemed terribly surprised, almost as if they'd been expecting it. Everyone hugged and talked at the same time—like they were already on the road to becoming one big happy family.

"And I want you both to be in the wedding," Daphne told them. "Jenna, will you be my bridesmaid? And Mabel—my flower girl?" They both happily agreed and were pleased to hear the wedding would be happening so soon.

"That's way better than Sabrina's wedding," Mabel told Jenna. "Hers won't be here until Christmastime."

"So we'll all live together?" Jenna asked hopefully. "In *this* house?"

Daphne looked at Jake. "Well, we haven't really discussed where we'll live yet. But there's certainly plenty of room here. What do you think, Jake?"

He looked at the girls. "What do you ladies think?"

Both Jenna and Mabel declared, "Here!" simultaneously.

"How about you?" Jake asked Daphne with a twinkle in his eye.

"I think you know where I want to live."

"Then it's unanimous," he told them.

By the next day, Daphne felt slightly overwhelmed. Was it even possible to plan much of a wedding in such a short amount of time? Even a simple one like she wanted? Olivia had called the previous day, insisting that Daphne take Wednesday off. "You need to meet with Sabrina tomorrow," Olivia had insisted. "She and I put together a list. Just answer her questions. And then trust us, okay?"

"Okay," Daphne had agreed tentatively.

"Besides that, the only thing you really need you to do is to make a guest list," Olivia instructed. "Sabrina and I will take it from there."

So with Jake, Jenna and Mabel's help, Daphne had put a list together last night. And since she and Jake wanted to keep the gathering small—less than fifty guests counting the wedding party—it didn't take too long either. It was only family and close friends—period.

Because Jake had scheduled to meet with Warren Thornton in the morning, Daphne invited Sabrina over to discuss the details. Daphne was determined to fully cooperate with her two enthusiastic wedding planners. And really, she decided as Sabrina walked into her house with a notebook that said *Daphne and Jake's Wedding* on the front, this was the perfect way to plan a wedding.

"What's your favorite color?" Sabrina began as soon as they were settled in the living room.

"Green."

Sabrina wrote this down. "So you'd like your bridesmaids in green?"

Daphne considered this. She'd already asked Olivia and Sabrina to be her bridesmaids, along with Jenna. But somehow she just didn't envision her bridal party in green.

"You know," Daphne said wistfully, "call me old fashioned, but I always imagined my bridesmaids would wear blue."

"Blue?" Sabrina crossed out green. "What shade of blue?"

"Cornflower blue."

"Hmm?" Sabrina wrote it down. "I like that."

"But how can you possibly find bridesmaid dresses in just a few—"

"Remember the rules?" Sabrina held her pen in the air like a first grade teacher.

"Ask you no questions, and you'll tell me no lies," Daphne repeated the vow that Olivia had made her take yesterday.

Sabrina giggled. "And just trust us, okay?"

"Okay." Daphne smiled happily. "The truth is, we could all wear gunnysacks for my wedding and I wouldn't even care. As long as Jake is my groom, I won't complain."

Sabrina looked back down at her list. "Your favorite kind of cake?"

"Lemon...or chocolate."

"Favorite sort of wedding music?"

She considered this. "Well, Jake loves jazz—and I like it too. But that's probably not appropriate for a wedding. I do like classical music. But nothing too auspicious or complicated, you know? Maybe I could give you a list of songs I like."

"Perfect. Now what about flowers? Olivia thinks you like old fashioned flowers." Sabrina looked doubtful. "She wants to do arrangements that look like wildflowers gathered from a field."

"I would totally love that!"

"Okay." Sabrina made another note. "I've already checked with our church, and it's not available that Saturday evening, so Olivia is checking on—"

"Oh, Sabrina, I wish I could have the wedding right here." Daphne waved toward the staircase. "Ever since I was a little girl, I always dreamed of coming down those stairs. Do you think it would be too much work?"

"I don't see why." Sabrina made note of this. "I'll check with Olivia though. And you still want an evening wedding, right?"

"That's right." Daphne nodded.

"But not too late that we can't have dinner afterwards?"

"I hadn't really thought about dinner." Daphne frowned.

"You have to do a wedding dinner," Sabrina insisted. "Ricardo will be heartbroken if you don't."

"Oh?"

"Besides, you're not supposed to question us, right?"

"Right..." Daphne nodded nervously.

"So what if the wedding was scheduled for 6:30? That means we'd have dinner around seven."

"That sounds good. Do you think that's too early for candles? I always imagined a candlelit wedding."

"I think it would be okay. Olivia is in charge of the decorations. I'll let her know you want candles."

Sabrina asked a few more questions and then brought up the subject of food again. "Ricardo wants to coordinate the dinner with Truman Walters at The Apple Basket. Are you willing to trust their decisions or do you—"

"I absolutely trust them," Daphne declared. "I love that he wants to include Truman."

"So you don't mind being surprised by the menu?"

"Not in the least."

"Great." Sabrina closed her notebook. "Well, that pretty much takes care of it. If we have any more questions, we know where to find you."

Daphne handed over the guest list. "And I really don't need to do anything?"

"Nope." Sabrina stood. "Just trust us."

"And you'll keep my budget in mind." Daphne handed Sabrina the check she'd written out this morning, a check that pretty much emptied her bank account but was actually pretty meager for a wedding budget.

"Just call us miracle workers." Sabrina grinned as she slipped the check into a pocket of the notebook.

"I don't know how to thank you." Daphne walked Sabrina to the door. "You and Olivia both."

Sabrina beamed at her. "Are you kidding? We're thrilled that you're allowing us to handle it. By the way, did Olivia tell you that she wants to hire a new part-time lady?"

"No." Daphne felt a wave of relief at this news. "Does that mean she's letting me go?"

"I guess you'll have to ask Olivia about that. But I hinted to her that you might not need to work there anymore. I didn't mention anything about your inheritance. I just made it sound like you'll be pretty busy. Plus there's the newspaper job in June."

"Good point." Daphne thanked her again and then, after she was gone, Daphne called Olivia. First of all, she thanked her for working with Sabrina to plan the wedding. "It's so amazing. I feel like I don't need to do anything."

"You really don't. Well, unless you want to."

Daphne laughed. "You know how I feel about weddings. Having someone else manage it is fine with me. As long as it's kept simple and sweet."

"Which is exactly what we plan to do."

"And on budget. Even if it seems a very tiny budget."

"We understand."

Daphne mentioned what Sabrina had just told her, and Olivia quickly explained how a woman who used to work for her had come in during the weekend. "She really needs a job," Olivia said apologetically. "I haven't called her back yet, Daphne, because I wanted to talk to you first. But I'm guessing you'll have your hands full. Being a mom to two girls and a new wife, well, I'll totally understand if you need to quit."

"As much as I appreciate you giving me work, I think you're

right, Olivia. But if you ever need me to fill in for you, please, call."

"I promise I will. But you have to promise me something too, Daphne."

"What's that?"

"Promise you will try to relax and enjoy this time before your wedding. Okay? I've seen you sort of running yourself ragged lately. Taking care of the girls. Working for me. Babysitting Bernie. Just being generally helpful to everyone around you."

Daphne laughed. "Well, you make it sound like more than it is. But, hey, you will hear no complaints from me. I don't mind having some down time."

Of course, after she hung up, Daphne was sorely tempted to break that promise. Especially since her house was overdue for a thorough cleaning, something she'd neglected due to working at the flower shop. But instead she decided to simply relax. She would work on her column then spend some time getting herself ready for her big date with Jake. Their plan was to enjoy a nice dinner at The Zeppelin before he had to return to Miami on a redeye flight. It would be their last chance to be together before the wedding. And, as much as she hated to see him leave, she wanted him to have this time to finish preparing for the trial and to pack things up as he prepared to leave Miami for good.

Although Daphne didn't feel particularly busy or stressed, the days leading up to her wedding seemed to whirl past. And whenever she offered to help Sabrina or Olivia, they simply assured her that everything was under control. And so Daphne had spent part of her time working in the yard. To her surprise, Mick had insisted on helping with it. "I just know it's something Dee would've wanted," he explained on the first day he came over. "And Dee was so good to me, helping me establish my business, selling me that farm. Well, I feel like I owe it to her."

Daphne did not argue with him. And when Julianne brought over fabulous pots of flowers to place here and there, Daphne figured that they would eventually send her a bill. Hopefully after the wedding. But as a result, the yard now looked spectacular. Better than it had ever looked before. Daphne also spent a fair amount of time getting her house in apple pie order. She didn't feel she was breaking her promise to Olivia, because she was so enjoying herself. For the first time in a year, it felt like this house was truly hers—or that it would soon be hers.

She'd even gotten an estimate from Tommy Troutman for clearing out and painting the basement. "I want this to become a great space for Jenna and Mabel," she explained to him. "Maybe with a pool table and a TV area. You know, a fun place to have friends."

Tommy promised to get back to her with something. "After you and Jake get back from your honeymoon." He winked. "Where you kids going anyway?"

"The truth is, I don't even know." Daphne blushed. "I'm not even sure I care—as long as it's with Jake."

Tommy grinned. "Now, that's the right attitude."

As she thanked Tommy, she was glad that she'd put him on the guest list. Sure, he wasn't one of their closest friends, but he'd always been a good one.

Between the house and the yard, Daphne kept herself moderately and happily busy, and the rest of her time was spent enjoying Mabel and Jenna. And, of course, her nightly phone calls with Jake.

"Someone asked me about our honeymoon plans," she told him a few days before their wedding. "I had to confess that I don't even know."

"Do you want to know?"

She laughed. "Not particularly. I trust you, Jake. Wherever you take me, I'm glad to go. I'd even imagined spending our honeymoon in your cabin at the lake."

"Seriously? You'd want to do that?"

"Of course."

He chuckled. "So should I see if I can return our tickets to Maui?"

"Maui?" She let out a happy shriek. "For real?"

He laughed. "I was hoping you'd like that. And, just so you know, Sabrina already offered to play housemother while we're gone. I mean, Jenna could probably handle it on her own...but I'm just not a fan of leaving teenagers home alone."

"Neither am I," she said eagerly.

By the time Friday night arrived and it was time to go through the wedding rehearsal, Jake was missing. "His flight was supposed to arrive at five," Daphne told the rest of the wedding party. "But he hasn't called. And I tried texting him, but he hasn't responded."

"I was talking to my mama today, and it sounds like they're having some severe weather in the south," Sabrina told her.

Daphne felt a wave of concern.

"Do you know his flight number?" Ricardo asked. "We could check online."

Daphne was just looking for it on her phone when it rang. To her relief it was Jake.

"Sorry not to be there," he said. "But my flight got—" His voice broke in the static of a bad connection. "In Memphis—can't make it out until the storm passes—maybe as late as ten o'clock."

"Don't worry about it," she told him. "Just be safe, okay?"

"Will do—" The connection crackled with static again. "I love you, Daphne."

"I love you too," she said loudly. "I'll ask everyone here to pray for you to have a safe trip. Okay?"

"Thanks! I'll see you tomorrow. Even if I have to take a bus."

She hung up and then turned to her friends. "Well, I guess you guys heard. He's stuck in Memphis."

Sabrina pointed at Ricardo. "You can stand in for the groom."

Ricardo chuckled. "I guess it'll be good practice."

Although Daphne was sad that Jake was stuck in Memphis, she didn't really mind that he missed the rehearsal. In her opinion, a rehearsal was a waste of time. Plus she didn't want to steal the thunder of her coming down the staircase by having him witnessing it the night before. No, as long as he made it here in time for the wedding, she was just as glad he wasn't here tonight.

Pastor Andrew did a good job of putting them through their paces. The living room, completely cleared of furniture that was currently stored in Sabrina's garage, had been rearranged into two sections of white folding chairs. It was definitely tight, but as the wedding party took their places near the dining room entrance, it seemed to work.

Later on, when they went across the street for a dinner prepared by Sabrina and Ricardo, Daphne looked around the full table, taking in the dear people surrounding her. From Mabel and Jenna, to her dad and Karen, to Olivia and Jeff, Ricardo and Sabrina, and even Jake's groomsmen—they all meant so much to her that Daphne felt a lump in her throat. She never could've imagined this moment just one year ago. And yet here it was. The only thing missing was Jake.

"Oh, sweetie," Sabrina said kindly. "Are you sad about Jake not being here?"

Daphne used her napkin to dab a stray tear. "Well, yes, I do wish he was here. But besides that I was just thinking how blessed I am to have all of you. Thank you all so much." She looked at Pastor Andrew. "I'd appreciate it if you said grace."

Pastor Andrew bowed his head, asking the blessing, not only on the dinner, but on the upcoming marriage, and on

Jake's safe journey home tonight. Daphne echoed this in her heart. "Bring him safely home, Lord. Bring him home to me."

Chapter 32

After discovering that Jake had made it home and was staying in his friend Warren Thornton's home, Daphne got a good night's sleep. Feeling happy and energized, she got up early the next morning. It was odd seeing her house rearranged for the wedding, but at the same time it was exciting. And she knew there was much to be done today. According to Sabrina, Daphne's mysterious wedding dress—something Daphne had yet to see—was supposed to arrive this morning. Along with the bridal party dresses. "And don't worry," Sabrina assured her. "I have a seamstress on call in case anything doesn't fit quite right. But since the wedding gown shop already had your measurements for my bridesmaid dress, it should be perfect."

With the house still quiet, Daphne tiptoed to the kitchen to make coffee. Naturally, Lucy and Ethel felt it was time for their breakfast. As Daphne dished out their food, she warned them of the chaos that would take place today. "You girls will be safest in the laundry room while people are setting things up," she assured them. "After that you can have free rein again." She petted them both. "And you should be relieved that you don't have to go live at The Cat House after all. Even though you would've been treated like queens there. I know you're happier here at home."

As Daphne carried her coffee out to the front porch, she thought about Aunt Dee. More than usual, Daphne could feel her presence in the house. As if she were saying, "It's about time you did this, Daphne. Now let's get on with it."

Daphne sat in a wicker rocker, surveying the pretty yard and the flower pots that Mick had dropped by. It all looked so perfect for a wedding. She closed her eyes, asking for God's blessing on this special day. She was just opening them when she heard footsteps on the walk.

"*Dum, dum, dee-dum. Dum, dum, dee-dum*," Sabrina sang out as she marched up the porch steps with a white garment bag in her arms. "Time to try on the dress."

"When did that get here?"

"Just a little bit ago. The owner of the bridal shop drove it over herself." Sabrina nodded to the house. "Let's go see how it fits."

Daphne felt nervous as she set down her coffee cup. As much as she'd wanted to trust Sabrina and Olivia for everything, it had been difficult not to worry about her wedding gown. And despite Sabrina's constant reassurance that Daphne would like it, Daphne had endured a couple of dreams where she came down the stairs to the sounds of laughter. In one dream she resembled a giant marshmallow. In another dream she looked more like Frosty the Snow-woman.

Sabrina led the way into Daphne's bedroom, hanging the garment bag on the hook next to Daphne's closet and slowly unzipping it. She reached in and extracted a dress that made Daphne gasp—with relief. "Sabrina," Daphne said in wonder. "This looks just like that dress from the trunk show. The celadon gown that I loved so—"

"It is the exact same design. But in white." Sabrina peered at it. "Well, not white, white, but more of an ivory. I hope that's okay."

"It's perfect." Daphne felt the lace, shaking her head in

disbelief.

"Try it on."

Daphne hurried to get out of her sweats, letting Sabrina help her into the delicate dress. "Oh, Sabrina, it's just perfect," Daphne said as she stood in front of the full length mirror.

Sabrina pinched the sides of the dress, pulling it in tighter. "I think it could use a little tuck here. I'll call the seamstress and—"

"No," Daphne told her. "I like it just as it is. I don't want to feel like I can't breathe. I want it to be comfortable. You cannot have it taken in." She stomped her foot. "I won't let you."

Sabrina laughed. "Okay, then. You win." She stepped back to look at it. "And you're probably right. It looks better like it is."

Daphne hugged Sabrina. "Thank you for getting this for me. And if you went over my budget to get it, I don't care. I will pay you back for it. And it will be worth every penny."

Sabrina waved her hand. "If you want, we can talk about that later. After the honeymoon."

"What about the bridesmaid dresses?" Daphne asked with curiosity. "Do I get to see those too?"

"I'll run home and get mine to show you."

Before long, Sabrina was dressed in a sweet cornflower blue dress made of a lightweight silky fabric. Like Daphne's, it was tea-length with an uneven hemline. The short sleeves were soft and loose and the general feeling was one of elegant simplicity. "I love it," Daphne told her.

"I thought it was a little plain," Sabrina confessed. "But Olivia and the saleswoman insisted it would be perfect with your dress. And because it's not highly structured or fitted, the saleswoman assured us that we probably wouldn't need any alterations."

"I think it looks perfect as it is," Daphne declared.

"Ooh," Jenna said as she poked her head in the door. "Look at you guys."

"Can I see?" Mabel begged.

Both girls came in and admired Daphne's dress, then Sabrina led them back to her house to get their own dresses.

Soon all of them were standing in Daphne's room in their wedding clothes. "I love this flower girl dress," Daphne told Sabrina.

"I do too!" Mabel twirled around to make the skirt go out. Like theirs, Mabel's dress was a mid-length too, but the empire cut waist allowed for a fuller skirt. And hers was a pastel shade of cornflower blue, tied with a darker velvet ribbon.

"I picked that out," Sabrina said proudly. "It just looked like Mabel to me." She reached for her phone. "I'll tell Olivia to come by and pick hers up too."

After the wedding clothes were removed and hung in an upstairs bedroom, a large delivery truck arrived. "What's that?" Daphne asked Sabrina.

"The rental people. That's probably the awning and a few other things."

"An awning?" Daphne frowned.

"For the backyard. It's where we'll have the wedding dinner. The forecast was kind of iffy and Ricardo insisted we need it." Sabrina pointed to the Bernie's Blooms delivery van pulling up. "There's Olivia. I'll let her tell them where it goes." She looked back at Daphne, removing something from the pocket of her jeans. "And your job today is to use this."

"What is it?"

"You have some appointments. First of all, you have an appointment at the spa for eleven. For a facial and nails. And they'll provide lunch. Then you'll go to my hair salon, where Betsy is going to do your hair. And, don't worry, I told her you'll want something sweet and simple and natural." Sabrina winked. "And Lynn would like to help you with some makeup too. I told her just a light touch."

Daphne frowned. "There's no way my budget could cover

all this, Sabrina."

"This is from Olivia and me," she insisted. "We didn't have time to give you a bridal shower, so this is in lieu of that."

"But I—"

"Remember our agreement not to question us?"

"Yes, but—"

"Besides that, I plan to help Mabel and Jenna with their hair this afternoon," Sabrina added. "So I won't have time to help with yours. Plus, Olivia didn't want you underfoot while she's getting things set up in here. Really, it's just easier for everyone. You should be done before five. Enough time for you to come home and check it all out."

Daphne knew it was pointless to argue. Besides that, as more delivery people started unloading stuff, and coming in and out, she realized she would be happy to get away from it all.

"And don't worry," Sabrina reassured Daphne as she kissed Mabel goodbye, "we'll all keep an eye on little darling here."

"I'm not worried." Daphne ruffled Mabel's hair. "I can see that she's enjoying all this."

"Yeah!" Mabel nodded eagerly. "I'm in hog heaven!"

Daphne laughed. "Don't know where she got that." She playfully nudged Sabrina.

Finally, the big moment was here—and Daphne was so happy and excited she could barely contain it as she stared down at the amazing bouquet in her trembling hands. A sweet combination of white tea roses, periwinkles, cherry blossoms, and cornflowers. "Where did you find cornflowers?" she asked Olivia.

"It took some looking." Olivia grinned. "But don't you think it was worth it?"

"It's beautiful."

"You are beautiful," Jenna declared, giving a little tweak to the halo of flowers that Olivia had just pinned into Daphne's hair—a combination of the same flowers in her bridal bouquet.

"You look like a fairy princess," Mabel said with wide eyes.

"You all look gorgeous." Daphne smiled to see her four bridesmaids all looking so pretty in their blue dresses. She was just thanking them for being part of her special day when someone knocked on the door.

Mabel ran to open it. "Grandpa, you look so handsome."

He laughed. "You girls ready for a wedding?"

Strains of music drifted up the stairs, and Daphne suddenly felt slightly lightheaded. Was she really ready?

"Come on," Sabrina told Mabel. "You go first, and I follow."

Just like that, it began. And before Daphne knew it, her dad was offering her his arm. "You look beautiful, darling. But I always knew you'd make a gorgeous bride." He led her toward the stairs. "Aunt Dee would be so proud."

Daphne took in a deep steadying breath as she clung to his arm. "I can feel her with us, Dad. I really can."

He nodded. "I know. Me too."

Daphne looked up at the ceiling, saying a silent thank you as she listened to the music drifting up the stairs. It was simply a classical guitar solo, but it was well done and sounded absolutely perfect. As they came to the top of the stairs, Olivia had just reached the bottom and was being met by Jake's best man Warren. Then as Daphne's foot went down the first step, the guitar player transitioned into the traditional "Here Comes the Bride" song, but it sounded so sweet and pure that it nearly brought tears to Daphne's eyes. She had to take a deep breath as she and her dad slowly made their way down the stairs.

As they went down, Daphne was stunned by the beauty of the house. Old fashioned flowers and trailing ivy as well as lots of glowing white candles had transformed the space into a magical place. Seeing her friends and family all standing and watching her with such happiness was incredible, but it was the handsome, dark-haired man in a black tuxedo that took her breath away. Standing under a gorgeous arch of delicate flowers and greens that separated the living room from the dining room, Jake seemed like part of an amazing dream. But as she got closer, she saw that he was real. And, like her, he was misty-eyed too.

Her dad said a few sweet words as he delivered her hand into Jake's, and suddenly it felt like she and Jake were the only two people in the entire world. Pastor Andrew said a prayer then started to speak. But like she and Jake had agreed upon, the ceremony was short and simple and traditional. And before she knew it, Pastor Andrew was pronouncing them husband and wife, and she and Jake were kissing—passionately!

As lovely and perfect as this wedding was, nothing in her opinion was better than the bridegroom who stayed by her side throughout the following festivities. And judging by the look in Jake's eyes, he felt the same about his bride. Despite how much she was enjoying her wedding, Daphne would be ready to go whenever Jake said the word. She knew they were headed to Maui for a week but hadn't heard what time their flight would depart. Based on the late hour already, she suspected it would be a red-eye, which would be interesting since she'd never spent a night flying before.

Still, she didn't really want the celebration to end. It was delightful spending this time with their family and friends. And the big white canopy in the backyard, decorated with strings of white lights and flowers and candles, was so festive and pretty. After a delicious dinner, everyone seemed so relaxed and jovial. They were like one big happy family as they moved tables and chairs to create a space for dancing. Although there wasn't a live band, someone had rigged up a sound system with dance music. But as Daphne looked at the makeshift dancefloor, she felt uneasy. She knew Jake wasn't much of a dancer, and she did not intend to pressure him on their wedding day.

"Don't feel you need to dance," she whispered to him as the first song began.

"I'd love to dance," he said with a twinkle in his dark brown eyes.

"Okay," she said a little nervously.

Everyone clapped and cheered as Jake led her to the dance floor. And then, to her surprise, he actually led her in a pretty decent swing step. "I took a dance lesson last week," he confessed as the song ended. "Sabrina set it up and insisted I had to go."

Daphne laughed. Her little fairy godmother had done it again.

After a few more dances, Jake pulled her aside. "Ready to make our getaway?"

"Sure," she eagerly told him.

"Got your bags all packed and everything?"

She nodded. "Should I change for the flight?" She had her "going away" outfit all laid out in her room. Something Sabrina insisted she needed for their flight to Maui.

He shrugged. "I don't see why."

Daphne felt uncertain, but she could tell he was anxious to get going. As she hurried into the house, she wondered if he wanted to avoid the craziness that happened at the end of weddings. The decorating cars, throwing of birdseed, honking of horns, the chase and so on. Although it sounded sort of fun to her. Well, except for the chase, she wasn't a fan of that. Still wearing her pretty wedding dress, she zipped her traveling outfit into her larger bag, knowing that she could just change at the airport if she wanted.

"Ready to go?" Jake reached for her bag as she emerged from her room. "The gang's all out in front, waiting to send us off." He took her hand in his. "Brace yourself."

Together they ran out of the house, being liberally pelted with birdseed and loud farewells. They stopped by Jenna and Mabel, who were positioned by the SUV with slightly guilty smiles.

"Doesn't your car look great?" Jenna said to Jake.

He laughed. "Thanks a lot!"

"I did that one." Mabel pointed to the back where it said J + D in a big heart.

"Nice work," Daphne told her.

Jake and Daphne hugged and kissed both girls before they hurried over to the rental SUV, which was liberally decorated with slogans and balloons and streamers. Jenna and Mabel must've had fun. Daphne held up her bridal bouquet. "You girls ready?" she called as she got ready to throw, aiming for Sabrina and giving it a toss. Thanks to Ricardo who grabbed up Sabrina, hoisting her up while the crowd laughed and cheered, she caught it.

Everyone shouted goodbye as they got in the SUV, and Jake drove them away. Thankfully, no one chased after them. All was quiet, and Daphne was slightly stunned to realize it was just the two of them.

"Wow," she said as they came to Main Street. "That was a great wedding."

"It really was." He reached for her hand, squeezing it warmly. "I can't remember if I told you this already tonight, but I love you, Mrs. McPheeters."

She giggled. "Mrs. McPheeters...that sounds so right." She squeezed his hand. "I love you too, Mr. McPheeters."

As Jake stopped for a traffic light in the middle of town, a couple of cars honked and waved. "They must like our *just married* decorations."

"What will the rental car place say about all this?" Daphne asked with concern.

"Don't worry. I'll wash it first."

"Where will you do that?" Daphne was aware that their small town didn't have a car wash in it.

"I can do it at the lake cabin." He grinned at her. "We'll spend our first married night there, Daphne. Our flight to Maui isn't until Sunday afternoon."

"Oh, Jake," she exclaimed. "That is perfect."

"And so are you." Jake leaned over to kiss her. Before they were done, they were interrupted by more honking. Only this time it was to inform them that the light had turned green.

"Off we go," Jake said merrily as he stepped on the gas.

"Into the rest of our lives." Daphne leaned back, sighing with satisfaction and feeling like—at long last—their dreams had come true.

The Dear Daphne Series

Book One
Lock, Stock, and Over a Barrel
June 2013

Book Two
Dating, Dining, and Desperation
March 2014

Book Three
Home, Hearth, and the Holidays
October 2015

Book Four
A Will, a Way, and a Wedding
April 2016

You May Also Enjoy...

I Always Cry at Weddings
by Sara Goff

A spunky, urbane contemporary set in NYC to make you laugh, cry, and cheer for one woman who has guts enough to fight for her dreams.

Love, Lace, and Minor Alterations
by V. Joy Palmer
(June 2016)

This bridal consultant is getting annoyed with everyone else's happily-ever-afters. But she knows if she lets go of the bitterness of her past, she's going to have to relinquish control of her future to God. Minor alterations required.

Austen in Austin
Volume 1

These four heroines find love in historical Austin, Texas . . . Jane Austen style. Each novella is based on one of Austen's beloved books, bringing you familiar storylines with Texas flair.

CPSIA information can be obtained at www.ICGtesting.com
Printed in the USA
LVOW07s0324080616

491661LV00007B/350/P

9 781939 023735